# THE SPOILER

She was there in the darkness of the cabin. A slender figure wrapped in a rough blanket. Pale skin, dark hair, a girl barely in her teens. Inside, the harsh odor of hospitals, drugs and disinfectant.

As Stone stepped closer, the girl's eyes snapped open, wild but unseeing . . .

"It's all right," said Stone. "You'll be all right." As he said it, he heard movement behind him.

He was just turning when the force of the blow drove him to his knees. His flashlight spun away, and in its light the impressions were little more than clipped mental snapshots: a tall figure standing over him; an L-shaped scar on one side of the face; the long-barrelled Luger poised, about to descend.

As it crashed down, Stone's last clear vision was the full uniform and peaked cap of a World War II German U-boat commander . . .

*Also by Robert Rostand from Pinnacle Books*

THE D'ARTAGNAN SIGNATURE
THE KILLER ELITE

# ROBERT ROSTAND

# CROSS CURRENTS

PINNACLE BOOKS  NEW YORK

CROSS CURRENTS

*Copyright © 1985 by Robert Rostand*

An original Pinnacle Books edition, published for the first time anywhere.

Cover photograph by Suzanne Opton.
Background photograph by Jean Pierre Pieuchot.

First printing/September 1985

ISBN: 0-523-42358-6
Can. ISBN: 0-523-43361-1

*Printed in the United States of America*

PINNACLE BOOKS, INC.
1430 Broadway
New York, New York 10018

9    8    7    6    5    4    3    2    1

For those art-lovers, Jeff and the TNB

No one is spared except in dreams.

—W. H. Auden, *Herman Melville*

# CROSS CURRENTS

# Part I
## Point of Contact

# Chapter 1
## Sleeping Beauty

"There she is, skipper," said Devlin, pointing into the darkness.

But Stone had already seen it: the slender, crimson trail of a distress flare arcing across the night sky a few points starboard of *Pegasus*'s bow.

*Lost in the night.*

The memory came again to Stone as Devlin lowered the big 8 × 50 binoculars and looked over. A face of the sea: sunbleached eyebrows, skin lined by too many years of salt spray and windburn.

"Can't make her out, yet. No running lights. No nothing."

Stone wrote the time on the pad near the wheel: 2310 hours.

Exactly three hours and five minutes earlier the stationary blip had crept onto the top of the radar scope— an object dead in the water ahead of them. Like some beckoning star it remained there, suspended, as *Pegasus* drew closer.

"Better wake the Gabrieles," Stone said, reaching over to punch the starter button of the big auxiliary diesel. Immediately a tremor of power surged through the hull.

Alec and Hanna Gabriele were the charter, a couple in their mid-thirties who'd come aboard at Antibes.

"Hell, those two never sleep," said Devlin. "I tell you, there's something about that forward cabin and all this clean living."

He gave a malicious cackle that deepened the lines at the corners of his eyes. "A little hard booze and a soft woman . . ."

"Devlin!"

"Ay, skipper. Just reflecting, skipper."

"Reflect on it while you're hauling down the jib. Then get the Zodiac in the water, just in case."

"Yeah, I figured that."

Face set in his stock grimace of displeasure, Devlin ducked from the cockpit.

Stone again flicked on the VHF, fine-tuning the emergency channel. Nothing. A moment later Devlin was back, cocking his head as he tried to find comfort in the empty, static squawk.

"Shooting off fireworks like that, and no Mayday. Something ain't right, Davey."

"We'll find out soon enough."

Devlin peered bleakly ahead.

"Had my fortune told, I mention it? That old gypsy hag of Le Pic's came around."

"She tell you to stay out of the casino?"

Devlin's mouth bent into a mournful grin. "Told me to beware the darkness. Fifty francs to hear what any fool ought to know."

In the luminescent glow from the instruments, Devlin saw Stone's gaze shift. Masked by shadow, his eyes were dark, empty craters.

*          *          *

They sighted the boat a quarter of an hour later, an indistinct shape against the paler wash of night horizon.

"That ain't no strayed fisherman," said Devlin, bracing himself against the boat's driving pitch.

By Stone's calculation, the closest land was the southern tip of Mallorca a hundred miles plus to starboard. They were running roughly parallel with the northern coast of Africa off somewhere to port. International waters.

"Good heavens," a voice said behind them. "Something is out there."

Reflected in the windscreen, Stone saw Alec Gabriele step into the rear of the cockpit. One hand pinched a robe around his slender frame. Again, the voice made Stone wonder. Gabriele's accent was upper-class British, but a little off somehow, a little too rounded, something Stone couldn't put his finger on. His wife Hanna was a few years older, thirty-five or so, pretty in a tired way, with bitten-down fingernails and a nervous, horsey laugh. An odd couple, but as charters go, no trouble.

"That something is called a boat," said Devlin mildly.

"But I don't see any lights."

"That's because there aren't any."

Stone could sense Devlin's rising tension: too many things that didn't fit with the way forty years at sea told him things ought to be.

Stone added the absence of running lights to the other items on his notepad. He knew too well how an inquiry could pick apart the most apparently straightforward recollections, find every inconsistency and hole.

"Well, let's shed some light on our mystery," Stone said, raising the hand-held spotlight.

He took his time moving the narrow halogen beam from the vessel's high, stubby bow, past the squat unlighted wheelhouse, to a broad sweep of afterdeck mounting two heavy winches.

About a hundred feet overall, Stone estimated; military-looking except for a hull painted sea green.

"Devlin?"

Already he'd raised the binoculars and was biting tentatively at his lip. "Coastal minesweeper or something close," he grunted. "British built from the line of her."

"Armed?"

Behind him, Stone thought he heard Alec Gabriele suck in a tightened breath.

"Nothing showing. But judging from the radar mast, some powerful electronics aboard. Life rafts in place, decks empty." He looked up. "Whoever shot off that flare is sure playing it cagey."

"Shouldn't there be a name somewhere, Captain?" Gabriele asked politely.

"A name," croaked Devlin. "Flags flying, some running lights. A few little things like that."

Stone eased him a narrow look of rebuke and took *Pegasus* in a wide circle around the vessel's stern. Again he used the spotlight.

"*Sea Fox*," read Devlin slowly. "From Panama, it says."

Then his expression puckered as downwind the odor reached them, biting and acrid.

"Burned insulation . . . diesel oil." He looked over. "Fire aboard."

On a second circuit of the dark vessel, Devlin hailed her from the deck. After a moment he shook his head.

Stone made his decision. "Devlin, take the wheel. I'm going to take a look."

"You sure, skipper?" There was enough doubt in his voice for the two of them.

*Hell no, he wasn't sure.*

He wondered if any of it showed, the way his stomach was turning over at the possibilities. He doubted it. Stone, Stoneface, carefully cultivating that image over the years as a man might grow and trim his beard to cover a scar.

"Anything I can do?" asked Gabriele with a sudden bluster. "I mean if there is any danger . . ." He let it trail off.

"If Dev needs anything, he's not shy about asking." Then he forgot about Gabriele, speaking to Devlin. "Note the time I go aboard, then radio Palma marine. Tell them we're aiding a vessel in distress."

"You go easy, Davey," Devlin warned. "Just go damn easy."

Taking a heavy flashlight, Stone hoisted himself from the inflatable boat to the deck of the *Sea Fox* and turned to watch *Pegasus* veer off and begin another wide circle.

The rhythmic pounding of *Pegasus*'s diesel faded slowly, and he was suddenly aware of the groaning deep within the wooden hull as the dark vessel rolled in a light running sea.

Stone took a breath and mounted the ladderway to the bridge, playing the light across the dark windows before he entered. He pushed open the wheelhouse door and swept his light past the wheel and binnacle. The smell of burning was stronger here, and for a moment he thought it was emanating from the radar screen beyond the wheel.

He stepped to it and touched the grill. Warm. Warm enough to indicate that someone might have watched their approach until the *Pegasus* was close enough to signal by flare.

Stone turned quickly and went to the hatchway at the

rear of the wheelhouse. It opened on a combined wardroom and galley. A single bare table spanned its width. He was about to step inside when he paused.

Above the hatchway he could make out a patch of discolored paint in the shape of a perfect rectangle. The maker's plate, the bronze plaque with which a ship's builder signs his work, had been removed.

"That figures," said Stone aloud, the sound of his own voice giving him not the slightest comfort. But he didn't have time to add the absent maker's plate to his growing list of misgivings, for in echo of his own voice he heard a cry, below and farther aft. Not truly a cry, but something low in a human throat, cut off as it rose in pitch. Then silence again, so pervasive that Stone wondered if he'd heard anything at all.

He crossed the wardroom in two strides, pausing at the hatch leading aft. Beyond was a short companionway, ten or twelve feet in length, with two cabin doors on either side. At the far end, a ladderway disappeared belowdecks.

He tried the first door, pushing it open to find the small cabin empty, except for a single cot and bare mattress. Officer's quarters, unoccupied.

Then the sound again, that same mournful cry coming from the cabin directly behind him.

Stone whirled, the heavy flashlight ready as a weapon. He tried the door, found it unlocked, and slowly looked in.

She was there in the darkness. A slender figure wrapped in a rough blanket. Pale skin, dark hair, a girl barely in her teens. Inside, the harsh odor of hospitals, drugs and disinfectant.

As he stepped closer, the girl's eyes snapped open, wild but unseeing, and again the breathy metallic scream that drew back her lips in a ghastly grimace.

"It's all right," said Stone. "You'll be all right." As he said it, he heard movement behind him.

He was just turning when the force of the blow drove him to his knees. His flashlight spun away, its beam whirling crazily over the bulkheads and ceiling.

In its light the impressions were little more than clipped mental snapshots: a tall figure standing over him; an L-shaped scar on one side of the face; the long-barreled Luger poised, about to descend.

An appropriate weapon, really, for as it crashed down, Stone's last clear vision was the full uniform and peaked cap of a World War II German U-boat commander.

# Chapter 2
## The Axeman

In the two months since the disappearance of the *Pegasus*, the vision, hallucination, whatever they chose to label it, had visited Stone with agonizing regularity.

Even in the inquiry room he found the scene replaying itself, unrolling in his mind again and again like a piece of film snipped from the middle of the drama. It never altered in the slightest.

. . . *the girl's face pressing close in the darkness. The ragged fringe of dark hair above bright black eyes. Yes, a face he knew, but from where, when?*

*Diesel fuel, the damp wool of the blanket that covered him, familiar smells. Somehow he was back aboard* Pegasus, *the narrow crew's cabin aft. In and out of consciousness, a chemical taste so raw in his mouth that he gagged when he tried to speak. "Shhh," the girl whispered, her hands moving along his arms and legs. "You're free now. You must help us." But his extremities were powerless, as in a dream.*

*Then she was gone. Moments later, or seconds—he couldn't tell—the explosion, the shock wave throwing him roughly from the bunk. The narrow cabin tilting, beginning to slide away toward the edge of the earth. Always, as a child, he'd been able to wake himself from his nightmares, but that power too had abandoned him. He tried to pull himself upright. Hurry. Close by, the sound of rushing water. He had to move. He had to try . . .*

"Are you still with us, Mr. Stone?"

The impatient voice that rolled through the inquiry room belonged to Will Dunsteen, the silver-haired City of London solicitor who headed the inquiry board. From the opposite end of the large conference table he peered at Stone severely over the top of half-moon spectacles.

Between them a dozen curious faces waited for Stone's reply. Not impatient men, Stone couldn't fault them that. Underwriter's representatives, adjusters, investigators of one fashion or another, even a man from Scotland Yard, quietly making notes. All concerned, all careful to preface their probing: "I realize this must be difficult, Captain. But . . ."

The men waited.

The only sound was the gentle drumming of London rain on the high windows of the inquiry room, and the muted peck of the stenographer's machine as she recorded the proceedings.

"Sorry," said Stone. "Would you repeat the question?"

Dunsteen lowered his eyelids a fraction, like a great jowled lizard looking down from a rock.

"My question was did you wish to add anything to Mr. Black's testimony, regarding the loss of your vessel *Pegasus*?"

Stone found the portly figure of Nevil Black, representative of the Foreign Office, halfway around the table. His eyes shifted just enough to avoid Stone's gaze.

"I've nothing to add."

"You're certain, Captain?"

"I am," said Stone, an impatient edge to his voice.

Dunsteen's sigh was inaudible. He felt suddenly powerless and wasn't sure why.

A strong case could be made that the city of London was no longer the financial center of the earth. These days its banks and money men scratched for business like so many tradesmen. This wasn't the tourists' London of familiar names and attractions: Regent Street, New Bond, Picadilly. Here it was Lime Street and Guildhall, a somber London of bespoke tailoring and clerks and accountants to oil the machinery of commerce faltering or not.

Yet in one realm the Square Mile still ruled to the farthest corners of the globe: marine insurance. And it was a matter of marine insurance that had brought them here.

Dunsteen had a hard-earned reputation for firm-handed control, and in his opening remarks he wasted no time letting David Stone know exactly what faced him.

"Since the missing vessel *Pegasus* carried British registry, a flag favored by most of the Mediterranean charter trade, its insurance quite naturally was placed through Lloyds underwriters on the London market. Quite separately from the matter of filing criminal charges"—he paused for emphasis—"a Board of Inquiry is required prior to the settling of any claim. I urge your cooperation, Captain. The disappearance of a vessel with charter and crew aboard is a most serious business. Most . . . serious."

But as in the moments just past, with Stone's reticence apparent in every word and gesture, Dunsteen wondered if he was reaching the man at all.

Halfway along the table the gaunt, mantislike figure of

Robert Christian rose and bent formally from the waist before addressing Dunsteen.

"Since Captain Stone has nothing to add, I wonder if I might summarize the facts to date."

His voice had the rolling tones and modulations of a Roman orator; his intervention was as predictable as frost in December. Christian, the axeman.

Dunsteen nodded, offering a mild warning. "The facts, yes. But it is not the work of this board to speculate, not at this point. The facts," he said again for emphasis.

Christian accepted it with a deferential tilt of his head.

Given the peculiar circumstances surrounding the *Pegasus*'s disappearance, the underwriters had mounted their own investigation, bringing in Christian.

Tall and hollow-faced, he looked less like a former policeman than a schoolmaster, who, with his thoughts elsewhere, cared little for appearance. His graying hair was plastered close to a narrowish skull, his suit poorly tailored and in need of a good pressing. In one regard Christian and David Stone were the same. Next to the well-manicured men here in their serges and pinstripes, neither appeared to belong.

"Then," said Christian, "we shall stick with the facts. Fact . . . ," he began, referring to notes on the table in front of him. "At eleven thirty-two a.m. on the twenty-first of April, the British consulate in Tangier received a telephone call from the prefect of police in a small coastal village. A man speaking English had been found in a dazed condition on a nearby beach by a shepherd boy. He identified himself as David Stone, U.S. citizen and charter boat captain out of Cannes on the French Riviera. Are the facts correct so far, Captain?"

"So far," replied Stone, observing Christian blankly. Addressing the others, Christian said, "Captain

Stone's first questions concerned the whereabouts of his boat, *Pegasus*, and the safety of his charter and crew. All quite admirable in view of Captain Stone's injuries, an item I will come to in a moment. In response, local authorities dispatched a customs patrol boat, which searched the area with negative results. You were satisfied with their efforts, Captain?''

Stone nodded vaguely.

Damn, cursed Dunsteen silently. The inquiry wasn't a trial. But often enough the investigation into the loss or damage of a vessel evolved into a de facto judgment of her captain and his actions. And Stone was doing damn little to help his own case.

Granted, the man had been through an ordeal. Dunsteen himself had captained a frigate on convoy duty during the hellish winter of '42–43. He'd pulled aboard many a freighter captain with that inward look, men whose best judgments had been trumped by fate or a cunning beyond their understanding. In the past week Stone had visibly aged beyond his thirty-three years. His tanned complexion had taken on a yellowish cast, and deep worry lines carved his face. If anything, the jawline had grown tighter, matching the set of his shoulders, tensed and ready, as though prepared to fight off a physical attack.

Wartime or not, a ship's captain crossed the path of chance more often than any of the men seated around the table could possibly understand. To these men, catastrophe was something encountered secondhand in an inquiry room or actuarial table. Perhaps Stone resented the fact that they weren't men like himself who earned their living upon the sea and truly knew the risks. For whatever reason, Stone was fighting them. And Dunsteen suspected that more than one around the table had reached a private conclusion: that Captain Stone had something damning to hide.

"Fact," said Christian, towering over the table as he continued to speak. "A later statement by Captain Stone claimed that he was knocked unconscious by person or persons unknown after boarding a vessel in international waters, a vessel named *Sea Fox* and displaying a Panamanian flag."

The Foreign Office's man, Nevil Black broke in with a clucking deep in his throat. He was an enormous round man whose chin receded into his collar top. Christian glared annoyed by the interruption.

In a thin, wheezy voice, Black said, "The Spanish maritime police in Palma Mallorca did report that a radio call was received and logged from the *Pegasus* at 2340 hours. The call advised that *Pegasus* was aiding a vessel in distress."

"At a point two hundred and thirty nautical miles distant from where Captain Stone was later found," said Christian, again referring to his notes. "An elapsed time of thirty-six hours, during which Captain Stone claims to have no clear recollection. Is that so, Captain?"

"I've said it all before," replied Stone evenly.

Dunsteen said, "I fail to see where this is leading us."

Acidly, Christian responded, "We have heard a great deal of testimony, some of it important, some of it not. I have questions to ask. But I want all of us, particularly Captain Stone, to have a few essential items in mind. After all"—he straightened and smiled suddenly—"the purpose of a Board of Inquiry is to inquire. Is it not?"

"You may continue," said Dunsteen icily.

"I wish only to add that thanks to action by the British consul, an extensive air and sea search for both vessels was mounted, but again with no success. After which a cable was drafted to Lloyds Intelligence Department. A day later the *Pegasus* was entered in Lloyds List as missing. Where it remains."

The untidy limbo of a missing vessel, thought Dunsteen. The healthy insurance claims on the *Pegasus* and her passengers, Alec and Hanna Gabriele, were pending. Morally correct or not, the raison d'être for the Board of Inquiry was money. Nothing would be paid until the *Pegasus* was declared officially lost, and the circumstances of her loss determined. Death certificates would need to be issued for passengers and crew, even if their bodies were lost at sea. All was in the hands of the board; in insurance terms, they had the power to grant life and death.

"Then, if we agree on these *facts* . . ."

Christian's hollow glance moved slowly about the table, inviting comment. There was none; only the mumbled acquiescence of agreeable men, most praying the afternoon's work would finish by cocktail time.

". . . I *do* have a few questions." He addressed himself to Dunsteen. "Questions for Captain Stone."

Dunsteen's silver head bobbed once, giving Christian the floor.

"About this vessel you boarded, Captain?"

"The *Sea Fox*."

"Yes, the *Sea Fox*. You are aware that our inquiries have shown that no vessel of that description and name is registered in Panama. Or anywhere else."

A balding insurance adjuster named Kellman whispered to one of the underwriter's men, "Makes it sound like the bloody *Flying Dutchman*." The underwriter's man was at that moment more interested in the shapely brown calves of the inquiry stenographer, a Miss Postlethwaite.

In reply to Christian's remark, Stone's shoulders lifted indifferently; again he said nothing.

"If this were a court of law," said Christian ponderously, "a good case could be made that the vessel does not exist."

Stone shot a hard glance toward Dunsteen, whose hand came down sharply on the tabletop.

"Dammit, Robert, I will not have implications of that kind in my Board of Inquiry. Facts," he hissed.

He gestured toward the stenographer to have the comment struck from the record, but the damage was already done. Christian had planted his seed of doubt.

Unruffled, Christian met Dunsteen's eyes levelly.

"Then the fact is that the *Sea Fox* is not registered in Panama. Nor is a vessel of that name and description registered anywhere else." With heavy courtesy, he added, "Those are the facts I wish to state and put on record."

"It doesn't matter," said Stone quietly. "The boat exists, whatever its name."

"For your sake I hope so, Captain," Christian said. "Which brings me to a second question. A point of judgment really." He waited until Stone met his gaze. The inquiry room was Christian's turf, and Dunsteen, as much as he disliked the man, admired his skill un using it—clubbing points home one by one until they accumulated in the minds of everyone around the table, providing the exact effect Christian intended.

"About the advisability of leaving a boat," Christian said, "in the hands of crew while the captain himself investigates a vessel lying dead in the water."

"*Pegasus* was hardly the *Queen Mary*. The only crew aboard was Devlin."

"Then why didn't you send Mr. Devlin?"

"Because the boat was as safe in his hands as my own. And because Devlin was afraid of the water."

"I see."

Christian found himself smiling at the incongruity with the others around the table. Judiciously, he decided not to pursue the subject.

"My last question concerns the report of the British doctor who examined you two days after you were found." He ruffled through the papers in front of him and removed his glasses. "Tell me, Captain, are you still having hallucinations?"

A murmur went around the table, but Stone spoke quickly, just loud enough to command attention.

"Hallucination was the doctor's term, not mine."

"But this business about waking up in a dark room with a girl asking you for help. The same girl, so you thought, you'd seen when you boarded our mystery ship." Christian's tone was clearly doubtful.

"I'm not sure what I saw. A dream, maybe. Hallucination. Something that occurred in a semiconscious state— or a drugged one. I can't explain it."

Dunsteen scored a point for Stone. He'd refused to let Christian bait him.

"The doctor reported you took a blow on the head requiring twelve stitches," Christian went on.

"It felt twice that, but I'll accept your word."

Christian ignored the jab. "And you later displayed symptoms of concussion that persisted for days. Headaches, dizzy spells, portions of recent memory gone blank."

The implication in his phrasing wasn't lost to any of them. A blow anywhere on the head could be self-inflicted, the symptoms of concussion feigned.

"The doctor also concluded that hallucination might be perfectly normal after such a concussion."

"You're referring to the girl."

"Yes, the girl."

The girl troubled them, Stone sensed. She was an errant bit of evidence, something that didn't belong. It was the kind of thing a careful investigator would seize upon as a clue to new lines of inquiry, and a bad one ignore because it didn't fit the case he was building.

Stone was thankful he'd kept his mouth shut about his blurred, final vision aboard the *Sea Fox*: a man in the uniform and cap of a German U-boat skipper. If the idea of a dark-haired girl made the Board of Inquiry nervous, a U-boat captain forty years too late in history would have taxed their credulity to the breaking point. Better to be thought a fool, as the saying went, than to open his mouth and remove all doubt.

Stone chose his words with care. "I am not a medical man. If the doctor believes hallucination was possible, that's his business."

"Clearly you think this . . . vision was something else."

Stone nodded. "I don't think it was a dream. Nor a hallucination. She was real. But I don't know what her presence means. Not yet."

They all heard the determination in Stone's voice. For a few seconds Christian held him in a rigid gaze; then he nodded and lowered himself into his chair.

It was late afternoon before Dunsteen asked Stone to give his opinion on what had happened to him that night aboard the *Sea Fox*. As the inquiry room fell silent, Stone rose and circled toward the map of the Mediterranean mounted on one wall.

# Chapter 3
## Lady

The Rose and Thorns was a homey pub, as Maddy thought of it. Not a place for rowdies, with its velvet walls, cut-glass mirrors, and cozy high-backed booths of dark old wood. Maddy Postlethwaite felt a lady there, especially when, at 7:00 p.m. precisely, she met her new lover in a dimly lit corner booth.

She slid into the booth, plunking down her large handbag, giving Red her best smile. She was dog-tired after a grinding day spent transcribing testimony, and knew she still carried the lingering masculine imprint of the inquiry room, the mixed aromas of tweedy cologne and stale tobacco.

Viewed as they were from the bar by a none-too-sober twenty-four-year-old postal worker, they were a handsome couple. Maddy was small and perfectly groomed, but full-hipped, with a pair of fine, well-shaped legs.

Her partner, Red, was fair-skinned with carrot-red hair and a strong, squarish face marred only by a scarred left eyebrow. Upon meeting, they didn't kiss or even touch.

Red eyed Maddy's large handbag. "You have the transcript?"

"I shouldn't be doing this."

"Come on, now. I thought we'd settled it."

As usual, Red was impatient.

"I just want you to know how I feel."

"Darling . . ."

"Don't start that 'darling' bit," said Maddy. "Transcripts are confidential. I feel like a spy."

"You're not a spy," Red protested, beginning the tedious but necessary ritual of helping Maddy justify her actions. "This isn't the government. And I've told you, some people think Stone is mixed up in something shady."

"But who are these people? Why won't you tell me that?"

"Because it doesn't matter. They're paying for it, aren't they? Paying *us*. Unless you want to forget about our trip to Greece."

"Is Red your real name?"

"With my hair, are you crazy?"

"There's so much about you I don't know," said Maddy, thinking it might have been a line she'd heard in a movie.

"Ah, but there's so much you do know."

Red reached over to touch her hand. When Maddy tried to pull it away, Red gripped it so tightly that she winced. Maddy still wasn't comfortable letting Red touch her in public. When Red brought the hand up, kissing it gently, she knew that crooked smile was mocking her. "You're a devil. A red devil." But she stopped trying to pull her hand away.

From the bar the postal worker observed the two of them and spoke to the bartender.

"Would you look at that?"

"Look at what?"

"Those two girls. A lover's quarrel. Bloody disgusting."

"Enjoy your pint, mate," said the bartender, who couldn't care less.

"Bloody disgusting."

In the booth, Red smiled and asked, "How much longer will the hearing last?"

"It's not a hearing. It's a Board of Inquiry."

Red looked at her; the poor little twit.

"How much longer?" she repeated.

"Another day or two. Stone is giving testimony now. Those crowing buggers are out to smear him, you can just tell. Especially Christian. He's the insurance investigator and a real snake. He even looks like a snake, all thin and shiny."

"And you've plenty of experience with snakes."

"Are you laughing at me?"

"Order us drinks, darling, while I have a peek." Red took the transcript.

"I like doing things for you, you know that," said Maddy.

"I'll take a whiskey. And if that cheeky monkey at the bar makes any remark, tell him I'll come over and put him on the floor."

Maddy beamed. "You would too, wouldn't you?"

"For you I would."


Red studied the photocopied papers, a rough draft of that day's proceedings. Here and there Maddy had penciled in a remark to be expanded in the final form.

It began with Dunsteen, head of the inquiry board, speaking to David Stone:

> Now, from the time you boarded the *Sea Fox*, your own thoughts, Captain. No need to be formal.
> Stone: I believe the vessel was on a mission. A smuggler most likely, but headed where and with what I don't know.

Christian (insurance investigator): A mysterious vessel on a mysterious mission.

Kellman (insurance adjustor): Perhaps to the north coast of Africa, where you were found.

Stone: A reasonable guess that might be 180 degrees wrong. The *Sea Fox* could have been outbound, headed anywhere. But here . . . (Stone points to map) a fire in the engine room stops it dead.

Christian: You saw evidence of fire aboard?

Stone: Downwind we smelled burned oil and insulation. My crew man, Devlin, was a former U.S. Navy chief engineer. His conclusion was fire, and it wasn't the kind of thing he would be wrong about.

Christian: I admire your confidence, Captain. Still, if the vessel was in trouble, why not a radioed Mayday?

Stone: Because it might have brought the wrong people. A patrol boat from Algeria, for example, or one of Colonel Khadafi's corvettes.

Christian: How did they know *you* weren't a patrol boat?

Stone: The *Pegasus* was sixty-three feet and moving slowly under sail. A good radar man would have guessed what we were or weren't. When we were close enough, they drew us in with flares. They played it well, all of it.

Christian: The sound of experience, Captain.

(Stone doesn't answer; Christian addresses Dunsteen.)

Christian: Captain Stone's expertise in such deceptions might be related to the fact that he spent eighteen months in an Italian prison. Accused of smuggling.

(There is some disorder here.)

Dunsteen: Come now, gentlemen, give the Captain a chance to explain.

Stone: There's nothing to explain. It's true. *Accused*—and released before trial.

Dunsteen: Accused of what?

Stone: An incorrect manifest that didn't fit a cargo of water pumps from Rijeka to Brindisi and the illegal importation of firearms.

Christian: In simpler terms, gunrunning.

Stone: Four Turkish Mauser rifles no one would bother smuggling. They were found among cargo in a vessel under my command. I was the first one the police grabbed. By the time I was brought to trial, the weapons had disappeared from an evidence vault and they dropped the case.

Christian: How miraculous.

Stone: That was six years ago, before the *Pegasus*.

Christian: You were doubtless innocent.

Stone: Innocent of everything except stupidity. My boat was being used as a decoy. While someone tipped the police about a gunrunner, the real smuggling operation went on elsewhere. Not the newest trick around the Med, but I didn't know it then.

Christian: Older and wiser, but still not wise enough to keep your vessel *Pegasus* from being hijacked.

Stone: A captain has a moral obligation to aid a vessel in distress.

Christian: "So you . . ." (In mid-sentence Christian stops. He looks faint but catches himself on the edge of the table, then continues as if nothing happened. He'd done it once or twice before.) "So you boarded her and were knocked unconscious?

Stone: Then used as a hostage to get the *Pegasus*. After that I'm not sure."

Dunsteen: But you've a guess, Captain.

Stone: One possibility is that they used *Pegasus* to tow the *Sea Fox* to her destination. A second possibility was to send *Pegasus* off to finish the *Sea Fox*'s work, while someone stayed aboard to repair her enough so she could limp home. Wherever that might be.

Dunsteen: And which theory do you favor?

Stone: The second. That is, *Pegasus* used in place of the *Sea Fox*. A tow from the point we made contact would have meant a long, daylight run across open sea, something I don't think the *Sea Fox* wanted to risk. Either way it ends the same.

Christian: How so, Captain?

Stone: With *Pegasus* sunk in deep water, and those aboard disposed of.

Christian: Murdered?

Stone: Easier than leaving them alive to tell the story.

(Dunsteen needs several minutes to calm the room.)

Dunsteen: A most serious charge, Captain.

Stone (addressing the board): I realize how difficult it might be for you gentlemen to think like smugglers. Why sink an expensive boat like the *Pegasus* when, with care, she could be sold in the worldwide market for stolen yachts? All easy enough if stealing yachts is your business. But it wasn't the business of those aboard the *Sea Fox*. Selling a stolen yacht wasn't worth the trouble. Letting those aboard live to possibly tell this story was too big a risk.

Christian: A rather high price for whatever the *Sea Fox* carried as cargo.

Stone: Very. You wanted my opinion.

Christian: And something else. An explanation for your own good fortune. Why you are here to tell the story, as you put it, and not with the *Pegasus*.

Stone: I have no rational explanation.

Christian: An irrational one then. Or is that your girl who comes in the darkness to free you at the opportune moment?

Stone: I've made my statement.

Christian (getting to his feet, face very red): Like the explanation, rational or irrational, for the loss of your first boat, Captain. Off the coast of North America seven years ago, in similar circumstances?

Dunsteen: I say, Robert . . .

Christian (to the board): I think we'd all be fascinated to hear about that. Won't Captain Stone be kind enough to tell us about the loss of the *Mary Anne*?


It was the final item on the transcript. Red looked across the pub table at Maddy sipping her drink.

"That's all?"

"I'll let you see the rest later."

Red understood: the blackmailing little snot.

From the bar the post-office worker watched them rise to leave, the redhead helping the other on with her coat.

As Red passed close by, she whispered, "Eat your heart out, dearie," and protectively accepted Maddy's arm.

# Chapter 4
## The Shadow Man

Scarcely ten seconds had passed since the insurance investigator Christian challenged Stone, in front of the inquiry board, to explain the loss of the *Mary Anne*.

As he turned from the map of the Mediterranean, Stone's hard gray eyes fixed on Christian. But it was Christian who spoke first, goading Stone, refusing to let him take refuge in silence.

"Come now, Captain, if I'm mistaken I'll apologize. A sinking off the California coast, wasn't it?"

"You're not mistaken, and you damn well know it. The sinking of the *Mary Anne* is public record. I made a disclosure about the loss when I applied for the *Pegasus*'s insurance."

"A disclosure I wish added to the minutes of this inquiry."

Losing patience, Dunsteen spoke angrily from the head of the table. "For heaven's sake, Robert, make your point and be done with it."

Christian spun around, regarding Dunsteen with a fiery stare. "My point is that Captain Stone, in the span of seven years, has lost two boats without a trace. Each with apparent loss of life."

"In entirely different circumstances," said Stone. His voice was controlled now, almost too much so. "Different in every way, except the night. They both happened at night."

Christian's glance jumped toward Stone. "And in each circumstance the sole survivor was the vessel's captain."

"It was my own boat," said Stone, as though not hearing Christian. "I'd designed and built her."

"There was a loss of life, Captain?" Dunsteen asked.

Stone's head dipped in affirmation. "My wife."

During the Coast Guard hearing, he'd tried inadequately to describe the sequence of events, more precisely the sequence of sensations because there was nothing visual to report.

About midnight. Sailing north from Ensenada, some four miles off the California coast. Conditions calm, a light offshore breeze, no other vessels in sight.

He'd been given a few seconds' warning, had there been anything in his experience that would have allowed him to recognize it as such. An empty sea in all directions. Then to starboard, the sudden hiss of something cutting through the water, the impact, and the sound of tearing fiberglass as the *Mary Anne* was sent nearly keel over.

Even as he called his wife's name, he'd found himself in total darkness, the cabin lights out, water rising already knee-deep. Looking down through the companionway into the galley where his wife had been making tea a moment before, he saw nothing but angry green water bubbling up toward him. His heart squeezed in shock as he understood. The *Mary Anne* had been sheared in two. The sloop's front half was gone, and

Stone was riding the aft section down like a sinking piece of concrete.

Later he found the raft and its blinking beacon light. He spent the rest of the night alternately diving, praying his hand would touch something solid, and calling out her name until his voice gave out.

In the morning light, nothing. Gone. All of it, without a trace.

Now, in the quiet of the inquiry room, Dunsteen asked, "A collision with another vessel?"

Christian was seated again, head cocked to catch the small things hidden in Stone's voice.

Stone drew the exact wording from memory: "The official conclusion was that the *Mary Anne* was struck by a whale or other large object . . . unidentified. A freak accident brought about by a juxtaposition of incidents unlikely to occur again."

"Did you agree?"

"In a general way."

Dunsteen's brows ridged in question.

Stone said, "I didn't think it was a whale when it happened. Later, when I researched their behavior and the record of collisions at sea between whales and small boats, I found nothing to change my mind."

"But such collisions are not uncommon."

"The instant of contact was too sharp," countered Stone. "Hard surfaces meeting hard and at speed."

"Thus you concluded . . ."

Stone glanced around the room. The faint smile again. He doesn't expect to be believed, thought Dunsteen.

"The sail of a submarine. One partially submerged or running shallow. It's happened before: the *Nissho Maru* struck by the *George Washington*, for example. My case wasn't that good. The Navy made its own investigation, then refused to comment. But I knew." Again he fell silent.

Dunsteen understood then, heard it in Stone's voice. Stone was fighting the Board of Inquiry because he saw it as powerless or unwilling to give him the answers he needed, perhaps for his own peace. He counted upon them not at all. To Stone they were shadow men who didn't matter. He didn't seek their approval, and would survive their judgments even if they ruled against him. Void his claim to insurance, even recommend criminal charges, and they still couldn't touch David Stone.

Exiting the inquiry room, the Foreign Office man Nevil Black found Christian looking drawn and exhausted. "I'd say you've put the spike into Captain Stone," Black observed.

"Have I? You know, Nevil, I have this unfortunate habit of not sleeping nights if I think someone has gotten away with something. I take it personally."

From behind them, Stone's voice cut like a knife. "So you want to believe I sunk my own boat for the insurance."

Black turned and took a step backward. Something dangerous in Stone's manner warned him not to take chances.

"It happens," Christian replied, unruffled. "Insurance from the *Mary Anne* put a down payment on the *Pegasus*, did it not?"

Stone stood motionless a moment. "You're thorough, I'll give you that. But stay out of my way."

"While you pursue your own investigation?"

"I've spent too long listening to everyone tell me what I already know. Hell, I know the *Pegasus* is gone."

"It's the law, Stone. The way things are done."

"But the law and a table of curious men hasn't found

my boat. Or told me who took her. Or why. I don't begrudge your efforts to save the underwriters' money."

Defensively, Christian said, "It isn't my job to save anyone money. My job is to investigate, wherever that might lead. I work my own way, Stone. And it doesn't require giving you the time of day."

"Which suits me fine."

As Stone turned away, Christian called after him. "But don't be surprised if our paths cross, yours and mine."

"I dread the moment," Stone replied and was gone.

Two days later, the Board of Inquiry recessed for an indefinite period. Stone wasn't surprised. By delaying a ruling, the underwriters hung onto their money—at least for the moment. Christian was given more time to try and find evidence to hang the *Pegasus*'s captain, while Stone's reputation remained suspended over the boneyard. But the delay meant that he, too, had borrowed time. And he intended to use every bit of it.

# Chapter 5
## Ultra Deep

*Two*.

Standing on the promenade above one of Cannes's seedier public beaches, the two men suggested an unlikely meeting between Michelangelo's *David* and a nautical Santa Claus.

The *David* was in fact a twenty-two-year-old Australian named Pino—tall, sun-bronzed, and whippet-lean, with fine silky hair that curled fashionably at the back of his neck. What remained of his partner Yank's hair was a shaggy white fringe around the back of the skull; his eternally sunburned dome was covered by a Greek fisherman's cap cocked at a jaunty angle.

Yank was a head shorter than Pino, carrying considerable weight and power in his torso. A jolly grin, when he chose to employ it, crinkled the corners of his pale blue eyes.

"That's them," said Pino, nodding to the two girls sunning themselves on the sandy beach below. "The plump one's name is Wendy. Ready to jump, you might say. Her friend Robin is the trouble."

"Reluctant Robin," said Yank. Then, thoughtfully, "We'll see what can be done."

From the beach the girl Wendy waved, her inviting smile directed toward Pino. Sixteen or seventeen at most, Yank estimated, although she'd told Pino twenty. A large, thick-boned girl, plain except for her magnificent breasts, milky white and pink tipped. Her friend Robin was small, but equally pale skinned, with a sweep of chestnut-colored bangs across her forehead and deep, dark eyes. Robin had modestly chosen to keep her bikini top in place, a minority preference that year on France's Côte d'Azur.

Yank caught the secretive something in Wendy's smile and looked sidewise at his young companion. "Been sampling the goods, my lad?" His tone was not at all scolding.

Pino returned Wendy's smile, revealing a line of fine white teeth. "Like wrestling a bloody cow," he said, continuing to smile.

To Yank, Pino's malevolence was a constant reassurance. An absolute need to conquer plus the required physical equipment were his contributions to the team. Most operations like theirs needed a lover-boy.

"Well then," said Yank, "let's go to work."

Later, over drinks aboard the boat, Yank eased into his pitch. He could see this pair would be no special problem. Once aboard the boat, a sleek Italian built forty-six-foot power cruiser, problems were rare.

"Yum," said Wendy, appraising the plush main cabin.

Pino had met the two girls the night before in a bar named The Swan—not exactly by chance, as the song went.

Despite the self-conscious attempt to emulate a British pub, complete with dartboard and football pennants, The Swan was hidden away on a narrow street in old

Antibes, not far from the arches that led to the port.
There were other bars like it along the French and Italian
Rivieras and, from Yank's experience, the world over. A
young clientele, largely English-speaking, who liked the
trappings of home with their adventure.

Near the pub's door a bulletin board displayed various
cards and slips of paper all telling much the same story:
*Young person, experienced, seeks work afloat.* Usually a
tag word or two was a fair barometer of the seeker's
desperation. That the "experience" mentioned was
largely illusory had never bothered Yank in the slightest.

It was just such an announcement and the notation
"anything reasonable considered," with a request to
meet "interested parties" the next night at eight (signed
Wendy and Robin) that had caught Pino's eye. Drawn
instinctively, in a manner Yank found uncanny, to the
most vulnerable creatures in the pack, Pino went to the
pub a little before eight to check out the talent.

Conversation with the two girls had come easily.
Especially when Pino mentioned a friend with a boat
who might be looking for a crew. "Fantastic," Wendy
crooned. Her eagerness had already promised that a
score of one kind or another was Pino's for the taking.

And now, aboard Yank's boat, her meaty thigh pressed
against his beneath the galley table. He wanted to tell his
partner to save the energy, but already Yank had swung
into his pitch.

"You sure you have experience?" A thumbnail
scratched his chin in doubt.

"We've lots," said Wendy quickly. But Yank noticed
the other girl, Robin, avoiding his eyes.

"You two don't look old enough." By now his tone
was unmistakably suspicious.

Yank had learned his trade in the fat years following
World War II, from the best: the silky-smooth Parisian

Jew known as the Cadillac Man, so named less for his preference in automobiles than for the quality of goods he delivered.

His approach was based on a universal verity: in a buyer's market—and Yank was certainly a buyer where talent was concerned—the more reluctant to buy he appeared, the more anxious to sell the seller became. In doing so, eagerness replaced good sense, obvious questions went unasked. Uncover the greed hiding in everyone, the fear of missing a "once-in-a-lifetime" opportunity, and Yank knew the seller would hand herself over willingly, like a princess expecting the slipper. It was the basis of every scam.

Wendy chirped, "And Robin's a terrif cook, aren't you, Rob?"

"Oh, come on, let's get off it. Tell the truth for once." She looked directly at Yank, her bright black eyes disconcerting. A tough little nut, this one, Yank sensed. She'd need special treatment. "You'd find out soon enough anyway," she said.

The truth largely consisted of the fact that the two girls were from a cold, hard city in the British Midlands and neither knew forward from aft.

Yank appeared to waver, touched as were all good men by a young girl coming forth with an honest confession.

"I don't know," he said, looking troubled.

"Just a chance," pleaded Wendy. "A few days' trial and you'd see."

"Work aboard a boat is hard and dirty," Yank said sternly.

Sensing his softening resistance, Wendy said, "I've plenty experience at that, you can bet."

"And I don't want your folks howling when they don't get a postcard home once a week." Yank looked from Wendy to Robin in question.

"Not from mine," Robin assured him. "Don't worry."

"Let's leave parents out of this," said Wendy, with sudden bitterness. "My life is my business."

Pino looked into her eyes and pressed his leg more tightly against hers.

Yank winked at the two girls, nodding. "What the hell, we'll give it a go. Pino, some champagne for my new crew, the special stuff."

Special indeed.

"Beaut," said Wendy.

"Lovely," said Robin.

And Yank grinned his jolliest.

*That's two*.

At a depth of fifteen hundred feet Kits Maitland knew *Lady Bug* was in trouble. The craft was a forty-two-foot aluminum submarine, the latest enterprise of a company known principally for its corporate jets. Designed as a deep-diving reconnaissance vehicle—a DREC, as it had been acronymed by the project director—the company was patting its own corporate back for its intended service in the interest of pure research, exploring the mid-ocean rifts at depths of eight thousand feet and more. All the while Kits knew the military was watching silently from the wings with lucrative contracts waiting in their pockets. Hypocrisy was the company's business; making *Lady Bug* work was hers, and the vehicle was plagued.

"Same problem, Ray. I can't hold a steady depth."

Though alone in the craft's contoured pilot's seat, Kits spoke aloud. The vibrations of her voice over the throat mike automatically triggered recording equipment aboard the twin-hulled mother ship a quarter of a mile above.

"Instability below fifteen hundred feet," she said. "Don't know if it's the ballast problem again or a faulty vertical driver."

The *Lady Bug* was intended to be state-of-the-art in every way, a swift submarine that would, in the words of French aquanaut Jacques Picaud, go on its own where the eels spawned in mid-ocean, follow whales, or plumb the Sargasso Sea.

"The problem is," confessed Ray Hammer, *Lady Bug*'s designer and head of project, "we are at about the same stage in designing undersea vehicles the Wright Brothers were with aircraft."

Ray's familiar voice cracked at her now in the earphones.

"Are you in control?"

"You ought to know," replied Kits.

Sensors in her flight suit sent information on her body's vital signs topside.

"It reads like you're walking the baby. You are the ice queen, sweetheart."

*Am I, now?*

They were still learning how the human body reacted to stress situations undersea, even in a one-atmosphere system like the *Lady Bug*. Inside the craft's pressure hull, she was functioning at an air pressure equal to sea level, avoiding problems with nitrogen absorption in the human body or the alternative of a helium-charged interior.

Outside, through the narrow acrylic viewport, the water was a barely penetrable bath of deep indigo. At that depth, the pressure on the craft's six-inch molded skin was fierce enough to challenge every facet of its design and construction. Found wanting, both submersible and pilot would instantly compact into an erratically shaped modern sculpture several square yards in volume.

Kits Maitland once calculated she'd spent more than

three thousand hours undersea. From the early years of free diving and scuba to the later highly financed research ventures: Ed Link's man-in-the-sea program, the behavorial studies at Scripps, her own biological work on a wide range of subjects from aggression in whales to chemeosynthesis—the process by which the ecosystems that existed in the dark ocean depths had replaced photosynthesis. Only lately had come the lucrative projects for private industry that more and more often were taking her out of the laboratory and classroom.

But she'd never stopped learning through any of it: about the sea, about herself, the two entwined so long now that they were inseparable in her mind. Somehow, though, the magnitude of the game had changed with dizzying speed these past couple of years. The fee she would collect for the *Lady Bug* test program seemed almost indecent.

Until the moment arrived, as it had now. The moment when she felt the familiar surge of fear threatening to give way to panic and she had to summon every trick of self-control to force it down. No different now in the cockpit of *Lady Bug* with a quarter of a mile of water above her than when she was nineteen. Diving in twenty feet and feeling the tug at her side as an eight-foot blue shark ripped away the pouch of abalone dangling from her hip. These days she was paid not for those lazy moments when all ran well, but for the times of crisis that only she could handle.

"Ray, I'm going to take her deeper. See if I can coax the lady out of her problem."

"No you're not," came back the sharp response. "You're bringing her up."

"I am not in trouble."

"Just bring her up, Kits. Humor old daddy, Ray."

It was his growly-bear mode. He thought it hid the fact that he worried intensely about one smallish, well-muscled woman no longer quite young, who calmly took his creation touring around the ocean floor. He'd been hell since they stopped using the umbilical, the safety cable that linked *Lady Bug* to the mother ship.

"Come on, Kits, I said bring her up."

Suddenly she knew.

"Pour me a cognac and start running a bath."

She dropped enough ballast—tiny lead pellets kept in tanks inside the hull—to begin an easy two-degree ascent.

The last time she'd heard that particular something in Ray's voice was sixteen months before. When she'd scrambled through the hatch of *Lady Bug*'s predecessor, he had broken the news: her ex-husband Burt was dead. A diving accident in the North Sea.

About bad news, this time she hoped she was wrong. She wasn't.

Twelve hours later she was on a Swissair DC–9 taking off from London's Heathrow Airport for Geneva, Switzerland.

# Chapter 6
## Little Girl Lost

The Leman International School was ten miles from Geneva, on the sloping north shore of the lake. The school building was a six-story chateau built on a seven-acre park surrounded by vineyards. To the south was a splendid view of water and a jagged line of Alpine peaks, still covered by late snow. The Leman School—or Lemon, as it was called by its English-speaking students—provided a traditional education for 150 young ladies of varying nationalities between the ages of fourteen and twenty. Not yet had courses in Cordon Bleu cookery and "*savoir-vivre*" crept into the curriculum.

In winter there was a mountain chalet with skiing instruction; in summer, tennis, sailing, waterskiing, and horseback riding. The school had sounded like an earthly paradise to Kits Maitland. Yet for some reason she never could understand, it had made her uncomfortable from the first moment she'd entered its high, carved wooden doors with her then thirteen-year-old daughter, Polly.

"What in hell do you mean missing?" Kits demanded angrily.

40

The office of the school directoress, Madame Berthois, looked out on thick forest; beyond was the lake sparkling in bright sunlight.

"I understand your concern," the directoress replied with what seemed to Kits too damn much calm.

"But what exactly do you mean, missing? Kidnapped, in jail, what?" Kits waited.

"I'm afraid we just don't know," Madame Berthois replied. Her manner, in good Swiss fashion, signaled a refusal to be caught up in the emotion of the moment.

Kits fought to keep hold of her considerable temper. Her brain was still running on Los Angeles time. She had traveled east and west enough to know she must allow for jet lag. Mark, her future husband and business manager—Mark Tyler—said she needed to learn to cope the way diplomats did: put up a good front and be tougher than the opposition whether you felt it or not; it was a technique she hadn't yet mastered.

"Suppose you tell me what happened," Kits said, trying to sound at least courteous. "From the beginning."

Madame Berthois rose and refilled their teacups. She was a big woman with square shoulders and a ponderous heavy-legged way of moving. Running a school for 150 pubescent girls had provided her life with a series of trials, among which the disappearance of Polly Maitland was unusual but not extraordinary. One day, she considered, she would write a book.

She had met Polly's mother twice, her father once, two months before his death. She was well informed of—and unimpressed by—Mrs. Maitland's celebrity. Fame and fortune had their place, but they were not of the slightest value in the administration of a school.

She put down her cup and began. "A month ago we took our spring recess. It is the custom for the girls who don't visit home to arrange sightseeing trips, of which we approve."

"Even girls fifteen years old?"

Kits was trying without success to remember exactly where she'd been a month before. A professional meeting in Chicago she thought. Perhaps. But time in the past year, busy as she was, had taken a strange subjective bending.

"Fifteen-year-old girls of proper breeding are well able to take care of themselves," replied Madame Berthois, "given careful guidance. Each holiday must be made in the company of at least one other girl, and their plans passed by our travel committee."

"Then how did Polly end up missing?"

"I am trying to explain." She spread her hands, trying to preserve the calm.

Kits was damned if she was going to apologize. She took a slow breath and waited.

"Polly and Victoria, a sixteen-year-old German girl, took the Europa bus to Juan-les-Pins in the south of France, a beach town quite popular with young people."

"I know where it is."

Kits had chosen Leman International School the year she'd been doing research on Mediterranean pollution at the oceanographic institute in Monte Carlo. Polly's father, Burt, had been in Scotland then, working on the rigs drilling for North Sea oil. It seemed an ideal compromise.

Polly had been the only thing she and Burt agreed upon at the end, and Polly adored him. Not that she had known Burt well as a father. He'd been up and gone from their lives by the time his daughter was six. She had viewed him as some charming, doting uncle who always showed up with good stories to tell and a bagful of gifts that never emptied. Whatever Burt had or hadn't been, he'd filled a room when he walked in and he was never boring. Burt's death had shaken Polly more than Kits at first realized.

Now Madame Berthois was saying, "The girls were to spend ten days. When time came to leave, according to Victoria, Polly said she wanted to stay an extra few days to 'think things out,' as she put it."

"What things?"

"You might know better than I," she replied pointedly. "When school began again and Polly was absent, we began to worry."

"And about time."

"Mrs. Maitland, teenage girls these days are capable of all manner of . . . mischief."

"They always were, as I remember."

Madame Berthois chose not to comment directly, and went on: "At that point, although your daughter was breaking school rules, there was no need for undue alarm."

Kits leaned forward. "What I am trying to determine is when the alarm became due."

"When we called her hotel in Juan-les-Pins and were told Polly owed rent and hadn't been seen in two days."

The words struck Kits a hard, sharp blow.

Madame Berthois's eyes became hooded, preventing too close a scrutiny. "At that point we called the police, the U.S. Embassy in Paris, and you."

Later that night, from her hotel room in Geneva, Kits got through by telephone to Mark Tyler Associates in Los Angeles.

She owed her newfound celebrity, a word she'd heard often enough, more to Mark's efforts than to any change in her own way of doing things. It was a question of management, as he modestly put it. She'd once con-

sidered that her former husband, Burt, was a man
designed for another era, when time had mattered less
and the skills needed for success were in the realm of the
physical—brick laying always came to mind immediately. Or wrestling tuna aboard deep-sea boats, or hauling in
sail. Mark, however, had talents appropriate for the
times. In his late thirties, Mark Tyler had the rugged
looks of a Marlboro man, yet a careful, analytical mind,
a scientist's mind really. His considerable wealth had
initially come from representing sports personalities in
contract negotiations. Later he'd offered them complete
business management, eventually moving from sports
laterally into show business. He had both a law degree
and an MBA from Harvard, credentials he preferred to
let others discover on their own, and usually at some
expense. People came to him.

With the exception of Kits Maitland.

"You're a lousy judge of yourself," he'd railed at her
early on. "Don't you see what you've got going?"

"I guess not, to hear you tell it."

"The whole package. Brains, the right background,
and the looks to sell it to the media and public."

"Mark, I'm not sure I want to sell it, whatever *it* is.
I'm not sure I want to sell anything."

"I don't mean sell it like a box of soap. I mean put a
proper value on your work. Make your time count. It's a
matter of maximizing your own potential."

"You make it sound so damn important."

"These days, what *is* important?"

She hadn't an answer then; still wasn't sure she'd ever
have one that made sense to Mark. All she knew for sure
was that Mark's management had brought her more work
and more money than she'd imagined possible for a
woman whose interests lay mainly underwater.

She reached his private secretary and was put straight through.

"How are you holding up?" he asked directly.

"Mark, this business with Polly is serious."

She heard him hum, a neutral verbal response that was patently noncommittal. She reacted predictably, doing all the talking.

She visualized him, gazing from the large glass-paneled office in Century City out across the yellow layer of sludge beneath which lived the inhabitants of Los Angeles. There were moments when the entire city struck her as a massive, cruel experiment. Purpose: subjecting creatures to a wide variety of undue psychological and physical stresses in an attempt to find their breaking point.

She said, "The French police are looking for her, and I have an appointment tomorrow with the American Embassy in Paris."

"Tomorrow?"

"That's the soonest I can get there."

"Kits, you're speaking tomorrow night at the Explorers Club in New York. Black-tie reception at the Waldorf at eight p.m."

"Oh, Christ!"

"Eight hundred and fifty people are paying one hundred and seventy-five dollars a plate to hear you talk about humpbacked whales and such."

"I forgot all about it. Cancel it."

"Kits, I know Polly is more important. But you might do her more good in New York. In which case you nail down both birds and make everyone happy."

"Mark, darling, please don't begin negotiating this one."

"I only mean that by tomorrow night I'll have a pitch from a couple of the best private-detective firms in the country. And if you want it, a press conference to spotlight the issues."

"The issue is my daughter, Mark. I can't just get on a plane and leave."

"I want you to sit down and analyze it," he said. "Nothing emotional now. Just take the problem apart, imagine it's science. You'll see that one woman blindly wandering around some alleys in France isn't going to find Polly any faster than the best search organization in the world."

She sighed. Mark was persuasive precisely because so often he was 110 percent right, as he so often reminded people.

"I'll think about it."

"Cable your flight number and I'll limo you in from JFK."

"I said I'd think about it," protested Kits, but he'd already said he loved her and rung off.

# Chapter 7
## The Arena

The limousine was waiting at the airport as promised; Mark was not.

"Mr. Tyler will join you for dinner," the driver announced, taking her single bag.

"Appointments?"

"He didn't say."

Kits was surprised at the relief she felt. Alone in the rear seat of the limo, she had a chance to think. Mark would have kept up a continuous stream-of-consciousness monologue, accompanied by distracting smiles and touches.

She hadn't yet come to terms with the exact nature of their mutual attraction. They worked wonderfully together in bed. Both were experienced and patient enough to satisfy the physical side. The moments were few, but always skillfully stage-managed by Mark. The right room in the right hotel; champagne, candlelight, and enough artful playmanship to convince her that there had never been another relationship like it. Relationship. Their *relationship*. His favorite word. So much for the intimate.

In the public realm, Mark had introduced her to levels
of society she'd scarcely known existed. Power and
money and the tightly knit world of people at the top who
enjoyed using both. They went out frequently and were
photographed often. They were a stunning couple in
print. With Mark she'd begun to understand the heady
attraction that show people and national politicians felt
for their public. To be recognized by total strangers was
an experience to which she still was not accustomed. It
was all she could do sometimes to keep the ravishing
things she read about herself in the arena of truth. To
remember that her brilliant quotes in *Time* or *People*
were the result of careful editing of her long, overprecise
explanations, a habit owed her scientific training. "We'll
work on it," Mark vowed. "You have to get to the point,
especially on television. Give people something they can
grab on to in every line." A challenge as Mark labeled it,
and she was trying.

Mark had sent one of her gowns with the limo. The
long black one with the low-cut back. His selection. It
was becoming easier daily to surrender even the smallest
decisions, to lean on him for every little thing. "Part of
the service," he said with a grin whenever she protested.
But she made a mental note to fight it, lover or not.
Lately too many mental notes.

Riding toward the city, panels of light filled the
windshield as the limo dipped into the Midtown Tunnel.
She kept thinking of the things Polly's roommate, the
German girl Victoria, had tried to tell her.

Madame Berthois had arranged the meeting with the
sixteen-year-old following classes earlier that afternoon.
So short a time ago? The flight, moving with the sun on
its return to New York, had stretched the day into an
eternity, with more to come.

Kits wasn't sure what she'd expected of Victoria.

Something more representative of a young schoolgirl: plaid skirt, horn-rims, that sort of thing. Instead, a tall, model-slender young woman had risen to meet her in one of the sitting rooms. As Polly's roommate held out an elegant hand, a diamond-and-emerald ring winked at Kits in the sunlight.

"Hello. I am Victoria."

Kits remembered herself at sixteen as sunbleached and peely-nosed with a body that hadn't quite lost its baby fat.

"Perhaps you would like to see our rooms. *Roommate* is such a funny word, yes?" She giggled then, dropping her worldly-wise mask for a moment, and Kits liked her better for it.

"I'd like to very much."

When Victoria told her they'd been roommates since the beginning of the school year, Kits realized guiltily that she'd seen Polly only once in that period—the three days they'd spent together in New York over Christmas. They'd missed connections on half a dozen trans-Atlantic calls; so busy.

The two girls shared a common living room overlooking the lake, with separate bedrooms leading off on either side. Uncomfortable, for reasons she couldn't pin down, Kits entered Polly's room and looked slowly around.

Taped to the door of the closet was the usual teenage panorama: magazine photos of pop stars, a couple of L.A. Rams football players, her favorite snapshot of Burt.

It took a while for Kits to put her finger on it. When she did, she experienced a nasty feeling deep within: not a single reminder of Kits—not one photograph or clipping, nothing.

Victoria watched her from the door.

"You are too much for Polly," she said finally. "To compete with, I think."

"Does she really believe that?"

"Yes, Mrs. Maitland. We have talked about it, greatly. At least Polly talks and I am the listener. You are a beautiful woman, a famous scientist, and well, as the French say, *un peu snob*."

"And as the Americans say, that's bull."

"Polly believes she will never be as pretty as you are. And never so successful."

The remark pained Kits all the more because it was probably true. In looks, Polly favored her father, large boned and thick hipped with plain brown hair tending to wildness. At fourteen she'd been taller than Kits, with legs and feet always tangling. They looked less like mother and daughter than Kits had secretly hoped they would. About the success, she didn't know. That meant luck in finding something that clicked, and not everyone had that.

"And you think this imagined competition has something to do with Polly's disappearance?"

"If you want the truth, Mrs. Maitland, it has everything."

In the back of the limo Kits slipped out of her traveling dress and into the gown, indifferent to the driver's appreciative glance in the rearview mirror.

Mark met her in the Waldorf lobby, and promptly at nine o'clock escorted her to the dais in the Grand Ballroom. There was applause from a crowd made up largely of men over sixty.

Later—she remembered little of the ceremony—there was a capsulizing of her career, with emphasis on her recent efforts on behalf of endangered sea mammals. A medal was awarded her "in honor of your exploration of the last frontier on earth—the ocean."

She gave a short speech Mark had written, shook countless hands at the reception, and was whisked away in a taxi by 11:00 p.m.

In the cab Mark loosened his tie and groaned in relief.

"How was I?" she asked, then wished she hadn't. His expression wrinkled, his mouth pursed. All she'd wanted were a few harmless, cheery words; but she was about to get a professional assessment.

"You must smile, darling. You've a great smile. Use it."

"I didn't feel like smiling. Did you talk with the private detectives?"

"Ah, yes. Expensive. I had no idea . . ."

"I meant about what they thought they could do. Polly's been missing five days, Mark."

"Now, Kits." He put a comforting arm around her shoulders.

"I don't know whether to hope she's alone or with somebody. The idea of Polly shacked up with some guy boggles my mind."

"A possibility?"

"At this point anything is a possibility. But her roommate Victoria didn't think so."

"And what *did* this Victoria think?"

Kits shrugged wearily. "Only that Polly has developed some sort of a competitive thing about me. Feels she has to prove herself in her own way."

"Normal," Mark intoned. "We all go through that stage."

"If only I could talk to her. Tell her there's no rush to find something. She doesn't have to prove anything to me."

"Doesn't she?"

"No, dammit! She's my daughter, and that buys a lifetime ticket."

"Look," said Mark, trying to calm her, "maybe a change of pace is in order. Get your mind off things."

"Like what?"

"A little club I know."

"I want to hear about the private detectives."

Mark accepted the rebuff, his voice becoming businesslike and suddenly cold. "They'll start tomorrow. I guess this happens a lot—teenage girls and such. They thought they'd have something in a week."

"A week isn't good enough."

"You need some sleep," he remarked casually.

"Hire them, but tell them just that. A week isn't good enough."

Mark leaned forward and told the driver to take them to the Sherry Netherland Hotel.

"Let's just call this one a night. A little champagne on ice, and your lover's special therapy."

"They'll both have to wait," said Kits. "Sorry, darling." She began slipping off the black gown, the New York cabdriver flicking her a glance that said he could care less.

"What the hell are you doing?" asked Mark.

"The first thing I'm doing is putting on some clothes that feel like me." She dug her traveling dress out of the suitcase.

Mark rolled back his head and gazed up at the roof of the cab. "Kits, don't start that 'me' business again."

"Then I am going to rush like hell for the airport."

"Oh, come on."

"Because I've a midnight flight for Paris," she said, "and I don't intend to miss it."

# Chapter 8
## Dead End

"Smugglers for sure," said Le Pic, stabbing an emphatic finger in the direction of David Stone. "What honor left these days when a once noble profession is taken over by thieves?"

They were drinking steaming mugs of morning *café crème* around a cigarette-scarred table in the back of Le Pic's Bar des Marines.

Across from Le Pic, Aggie Godwin said, "You should know about smuggling, you old crook. You've probably cached more gold bars aboard those junkboats you owned than anyone since de Rochefelt supplied half of India."

Aggie Godwin was Scots, as squarely built as any local fishwife, with iron-gray hair and a hardheadedness to match. Aggie's company, Nautilus Marine, had booked Stone's charters.

Stone started to interrupt, then sat back to let the storm run its course. If Le Pic and Aggie Godwin had ever had a normal conversation in their lives, Stone had not witnessed it.

"Don't talk to me about crooked, madame," said Le

Pic indignantly. "There is more crookery aboard those ragged yachts you charter than Le Pic would stand for. Thieving crews, jelly-kneed captains." He looked right through Stone, and touched upon the true source of irritation. "Besides, I take exception to you calling me old. You!"

Le Pic was small but deep chested, a keg with legs, sprouting arms like knotted rope, hard muscled despite the seventy years plus he admitted to. And *Niçoise* to the core—excitable, stubborn, given to passions that changed with the weather and friendships that didn't change at all.

It was Le Pic years before who'd arranged the disappearance of evidence—four Mauser rifles—while Stone languished in an Italian prison awaiting trial for gunrunning. He'd accepted repayment for the modest bribes involved, but asked nothing else of Stone and never would. Once accepted by Le Pic, it was without condition. Except the unspoken one that expected forbearance whichever way his emotional winds chose to blow. The Bar des Marines was his home and forum.

The food that came from the cook Basso's kitchen was from another era—*soupe des poissons*, *tripes*, and *daubes*, and when the fish were right, a *bourride* of exquisite tastes and textures Stone had given up trying to describe. Now, a little past eight in the morning, the half-dozen tables up front were already filled with fishermen bent over heavy lunches and coarse Midi wine. The day had begun here at midnight with breakfasts of strong coffee laced with *eau-de-vie*.

"Mark them well, David," Le Pic had once warned. "The last of their kind." The entire port knew the local fishermen were losing out to the big marketing cooperatives in Bologna and Paris. While they remained content to sell their octopus and bony plug-ugly fish from plain wooden trays in the city market, the large hotels and restaurants telephoned orders for neatly packaged fish from the co-ops. "Too proud to organize, except to play *petanque* and argue which politician is the biggest thief."

And yet Le Pic grudgingly admired their acceptance of what fate had dealt them, the way they still managed to take the best from each day as it came. But quiet acceptance wasn't Stone's way any more than it was Le Pic's; it would have been easier for him if it were.

"Well you *are* old," said Aggie, refusing to let Le Pic escape unscathed. "And a goat besides."

A casual observer might have judged them bitter enemies. But Stone knew that to question their friendship aloud risked a double peril. God help the person Aggie and Le Pic attacked in tandem.

Le Pic leaned toward the Scotswoman, squinting with hard blue eyes. "Then perhaps you'd like to test the age of Le Pic in time-honored fashion, eh?"

Aggie roared with laughter. "That will be a colder day than I've ever had."

"And one you'd remember, woman."

"They'd hear your bones rattle in Toulon."

"I . . ." Le Pic sputtered, face reddening. Before he could shift into high gear, Stone put his hand on the table between them.

"Enough, you two. All I wanted was an opinion, not a civil war over coffee."

"A smuggler for sure, this *Sea Fox*," said Le Pic. "I can feel it in my"—he cast a dark glance toward Aggie—"bones."

Aggie sighed. "I hate to admit it in Le Pic's presence, but I agree."

"Ah," said Le Pic with a sudden grin. Content with

his small victory, he reached down to stroke the nameless dog that was never far from his feet.

Some long ago accident had left the animal mobile but missing a hind leg. Le Pic claimed he kept it as a watchdog because there was nothing to equal the foul temper of a three-legged dog that was French to boot. To admit a fondness for the creature was a little too simple.

"The question," said Aggie, "is smuggling what? You don't need a boat the size of this *Sea Fox* to transport cigarettes. Or run in a couple of kilos of heroin, since that's all the local papers are full of these days."

"What do you know about the drug trade?" argued Le Pic. "Or about smuggling TV's or refrigerators to the Arabs?"

"I give up," said Aggie, looking toward Stone in appeal.

"The boat is the key," said Le Pic firmly. "That kind of boat."

Frowning, Aggie said, "Why not go over it again, Davey. That business in London."

Even while the Board of Inquiry was still grinding on, Stone had begun his own investigation.

The first discovery came too easily.

A morning in Guildhall Library, leafing through back copies of *Janes* produced the mystery vessel *Pegasus* had encountered that night, at least in type. Length, tonnage, the same boxy wheelhouse with radar mast amidships, heavy winches aft. Everything fitted. Devlin had been right. An inshore minesweeper, British built, of the "Ham" class.

The downside of the discovery was that between 1952 and 1959 a total of eighty had been built for the Royal Navy. It took an additional three days on the telephone to the Ministry of the Marine to learn that only three were still in navy service.

"What happened to the others?" he asked the voice on the telephone.

"You might try Thornelow," he was told. "He'd know if anyone would." It was said without much admiration.

When Stone entered a small, paper-cluttered office in the Ministry of the Marine, he felt his hackles rise uncontrollably. His dealings with bureaucracy in one form or another seemed to have occupied the larger part of his life: the U.S. Navy, in his investigation of the *Mary Anne*; the Coast Guard; the yearly battles any charter-boat captain working out of a French port fought with Excise and Customs, who wanted their slice and then some. The days sitting in the inquiry room had been his most recent test, and when the nondescript sandy-haired man of indeterminate middle-age glanced up from behind his desk, Stone steeled himself. Thornelow had that bureaucrat's look—from paunch to poochy skin beneath the chin, to the vagueness of gesture when he waved Stone toward a chair.

He rose slowly to shut the office door, massaging the small of his back. Stone turned to find Thornelow observing him with a steady questioning look, followed by a smile that was quick and direct, as though a surprise to himself.

"How about a drink," he said. "I could use one, and from the look of it, so could you."

Without waiting for Stone's answer, he produced a bottle of straight malt whiskey from a cabinet, two fine crystal glasses, and a bottle of Malvern Still water. "I've a hangover to cripple an ox," Thornelow remarked. "It always happens when my wife's family comes to do London. Odd, isn't it, the abuse a man endures for love? Puts us a step one side or the other of the animal kingdom, only I'm never quite sure which." He poured a measure of whiskey for Stone and handed him the glass. "Now what can we do for you?"

Stone told him exactly, all of it, about his missing boat and its encounter with the *Sea Fox*. Something in Thornelow's uncalled-for openness disarmed him.

"Imagine," said Thornelow, bemused, "an old Ham ripping about the Med like some eighteenth-century freebooter."

"You know those boats?"

"Indeed. The whole construction program was a typically military sort of thing: today's absolute necessity becoming tomorrow's obsolete white elephant. They were supposed to be a new breed of vessel, designed from experience gained in the Second World War and Korea. They cost three hundred thousand pounds each to build, and before the last one was even delivered, NATO scrapped the whole concept of inshore minesweepers. So there we were. Stuck with an unusual vessel."

"Unusual how?"

"Wooden hulled, and with an extremely shallow draft. Less than six feet as I recall. Built for work in rivers and estuaries."

Stone wondered if a shallow draft had any bearing on the opposite ends of the *Sea Fox*'s intended journey that night: the place it called home or its final destination.

Thornelow took a sip of whiskey, probing his neck as he tried to recall.

"Never a very likable craft, as I remember. Full of minor vexations, mainly their engines. Packman diesels. Moved the craft along at nine knots or so when they were on form, but few ever got over their teething problems before they were given away or withdrawn from service."

"What sort of problems?"

"Overheating. More than an occasional fire."

"I want to know what became of them."

Behind the thick glasses the eyes grew wider. "All eighty?"

"It's important."

For a moment it seemed that Thornelow was about to deny Stone's request. He held up the bottle, offering more whiskey. When Stone declined, he added a drop to his own glass and smiled, that same quick smile, unexpected but welcome.

"Strange the sudden interest in Hams. Just this morning I received a request much like your own, passed down through channels from the top."

That would be the insurance investigator, Christian. Stone was certain.

"But first things first," Thornelow said. He rose and returned the bottle to its place in the cupboard, his movements spare but precise, a ritual finished.

"And we'd best get started. I'm afraid you've given us quite a tangle of string."

Tangle of string. It was that all right. And by the time they'd unraveled it, Stone had also picked himself up a tail.

While he and Thornelow plowed back through the ministry's microfilmed records, Stone moved from a cheap hotel on Red Lion Square into a cheaper one in Victoria.

As he immersed himself in the problem of which among the eighty Ham class minesweepers strewn around the world now like so many feathers had become the *Sea Fox*, his routines would have made following him a cinch.

Returning from the ministry each evening, he habitually bought an *Evening Standard* at the same kiosk near

Picadilly. But this night, walking on, he turned about to go back for a French paper, the *Nice-Matin*.

She was fifty feet behind him, a tall woman, nearly his height, with carrot-red hair peeking out from a scarf tied over her head. She reacted quickly and was gone down the entrance to the nearby underground before Stone made the connection.

He'd seen her the night before in the pub where he'd taken dinner. Stone doubted the coincidence, wondering if the redheaded lady was more of Christian's work.

"Thornelow and I checked each boat in the Ham class, one by one," he told Le Pic and Aggie at the table in the Bar des Marines.

"A lot of boats," said Le Pic.

"Most turned to scrap."

"*Merde*," spat Le Pic in reply, glowering at the two of them. Le Pic had spent his life in marine salvage, but the idea of good boats finished before their time offended his sailor's instincts.

Stone told Le Pic, "Between 1959 and 1967, twenty-two of the Ham class went to the scrapyards, and another sixteen since. Thirty-three vessels were transferred to foreign navies—Australia, Malaysia, India. One became a reserve training ship, another was fitted out for fishery protection."

Le Pic dismissed them with a wave of a meaty hand.

"Where does that leave us?" asked Aggie dispiritedly.

"With four: *Reedham*, *Sidlesham*, *Darsham*, and *Westham*, all put on the disposal list in 1964."

"Disposal list?" Le Pic frowned.

"And subsequently sold by the Board of Trade at public auction," Stone said.

"There's your smuggler," cried Le Pic, "one of those boats."

"Le Pic, it's twenty years since those boats were auctioned. It's a cold trail."

"But even the English keep records," said Le Pic.

"Of the original buyers, yes. Not one of those boats is still owned by the party who originally bought it. Sold, resold, renamed."

"Easier to lose a boat than most people think," said Aggie, "even in the Med. Steal a boat here, sell it off there. The *Pearl Isle* goes missing in Greece and ends up the *Palmyra* in the Bahamas."

"Well, think, woman," badgered Le Pic. "That's your business."

"Oh, shut up," she said, appearing to study the far wall behind Le Pic. Beneath Aggie's flamboyant exterior was a tidy, orderly mind.

Between Gibraltar and the Greek Islands were more than a thousand boats for charter, and not more than half on the right side of reputable. Aggie knew the lot. Knew which were manned by crews more hazard than help. Which were past their prime, or plagued by the owner-skipper disagreements that were the pox of the trade.

"Davey, if there's an old Ham in business legally anywhere in the Med, I haven't heard about it. I'll ask around, but don't get your hopes up. Even if we find it, the ownership of that boat might be so well hidden that you'll never discover who's behind it."

"The Med is big enough to lose any boat," said Le Pic, "if someone wants it lost. Too damn big."

A big ocean. And on it somewhere, Stone was betting, a former Royal Navy minesweeper and his boat the *Pegasus*.

On it, or under it.

# Chapter 9
## Mare Nostrum

"The skipper aboard?" Stone called out. Above him, on the bridge of the *Wunderkind*, a uniformed deckhand was chipping paint. At Stone's question he waved airily toward the line of luxury hotels across the harbor, presenting an almost solid, bright facade to the sea.

Stone found Dolph Hess on the poolside terrace of the Hotel Majestic, indulging his Sunday ritual of straight-up martinis.

Dolph skippered the *Wunderkind*, the largest boat in port and plaything of a Bavarian industrialist who came aboard only a few weeks a year. He was a regular figure in the bars around the port, more unforgettable than most. A blond bear of a man, his charm and courtly manners belonged on the Côte D'Azur of a half-century before, as did the pale twill trousers, foulard, and blue blazer. "And what is a man my age to do?" he insisted. "Prowl the discos in tight jeans and shirt open to my navel?"

He raised his glass in greeting as he saw Stone from across the terrace. It looked like a twig in a bear's paw.

"Absolutely magnificent," said Dolph, happily scan-

ning the extraordinary array of women poolside. Some
young, some old, all tanned, all, in one fashion or
another, expensive. "When I can no longer appreciate
this, I will one night step from the stern of the
*Wunderkind* into the briny." His heavy accent made
English sound like a German dialect. "But I don't
suppose you've tracked me down to share my pleasures.
Sorry about the *Pegasus*, David. Bad luck."

"Luck had nothing to do with it. But thanks."

"The story is everywhere in the port. No secrets here,
my friend."

"I have one," said Stone, letting his eyes drift over
the crowd. In a vague way he wondered if the investigator Christian would trouble to have him watched in
Cannes. "A little part of the story no one else knows."

"Not even Le Pic? He'll be destroyed."

"If I'd told Le Pic, we'd have fought the battle of Le
Muy again in the back room of the Bar des Marines."

In World War II, Le Pic had served with an OSS
Jedburg unit assigned to liaison with the French underground during the Allied invasion of the French Riviera a
month following D-Day. Each anniversary he marched
with old comrades, laid his wreaths, and like the French
of his generation, refused to forget. One word about the
man with the Luger in the uniform of a German U-boat
skipper and Le Pic's blood pressure would have red-
lined.

When Stone told Dolph Hess, the big man listened
with no discernible emotion.

Dolph seldom spoke of the war. Although a bit here,
an item there, gathered in the six years Stone had known
him, all pointed to an impressive battle record.

He'd been a young torpedo lieutenant aboard Guggen-
berger's U-81 when it surfaced off the coast of North
Africa, glimpsed a shadowy target, and loosed a four-

torpedo salvo that sunk the British aircraft carrier *Ark Royal*, one of the two biggest scores of the Mediterranean war. Later he'd received his own U-boat, only to lose it to Allied aircraft during the saturation bombing of German vessels based at Toulon. He ended the war in a second command in the North Sea, long after the hunters had become the hunted. Once, late at night and drinking, Dolph had said, "I survived, but there were no survivors."

Now he shrugged and forced a smile. "Too many people hang onto that war like their best friend. Some like uniforms, Luger pistols too. It means nothing."

Across the terrace, a lovely almond-eyed girl seated with two men caught Stone's eye and waved. Dolph looked around at Stone, not without admiration.

"And what about the scar," said Stone. "L-shaped on one cheek?"

"A dueling scar?"

"Wouldn't that mean something?"

Dolph waved it away. "Fifty years ago a young officer of a certain kind would earn himself a scar like that as a badge of honor. Today it's tattoos and God knows what next. Don't argue with fashion."

"But you admit it was the kind of thing a former German naval officer might have."

"Ah, David . . ." Dolph rubbed his eyes tiredly.

"Just suppose the man aboard the *Sea Fox* was a former U-boat skipper—the gun, uniform, scar, all of it on the level—how do I track him down?"

"To what end?"

"If I find him, I'll find the *Sea Fox*."

"David, listen to me. Forty thousand men served in U-boats during the war, and do you know how many survived? One out of four. In 1941 if you were in U-boats and were twenty-two, as I was, you'd already seen too much. If you were still alive at the age of twenty-five you were finished for a normal life, this I promise you."

It was painful for Dolph, and Stone tried to push it gently. "Which meant how many former skippers to survive?"

"Four or five hundred."

"We'll never trace that many. How about those who served in the Med?"

Dolph ordered them both martinis then leaned back and looked at Stone directly. "Until mid-1941 it was Mussolini's war, his *mare nostrum*."

"But you served here."

"Yes. After the German command realized Mussolini could do nothing he promised and Hitler ordered a few submarines diverted from the Atlantic. Thirty-five, forty at most."

"That would narrow it. One tall U-boat skipper with a dueling scar."

Dolph's rough hand tightened on Stone's arm.

"Do you know what you are asking me?"

"For help, old friend."

"To look back. Is there nothing you'd like to forget?"

"Try, Dolph."

Hess sighed heavily. "Von Richert might know something. A drinking friend from the old times who was on the staff of the German naval command in the Med."

"Can you find him?"

"Find him?" Dolph laughed. "He has populated half of the Italian Riviera with his bastard offspring. Finally married an Italian woman out of guilt and settled in San Remo. I'll pay a visit. For you, David."

"Soon, Dolph."

He shook his head, remembering. "Von Richert and I

used to see each other often, but it's harder now. You know why?"

Something behind Dolph's eyes spoke of martinis in full flood.

"Because he's so damn happy. Him with that Italian wife built like a bus. And grandchildren. A man at peace with his choices. Not like us, David. We're searchers, you and I, never at peace."

Stone didn't argue it.

"I'll go. For you I'll go. If you tell me who is the girl. The Polynesian one that keeps looking our way with the almond eyes."

"You might not want to know."

Dolph grinned, misinterpreting it as a challenge.

"So, you're worried about a little competition. You flatter me."

"Flatter you hell. I know that look."

"The name, David, don't torture me."

It was Dolph who'd once observed that on the Côte d'Azur any sea captain of average looks and modest appetites could sleep with a different woman each night if he wanted to.

In the early years, Stone had found himself testing the assumption with too many women whose passion was equal parts wine and sea air and the danger provided by husbands or lovers never out of sight for long. They blurred in his memory. Hungry mouths, and buttocks pressed against every flat and convenient corner of *Pegasus*'s teakwork. On bunks and beaches, salt water mixed with sweat and a hundred different blends of perfume and woman, all of it somehow draining away his spirit.

Dolph had been right, but he'd missed the essential corollary as it evolved for Stone. On the Côte, a sea captain of average looks and modest appetites could find himself with a different woman each night even if he *didn't* want to.

"Her name is Nani Terangi," said Stone.

"And the two men?"

"Don't know. And guess Nani will forget by tomorrow."

Dolph frowned inquiringly.

"Nani is pure cat," said Stone. "She'll let you feed her and share your bed if she's attracted. But when the mood strikes her, she's gone. For Nani, it's a new life each sunrise."

Dolph looked over at Nani, humming beneath his breath. "I must make the lady's acquaintance."

"The word *hello* will probably do. But Dolph . . ."

"Yes, David."

". . . you'd better be strong."


When he left Dolph Hess, Stone walked the old port, then out along the Plage du Midi. One by one the beach clubs were coming to life, wood paneling and bright canvas sprouting from what only weeks before had been barren sand and a few concrete slabs. The late Easter holiday had brought the first waves of pale tourists down from the overcast north, blinking in the sunlight like nocturnal creatures, and testing the water the local Cannoise wouldn't enter until midsummer.

He cut away from the beach and climbed back through the Suquet, stopping twice for a *petit rouge*. Finally he admitted that if they were any good, he wouldn't know if he were being followed or not.

At least no visible redhead, of that he was certain. Maybe Christian had given up, but Stone wouldn't let himself believe it.

Poor Dolph. Dragging the past along like a trap on his ankle. And you, Stone, grinding it in, needing your answers. Everyone's pal, taking their best and offering little in return.

He said to hell with the wine and had a large *vieux marc*, trying to convince himself that the payoff was always worth anything you did to get it.

# Chapter 10
## Claimed Freight

She awoke to the rhythm of powerful engines.

In the cramped forward cabin the smell of diesel fuel hung in her nostrils, coated her mouth. Her lungs cried for fresh air, but when she tried to move, an invisible hand turned a spike in her head and she felt nausea rise.

She thought they'd bound her hands and feet, but when, with great effort, she moved her head around, she saw that only her right hand had been handcuffed to the bunk.

If she could get to her feet, her mind might stop turning. But as she tried to roll from the bunk, the cabin door opened. "Hey, you'll hurt yourself."

"Creep," she almost managed, but it stuck somewhere behind her tongue.

Carrying a cup of something, he came forward wearing only a narrow bikini.

"Your medicine," Pino said with that beautiful empty smile. "You'll feel better when you drink it."

He looked earnestly into her face, stroked her hair, then moved his hand to her breasts. He lifted her head to help her take the liquid. When she had a good mouthful, she spat it into his face.

His fist cracked across her jaw. The next thing she knew he was pulling down her jeans, turning her over. She heard her panties tear away. Immediately came the sharp sting in her buttock. As the nausea became a floaty numbness, Pino shifted her onto her back. Blurry and distant, she watched helplessly while he stepped out of his bikini. Then he moved next to her, rubbing himself against her bare thigh until he grew hard. "A little kiss and tickle, huh Pol. You feel me, don't you?"

*I don't want to.* She tried to scream, but he smothered her mouth with his. Then he laughed, a malicious laugh that showed perfect teeth.

"Can you feel it, Pol? Can you?"

She didn't answer. She gave in, let his body blend with the nausea, all of it a sickness that one day would pass.


On deck, Yank squinted through the cruiser's windscreen at the ragged coastline ahead.

Still ten miles distant it looked like a collection of purple building blocks in the pre-dawn light. Despite their speed, hammered along by twin turbo diesels, he damned himself for not starting sooner.

Yank always worried. Even when there was no good reason. The bloody island was a nest for cuckoos, mountain men who turned their back on the dark coast ahead. The nearest customs boat was 150 miles to the south, and they'd passed so much juice around through the locals that they could have hidden a stolen aircraft carrier without any trouble.

Still he never made the run with more than one item at a time. Easier to get rid of one, if necessary, than a cabinload. He'd let Bunnerman worry about cabinloads.

From below, Pino climbed up into the main cabin, the bulge in his swim suit abnormally apparent.

"You been stuffing in hankies again?" chided Yank.

"I don't need hankies."

"Just don't bruise the merchandise," Yank warned. He always delivered his items in top shape. God knew what they'd be like when they finally ended up wherever they ended up.

"She's okay," Pino assured him. "Just fine."

"What does it mean?" asked Yank.

"What does what mean?"

"The earring?"

Always right in style, Pino was. If butterflies tattooed on your ass came into fashion, Pino would have one an hour later. Pegged pants, white shoes, whatever was going—Pino had an underground telegraph, the right thing in the right place by sundown.

The latest was a gold earring with a pink stone dangling from a short chain studded in one ear.

Pino tried to shrug off Yank's interest. "It's just, you know . . ."

Yank's eyes were locked on his now. "No, I don't know. Tell me."

"Decoration."

"I thought only fags wore earrings."

"That's in the other ear."

"You sure?" asked Yank. "I think you got your ears mixed up."

A shadow of doubt crossed Pino's eyes. "Get off it, Yank."

"It's pretty anyway. What is it, jade or something?"

"I think so. I don't know."

"Where'd you get it?"

"Bought it in Cannes," said Pino.

"Where in Cannes? Maybe I'll get me one. We'll look like twins."

"Just a place." Pino looked out at the island growing nearer.

"Pino, are you happy in your work?"

"Sure, Yank."

"Good money, right? You'd never earn anything close hustling old broads in the casinos."

Pino was more than uneasy. He didn't understand Yank. Only that there was something bad about him, something you could feel. Really bad.

"Sure I like the work. What are you talking about?"

So smoothly that Pino barely noticed, Yank reached forward and flicked on the autopilot. In the same motion he brought his hand around and struck Pino with the side of a doubled-up fist that might well have been lined with metal.

Pino started to sag. But Yank was already on him, jerking him upright by his hair. With his left hand he took hold of the earring and with one firm pull tore it through the lobe of Pino's ear.

Pino howled, blood pouring from the wound.

"I've always wanted to do that to one of you jerks."

"Jesus," whispered Pino, in pain.

"But you bleed on this deck and you'll lick it up."

Pino knew it wasn't an idle threat. Yank stood over him, waving the earring with its pink stone.

"You pinched this off one of the girls."

"I didn't."

"What did I tell you? Never to do that. Never."

"Okay, so once I did. Hey, I'm bleeding to death."

"You'll bleed all right." Angrily Yank tossed the earring into the sea. "You ever keep one thing that can tie us to any of those items and you'll find out how much you can bleed. Understand?"

"I understand, Yank."

"You think an ear bleeds. You figure out what that thing between your legs will do. 'Cause it's next."

"It was just an earring, Yank."

"You think about what I said."

In the aroma-filled kitchen of the Bar des Marines, Le Pic shoved a plate of cold sausage beneath Stone's nose and plunked down a bottle of *vin ordinaire*.

"A man needs to eat. And drink. The wine is very important."

Le Pic nudged the three-legged dog under a table piled high with sea urchin, and joined the cook Basso in cleaning them. Basso used the meaty veins of the coral-colored flesh to make fresh *rouille*, the peppery condiment to accompany his thick *soupe des poissons*.

"Le Pic, I'm going back to the place where I was found ashore."

"Why? To search for footprints in the sand?"

"Because I'm gambling that where I was found is close to the place they took *Pegasus* to finish the *Sea Fox*'s mission." He spread a chart of the western Mediterranean on the table. "Here's the point where I boarded the *Sea Fox*, and here is where I was found ashore thirty-six hours later."

"More than two hundred miles."

"I didn't swim it, Le Pic. Which might mean the *Sea Fox* was inbound when it had engine trouble. And how does a smuggler run?"

"He runs fast. He runs at night if he can."

"Which could mean a straight-line course between starting point and destination."

"It's possible."

"If where I was found ashore is close to the *Sea Fox*'s destination . . ." He traced backward from the coast of

Africa, through the point at sea where he'd boarded the
*Sea Fox*, and continued the line northeast across the
Med. The line touched the southern coast of Corsica.
". . . this could be home base."

"All well and good," agreed Le Pic. "Except, slide
your starting point a few miles one way or another and
your straight line puts you in Sardinia, or the Italian
mainland, or France. And if your smuggler didn't fly
straight like the bird, maybe Greece or Turkey, someplace where a little money in the right hand keeps the
mouth closed, eh?"

"That's the question, Le Pic. How I got where I did.
How far from there to where they sunk the *Pegasus* after
they were finished with her, with me, and with Devlin
and the Gabrieles bound up aboard. And I got lucky."

Lucky in the form of a shadowy figure of a girl coming
to him in the dark crew's cabin, freeing his bonds. Then
the explosion and the sound of in-rushing water.

"The only known item is the beach where I was
found, and I'm praying it puts me on the trail of
*Pegasus*."

"You hear him, Basso," Le Pic said, speaking to the
cook while his eyes remained on Stone. "This one man
trying to do this great thing by himself. Too proud to ask
his friends for help."

With a knife Basso deftly slit an *oursin*, not appearing
to hear. He was tall for a Frenchman, over six feet, with
sloping, slab-muscled shoulders and a brawler's face.
Calcium deposits puffed each eye; a thin moustache
covered a ragged scar. He wiped his hands on an apron
already smeared with flesh and bloody fingermarks and
dug another *oursin* from the basket.

For years Basso had slept in the city's parks and on its
beaches, when he wasn't a guest of the local police in the
small jail on the Avenue de Grasse. During the Algerian

War he'd been a para, a true warrior Le Pic called him. When the warriors were no longer wanted, Basso had made his separate surrender to *vin ordinaire*, until Le Pic found him and put him to work. The Frenchman was silent and withdrawn, and Stone could not remember ever hearing him saying a word, even under Le Pic's most barbed tirades.

"Maybe this sea captain thinks he is a warrior like you, *mon petit*," said Le Pic, continuing to speak to Basso for Stone's benefit.

Stone countered, "Or it could be I was remembering something a courageous salvage master once told me about the times in a man's life when it is better to do something, even if it turns out to be the wrong thing, than nothing. To act, that is the important thing, this man told me, and worth the risk."

"A thoughtful man," said Le Pic after a moment. "But I'm not sure I'd agree with him."

"Of course that was before he became settled in his ways."

"Old, you mean. The devil take you, David Stone!" Angrily, Le Pic tore off his apron and hurled it across the kitchen. He stood glaring a moment at Stone, hands bunched defiantly on his hips. "You'll need a boat."

"Aggie's working on it."

"A real boat," said Le Pic sharply. "You'll take the *Marie-Hélène*.

The *Marie-Hélène* was Le Pic's boat, a sturdy, double-ended motor sailor, small enough for Stone to manage singlehanded.

"It's settled," said Le Pic. "Or I add the best part of you to this fine *rouille*." He made a sharp, hooked stroke with his knife.

A refusal would have been halfhearted at best. The *Marie-Hélène* was a perfect choice and they both knew it. Le Pic waved him away, fearing the embarrassing spectacle of having to endure David Stone's thanks.

At that moment a fisherman stuck his head into the kitchen and jerked his head toward Stone. "Some people out here asking for you." He gave Stone a slow wink that brought a frown from Le Pic.

Stone walked into the bar to find a man he recognized and a woman he didn't. She was smallish, dark-haired, and in her early twenties, he judged. Until closer he saw the fine lines around her moss-green eyes, and something sure in them that young women didn't often have.

She watched his approach with a direct appraisal that seemed to learn something from his every stride.

"No, Mr. Stone, we've never met," she said. "I'm Kits Maitland. I'm hoping we have something in common."

"There's one thing," replied Stone slowly, "but I'm not sure it's any way to begin."

The man with her, gaunt and waiting, was the insurance investigator, Christian.

# Chapter 11
## Little Birds

In the ten days preceding her entrance into the Bar des Marines, Kits Maitland had ridden an emotional roller-coaster, from terror to panic to frustration and back again. It had left her mistrustful of her own judgment as never before in her life, and scared stiff.

The turning point had been her encounter with a scruffy young Englishman named Kevin.

With as much calm as she could muster, she'd begun her search for her daughter at what seemed the logical place: the police station in the French beach town where Polly had last been seen. It turned out to be a waste of time, all the more painful because the police tried to pretend otherwise.

At the *hôtel de police* she was ushered into the office of a slim, uniformed officer who explained in broken English that the police of all France were searching for Polly. "But as yet . . ." Palms upraised, he gave that shrug she'd lately seen too much of.

He returned Polly's things, stuffed ajumble into a new suitcase with its lock broken. He gave Kits his calling card after jotting down a number he assured her was private. Then he suggested two other things: first, putting Polly's photograph in the national press. "I can arrange it. Many parents do this when their children are missing."

"You make it sound like a lost bicycle." She was angry at his matter-of-factness. She tried to rationalize it by arguing that the police dealt daily with tragedy. She was ready to give him the benefit of the doubt until the policeman's second suggestion: that they meet later for coffee.

Then there was the heated, trans-Atlantic phone call from Mark.

"Kits, listen, I've leaned on Al Meacham, and he is going to rattle somebody in the State Department to put pressure on the French at the highest levels of government."

Al Meacham was a congressman, and Mark's frequent golfing partner.

"I don't want the highest levels of government. I want somebody out on the street doing what I am doing. Most of all, I don't want publicity."

"Obviously you've thought this out."

"I've thought if somebody has taken Polly—"

"Now Kits," he broke in, "we just don't know."

"If she is in the hands of somebody, and they realize she's the subject of a big manhunt, they might . . ." She hesitated; to say it somehow made the possibility even greater. ". . . They might kill her instead of risking prosecution. I don't want it."

"Very wise." He gave her a report from the private detectives, which added up to nothing worth reporting. Plus the name of a local contact, an agency called Cabinet Jobert in Nice.

"But it takes time," he soothed. Mark seldom said the wrong thing, but the word *time* touched a nerve.

"Why is it I can't impress upon you or anyone else what time is worth."

"Easy, Kits."

"Each night Polly sleeps somewhere. She is out there, Mark, with someone, or alone and in trouble. I almost wish she had been kidnapped for ransom. It would be something tangible we could deal with."

With an audible sigh Mark said, "Look, I'll catch a flight over on the weekend."

"What's wrong with now?"

She knew she sounded the shrew. Nagging wasn't normally her tactic. But she was convinced that there were times in your life when you let everything and everyone on the periphery be damned, and took care of yourself and your own.

"I'll be there on the weekend," he repeated.

Thus had she set out on her own investigation, with only the vaguest idea of where to begin.

First, she went through Polly's things, item by item. She listed what she could remember seeing in Polly's school closet. She had hoped to determine what Polly was wearing, but soon gave it up as hopeless. So many of her clothes were new with French or Italian labels; it was like rummaging through the belongings of a stranger. And in a way it was. Almost six months had passed since she'd seen Polly, six months in the life of a fifteen-year-old, full of change and promise. They'd slipped by for Kits with scarcely a clear memory.

One thing she was positive about from their absence: a pair of pink-coral earrings, a gift from Burt for Polly's thirteenth birthday. They'd been fashioned from a coral branch Burt had basketed himself, when he worked for Maui Divers just after he and Kits were married. Polly never took them off. Lost, one girl with pink earrings.

Cabinet Jobert, the local private detective agency, was

on the third floor of a creaking office building near the Palais de Justice in the old part of Nice.

Jobert himself led her into his office, and gestured her to a chair with a courtly bow. He was in his fifties, with the heavy dark features so common in the south of France. As he seated himself across from her, his left arm remained straight at his side. He used his right hand to touch the papers, pen, and pack of cigarettes on his desk, as though making sure all were still there.

"You know what I want." Her unsatisfactory encounter with the police had left her patience in short supply.

"Of course, Madame Maitland."

"Have you learned anything about Polly?"

"At this point, nothing more than the police."

"Is finding a fifteen-year-old American girl wandering the Côte that difficult?"

Jobert looked up severely. His eyes were dark and feminine and, she thought, too sad-looking.

"You are making a great many assumptions, madame. If she were wandering the Côte, as you say, sooner or later the police would come upon her. An identity check among the young people that sleep on beaches . . . something."

"What are you telling me?"

"Only that it may be more serious than wandering."

"Serious in what way?" When Jobert didn't answer, she said, "Why is it I can't get anyone to tell me what they think?"

Jobert shifted in his chair. "Because very often the people who sit across this desk don't really want to know what I think, don't really want the truth. All they want are answers that absolve them from guilt. Answers that leave them blameless in the eyes of their neighbors. I am often lied to by people who claim they want my help.

France is a country of the rich, and the middle-class. No self-respecting Frenchman would ever admit to being poor. Pride, Madame Maitland, hides a great deal in France."

"Well I'm not French, and I don't give a damn about pretenses. I am trying to find out the truth. It's a simple question: What happened to my daughter?"

"The truth," said Jobert. "All right, I will tell you the truth."

"That's the most encouraging thing I've heard in days."

"Please reserve judgment, madame. Until I finish."

He turned and removed a thick folder from the table behind him and placed it in front of her.

"This is one possibility. Look for yourself."

Kits opened the folder, and spent a moment or so leafing through the pages. Each contained a photograph, some glossy, others cut from newspapers. Above each was the single word, *disparition*. The photographs were entirely of young girls.

"All missing?" asked Kits.

"Missing this year. Missing and cared about enough to force their parents into the embarrassing task of dealing with the police. A humbling experience for anyone." His remark was thick with irony.

Jobert gestured to other folders behind him. "That is last year, the year before."

"So many?"

"In western Europe an epidemic. Each year in round numbers, about fifty thousand young women between the ages of ten and twenty-five disappear."

"But why, who?"

"The obvious reasons, of course. Runaways, wanderers, as you say, who come home when the thrill passes.

Others slip away with bartenders or commercial travelers. Yes, it still happens."

"I don't believe Polly has run off with anyone."

"And there are those, like your daughter Polly, who just . . . disappear."

He waited, watching her with the sad dark eyes, estimating, she thought, just how much she could handle.

"And what happens to them?" Kits asked, holding her voice even. "I want to know. Terrorism, kidnapping, what?"

"It has the sound of the Middle Ages."

"I don't understand."

"*Traite des blanches*, we call it. White slavery. Girls, pretty young girls to fill the brothels of Africa and the Middle East. That's where too many of our *disparitions* end up."

"Abducted."

"Lured, Mrs. Maitland. Often by their own dreams."

"Oh, come on," said Kits, losing patience.

"Bogus employment agents promising money and travel. Poor girls hoping to become hotel maids in some distant romantic city. Ballet agents, talent bookers, the bait is endless."

"And after they've gone for the bait?"

"A pattern surprisingly similar. Break the will, in one fashion or another. Beating, starvation, and of course the drugs. Shall I continue?"

For a moment Kits was silent. "If she has disappeared like that, what are the odds of finding Polly before . . . it's too late."

"Not good," said Jobert. "You wanted the truth."

"How bad is not good."

"For every ten girls who disappear in this fashion, perhaps one will be found alive. After a few months in the hands of the sex slavers, Mrs. Maitland, most don't wish to be found."

She'd begun then, clawed at by a fear she'd never before known, not even in her most terrifying moments undersea. Fear, the iron spider, Burt had called it.

She started working her way along the Côte, seeking the hangouts where people of Polly's age passed their time. She felt foolish in the beginning, showing her daughter's photo to bartenders, waiters, anyone who would look and listen. Quickly she became more brazen, more direct. Polly was at risk and the knowledge fueled Kits with inexhaustible energy tapped from a source deep within.

She quickly discovered that even in the bigger towns, Cannes, Antibes, Nice, only a few discos and teenage meeting places appealed to tourists. These were little different in feel from their counterparts in Hollywood or Balboa, the places she'd haunted when she was Polly's age.

Initially she made a grave mistake, trying to dress young, to seem part of the scene by wearing jeans and a single thick braid down her back. She'd thought she was carrying it off pretty well. Until the looks she received told her she wasn't fooling anyone.

The charade ended when a waiter finally obliged in calling her mademoiselle instead of madame, but his voice said it straight enough. She was mutton dressed like lamb. There came a time, she guessed, when you had to accept the truth; that you are no longer of the younger generation, and age has built a wall of difference behind you. From her view of the current youthful lifestyle, she wasn't really sorry to be on her side of the wall.

At a place called the Ancre in Cannes she met the scruffy young Englishman, Kevin.

He listened to her story about Polly, more attentively than most, while consuming an enormous quantity of beer she gladly paid for.

"You seem like a nice person," he said, heavy with sincerity. He was twenty, perhaps, with dirt being the most notable element in his physical appearance. Dirty jeans, dirt beneath his fingernails, dirty blond hair seemingly cut by a lawn mower. When he smiled, the gap between his teeth gave him a canine look. If someone had told her just one week before that she would ever be desperate enough to offer her trust to Kevin, she would have known they were mad. "Look, I know this bloke who knows just about everybody. Let me have a little chat."

He took Polly's photo and returned a quarter of an hour later, giving Kits an encouraging grin. "He may have something. Come on, his apartment is close by."

If she'd been in the proper frame of mind to analyze it, she'd never have gone. As easy to talk in a bar as an apartment. But Kevin never left an idle second in the conversation to give her thinking time. At the stairway leading down from the cobbled street, he stopped.

Several small restaurants were still open. From the steps of a nearby building a *clochard* watched them, drink-reddened eyes staring out from a ravaged face.

"Down there." Kevin pointed. Stairs of uneven stone led down to another, even narrower, street.

"Picturesque, isn't it?" said Kevin.

"Very. What does this friend do for a living?"

"Oh, this and that. You know. I had to wake him up, so he'll probably want a little something for the trouble."

"What would you suggest?"

"A couple hundred francs, if you have it." He looked over in question. She nodded. Kevin grinned, his snaggletoothed grin. "But only if he's any help. That's fair enough, I reckon."

"Yes, it would be."

The friend was a tallish youth about the same age as Kevin. Olive skinned, rail thin, with unruly permed hair. He was waiting in the partly opened doorway of an old apartment building not more than a dozen feet in width. On the door was a brass knocker in the shape of a small human hand.

"This way," he said, nodding for Kits to enter. He stepped aside to let her pass. His cologne was heavy, sickening. "I've something to show you."

A narrow hallway paved with small colored tiles led to a curving stairway.

"Up the stairs?" she asked.

"No," he said. "Here will do."

He shut the door, leaving Kevin outside in the street. A knife in his hand pointed menacingly. "Your bag. If you scream I'll cut your throat."

A moment later Kevin and his thin friend were gone. Along with her purse and the equivalent of three hundred dollars, American.

She leaned against the building, the stink of her assailant's cologne still in her nostrils. She felt stupid and old and foolish. She wanted to cry, to let it out, but found she was too angry. The money was nothing; it was the lie about Polly, the hopes he'd raised, that hurt.

She went back to the Ancre praying Kevin, in his arrogance, would stop in for a drink of celebration. She wasn't sure what she'd do if he did, except raise holy hell.

She waited until closing, watching two young men from Kevin's same scruffy mold play darts, feeling utterly defeated. She didn't belong here, trying this.

"Sorry folks, that's it," the bartender called out in a

broad English accent. When she lingered on, he began to look at her in an appraising way.

She was reluctantly leaving when a bulletin board next to the door caught her eyes. She'd missed it in the earlier crowd, but now it jumped out at her.

Tacked up in the top right-hand corner was a note. A note in bright red ink, written in both English and French: "Young girl, experienced with boats, seeks immediate employment."

The handwriting was Polly's.

Early the next morning she went again to Cabinet Jobert, her mind racing with the thought that she had uncovered the first lead. Herself. She didn't intend to entrust it to the police.

Waiting in Jobert's office was another man. Tall, gaunt-faced, rising to address her in English when Jobert introduced them. "I thought you two should talk," the detective said.

# Chapter 12
## A Time For Whales

Now in the Bar des Marines, standing squarely in front of Stone, Kits Maitland held out her hand. The touch of a warm, moist palm left the barest scent of her perfume.

Le Pic emerged from the kitchen to watch the transaction narrowly.

"Your friends want coffee?" he grunted to Stone.

"Tea would be lovely," said Christian, mildly amused at Stone's surprise.

"Take the table in back," said Le Pic with a flick of his head. "I'll get the fine china."

"We've met before, in a way," Kits said.

Stone doubted it, but replied, "Have we?" He was sure he would have remembered.

The moss-green eyes never left him. Brown flecks in their irises caught the light like sparks set off from within; he had the impression she was aware of every second, every single thing that was happening around her. It was a bright quality that made him feel leaden and dull. Only her voice was a window to something darker within. It faltered at first, then grew in strength as though the very sound of it gave her reassurance.

"Some years ago you wrote to a professor I worked with, asking about aggressive tendencies in whales. I answered your letter."

"I do remember," said Stone, for a moment forgetting Christian's presence. "I learned more about whales in two pages than I had in weeks of prowling a library."

"Some things you can learn about in a library, Mr. Stone, but real aggression isn't one of them. I followed your story in the paper . . . about losing your wife and boat."

"It didn't stay news very long."

Christian said, "He has another quest these days, don't you, Stone?"

Stone turned on him. "What do you want here?"

"We've come to ask a favor," he replied mildly.

Le Pic arrived with tea in steaming mugs, and a coffee for Stone. He put a bottle of calvados and three glasses in the center of the table and retreated to watch, raising an eyebrow toward Stone that said *Beware.*

"Please, Mr. Stone," Kits urged. "It's important to all of us, and won't take long."

"I have some photographs," said Christian. "I wonder if you'd take a look."

He was already removing several thick sheets of paper from his briefcase. He pushed them across toward Stone.

Five photographs, two clipped from newspapers, all young girls with short, dark hair.

"I thought your dream girl might be among them."

Stone shot Christian a glance, but Kits touched his arm. "Please, Mr. Stone."

Kits felt the sudden tightness in her chest as Stone took a long moment studying the photos. His expression revealed nothing.

Christian strained forward.

"Is she there or isn't she, man? It may be the

beginning of what you're after, don't you see? What we're all after."

Stone touched one of the photos. "This one, maybe. Hard to tell from a photograph."

Visible relef swept over Kits. Stone wondered how it all connected: her presence, the picture of the girl, the disappearance of *Pegasus*.

Christian said, "Her name is Robin Worthing. Sixteen years old, born in Leeds, England. Disappeared two months ago with another girl named Wendy Asher, somewhere on the Côte d'Azur."

"The others?"

"These two are French, likewise missing." Christian chuckled, and tapped the final two photographs. "My nieces, both safe at home. I thought I'd throw a curve as you Americans say."

He caught Stone's doubtful look. "Listen, an investigator with his mind made up isn't much good. Before the hearing, and since, I've tried to tear your story apart. But it doesn't tear easily. I think you've stumbled onto more than you know."

"Have I?" Stone looked inquiringly toward Kits.

"My daughter is missing," she filled in. "One among many as it turns out. Fifteen years old, last seen in Juan-les-Pins. She was looking for work on a boat."

Stone could feel how much the admission pained her; the things omitted that might have included her own failings.

"Not an uncommon pattern," Christian remarked to Stone. "When I began investigating that story of yours, I had three channels I could follow. First there was you, your history. Then the boat you boarded that night." When Stone made no comment, he added, "And thirdly, the dark-haired girl. The girl seemed to be the thinnest item of evidence, but something about it haunted me. I had no idea then where it would lead.''

"And where has it led?''

"I understand your impatience,'' said Kits, anticipating him. Her eyes filled with anger, held in. "I know what time is worth, believe me.''

"I'm sorry,'' said Stone. "It's just that Christian here brings out the best in me.''

"Don't apologize yet, Captain. Wait until you find out what nasty work your boat was used for.'' Her glance jumped to Christian. "Tell him.''

Stone saw something else behind her eyes now, the glint of terror.

Christian said, "The sex trade, Stone, alive and well and flourishing in the Med. *Traite des blanches*, white slavery, whatever name you want to give it. The trade in young girls.''

"You mean the boat I boarded that night—the *Sea Fox*—was running girls?''

"That's exactly what I mean,'' said Christian. "The same cargo they transferred to your *Pegasus* before making for the coast of Africa.''

Kits felt her breath catch as she waited for Stone's response. She wanted Stone with them for reasons she hadn't yet fully analyzed. She felt the hope drain away when his head made a firm shake in the negative.

"I'm sorry, I can't help you.''

Christian flushed crimson. "Have you heard nothing I've said, man?''

"All of it,'' Stone replied levelly. "I've lost a boat. I intend to find it, just that.''

"But it's all related, don't you see?''

"Is it?'' asked Stone. "You're the one who said an investigator with his mind made up isn't worth a damn. One girl aboard the *Sea Fox* and you have her kidnapped and headed for the Bullring of Basra with a holdful of friends. Hell, she could have been aboard by choice, the captain's lady, anything."

From his vantage point, Le Pic saw something catch behind the gaze of the gaunt Englishman. He looked sick, Le Pic judged, a sick man. But, then, the English always looked sick.

"All right," Christian argued, "you've given me my words. Now I'll give you your own. From the inquiry, Stone. From the girl you've just identified, whispering to you in a dark cabin."

"I know what she said," Stone cut in, but Christian didn't falter.

"*Help us.* Those were her words. *Us,* Stone. Does that sound like a girl aboard a boat of her own choosing, and alone."

Stone rose, glaring down at Christian from his full height. For the first time in Le Pic's memory the Bar des Marines was in absolute silence.

"I'm sorry," said Stone, turning from the table. He pushed open the outer door and stepped into the bright morning sunlight.

Low and stunned, Kits murmured, "Why, the sonofabitch."

But Christian was already on his feet, swaying like a drunken man before he steadied himself against the table edge. "I will not accept that. Not this side of hell I won't."

As Kits started after the two men, she felt a hand gently grip her arm. "Let them go," said Le Pic at her side.

"But if there is one chance he can help find Polly . . ."

"Let them go," Le Pic repeated softly. "When a man's temper is like that, nothing good will come of it. Wait.

Let those two bang their stubborn heads together for a while. You understand this about men, I think."

"Among the things I wish I didn't."

"These whales you studied. I want to hear about them," said Le Pic.

"This isn't the time for whales."

"You tell Le Pic about whales," he said, "and I will tell you about David Stone."

# Chapter 13
## Alliance

In the bright, hard sunlight, Christian saw Stone walking fifty yards ahead near a low breakwater.

He hurried after him, heart pounding, then slowed as the strength drained from his legs. An ignoble end, to collapse on the pavement of some Riviera fleshpot like an aging tourist bounding up the Spanish Steps to a final coronary.

"Damn you, Stone! Give me a minute. It's worth a minute, I promise."

Ahead, Stone turned to face him. "Christian, you're worse than a case of the crabs."

"I wouldn't know, really. If you mean tenacious, I'll consider it praise." Christian's cheeks hollowed in an icy smile. "Odd, how we uncover the disturbing parts of ourselves in others and then chastise them for it. You've rather a dogged streak yourself, which is precisely why I want a deal."

"To do what?"

He moved closer, but stopped, not pressing too near. "A deal to quit fighting each other. We're chasing the same thing. Only there is more to it than we thought."

"You mean the missing girls?"

"Yes, and something more, something I haven't been able to uncover yet. The economics of the whole thing aren't right."

"What do you care about any of it?"

"The prerogative of a dogged old man. Who happens to work for himself. Stone, I have a story. Something to help you understand. About a Scotland Yard policeman I once knew."

"You were with Scotland Yard?"

"That's when I met him. A good family man, but strict. By the book on the job, and difficult at home because of it. It isn't easy being a policeman, or living with one."

Stone said nothing. Christian ran a finger across a gaunt cheek, not quite looking at Stone.

"Well, his daughter was sixteen when she ran away. He admitted he'd been stern, too much so. She wasn't abducted, not like the Maitland woman's daughter. But when a girl that age goes with nothing, no money, just the feeling that she has to run, the wrong people find her. They have a nose for it, can recognize a girl in flight the way my policeman friend could make a dealer on the street, or a junkie looking for a score."

"Then he knew where to search."

"But he didn't, don't you see? He never did find her. The first year passed, then part of a second. We all did our best for him on the street and through official channels, but the girl was gone." Christian stopped.

"Maybe that's the worst part," said Stone. "Not knowing what happened, no clean ending."

"I would have thought so. I can understand how you might feel that way, with the business about the *Mary Anne*. Never pinning the blame on anyone, no one brought to justice."

Stone was silent.

"But my policeman friend did find an end to the story. He was working vice, and one night he raided one of those porno shops that are taking the life out of Soho. It was run by a Chinaman who had turned his restaurant into a sex shop because his restaurant had been the last decent place on the street and he was going broke. Was he to blame?"

"What happened?"

"Do you know what a snuff film is?"

"I've heard about them. Someone, usually a girl, is brutalized and then killed on film."

"A lot of them are faked of course. Most come out of South America. The vilest part of the sex trade." Christian paused, but went on after a moment. "The Chinaman was selling snuff films, and it was my fellow officer's duty to view them and make his report."

"Don't tell me . . ."

"I'm afraid so. At first he didn't recognize her. Like so many of those films, it was made in a hut or a garage somewhere, with a girl, obviously drugged, being led into a room. Poor lighting, grainy film, the usual. Except this one was in Super Eight with sound."

"The policeman's daughter."

"Worn and puffy-faced from drugs and barely able to stand. They began by cutting off the fingers of her left hand. A man with a hatchet. One by one they—"

"You don't have to tell this, Christian."

"One by one they cut off both arms, two men working with hatchets and knives, and when she'd screamed herself out and become almost comatose and of no further dramatic value, they slit her throat."

For a full moment Christian said nothing, watching Stone with blank eyes.

"What happened to your friend?"

"It finished him. He knew if he tried to continue he'd be no good as a policeman. He would have become a vigilante in police uniform, using his position and his job to avenge. He left his wife and later turned to insurance investigation." He paused. "I know what you're thinking. But he was a friend, just that. The thing with being an insurance investigator, it's like a surgeon who has seen too much and becomes a dermatologist. The patients don't usually die. Do you understand? It limits your emotional exposure."

"Then why have you involved yourself in this? People are already dead, and it still isn't finished."

"Quite simply, because I can't help myself. Stone, don't you see, I distrust the law as much as you do. Not the law itself. There are enough laws to slice anything and anyone four ways from Sunday and even provide justice if those who administer it are so inclined. They're the ones I distrust. The good, solid people wanting their promotions and security and guarantees. Why should they take chances in someone else's interest?"

Stone's gaze was steady on Christian, that same disturbing intensity he'd seen during the hearing.

"You know the worst, Stone? They work nine to five. Punch in, punch out, get through the day, ignore what they must if it threatens. I'll say this for the people we're up against: they don't stop at nine to five. Just like you. You'll keep hammering at this the way you did with the sinking of the *Mary Anne*. Hammering away until something shakes loose."

"Sounds as if you've had a religious experience."

For an instant the fire went out of Christian's eyes. "Close enough. Does it matter? The important thing is that working our separate ways, but together, we'll get what we're after. All of us."

"Including Kits Maitland?"

"If there's a chance, if it's not too late. Sooner or later we'll have them, you and I."

"The elusive, ever-present *they*."

"Preying on human weakness, Stone. They traded on your sense of responsibility as a captain to come to their rescue. Look at their victims. Girls too young or too pained to know what they've stepped into, until it's too late." He paused, then said, "You're going back, aren't you? Back to where you were found." Christian's eyes were shiny with certainty.

Stone said, "If, as you claim, the *Sea Fox* was running a load of girls, then they were inbound, heading for the north African coast."

"I'm not offering you something for nothing, Stone. Oh, no. I've contacts among the police—informers, sources of information you couldn't touch in a year of trying."

"And what has it got you?"

"A line on this whole dirty business, for openers. You didn't see the sex-trade angle, didn't even suspect it."

Stone gave him a grudging nod.

"Second, I'm on the track of our mysterious *Sea Fox*."

Christian watched him carefully, laughing when he saw Stone's doubt. The laughter drew the skin more tightly across the hollows of his face.

Stone couldn't find anything about Christian to like. It was impossible to imagine him in a moment of passion, whispering to a loved one or trusting what he might hear in return. A solitary man—driven by what, Stone didn't know. A hundred years ago he would have been a bounty hunter, skilled and alone, trusting only his weaponry. The weapons were different now, but Christian was still a hunter.

"Chasing the *Sea Fox* is a dead end," said Stone. "I tried it."

"You didn't go far enough."

"Far enough to narrow it down to four boats sold at auction."

"I know," said Christian. "I've narrowed it down to one."

Christian stared out past the breakwater, seeing something other than ocean and blue sky. After a few seconds he shook himself, reaching into his memory with difficulty. "Of the four on your list, one is presently undertaking a marine survey for the Tanzanian government. A second ended up with an Italian company, supposedly working as a coastal freighter in the Adriatic. For three months it has been under impound by the authorities in Ravenna."

"Smuggling," said Stone.

Christian agreed. "Apparently Her Majesty's government built a handy little vessel."

"That's two."

"The third is in a Red Sea boatyard full of bullet holes. Found adrift. Naturally the owner refuses to claim it. Arab or Israeli, it hardly matters."

"Which brings us to number four." Stone waited.

Christian hesitated, uncertain for an instant. "I don't know where it is, physically. But I traced it from the original buyer to a Belgian industrialist who dumped it for a song two years ago."

"To whom?"

"A Swiss lawyer named Bertrand."

"The Swiss love expensive toys. But I'm not sure a one-hundred-and-twenty-ton minesweeper would be all that much fun."

"Acting on behalf of another party is my guess."

"What's Bertrand's reputation?"

"A lawyer is a lawyer, good fellow. Straight by all appearances. An office in Geneva. But unless he is caught in a swindle or murders his business partner, he is protected by Swiss law from idle investigation, as is his client." Christian shrugged. "I'll keep at it."

"A Swiss lawyer in Geneva is a long way from the *Pegasus*."

"Yes, but related and the very reason we should work together. Share what we learn, each from our opposite ends."

"And you'll do that? Share everything you find out, no matter how small?"

"Certainly." Stone could hear the mental fine print. They both knew that any alliance between them would exist only as long as it worked to the penalty of neither.

After a moment, Stone said, "On one condition. You call off the readhead. And her pals."

Christian's expression changed slightly. "I'm afraid I—"

"The one following me around London. And I've had a strange watched feeling here in Cannes."

"Describe her."

"Tall, my height. Thirty maybe. Not ugly, not pretty. Bright red hair."

"Or a wig. The easiest thing to change."

"It was red the two times I saw her."

"Why would I have you tailed? The things I've wanted to know weren't to be learned following you along a street."

"If she isn't yours, then whose?"

Christian sighed. "I suppose I'd better work on that as well."

* * *

The table was set for two. It rested with a handful of others on rough board planking spread out along the narrow beach in front of the Bar des Marines.

Kits thought food would be the last thing to attract her. She hadn't done more than nibble in days. But as she sat there across from Le Pic, the plates began to arrive, course by course, each with an aroma like nothing she'd ever smelled before. And for the first time in longer than she could remember, the pangs of honest hunger stirred in her stomach.

Here in the sun, a part of her was coming newly alive. Even before Polly, the work of the last year had driven a wedge between her body and mind. Now, giving herself over to the incredible smells and tastes, she began to rediscover her own senses—two of them at least.

When the big, slope-shouldered cook, Basso, served plates of grilled red fish, Le Pic watched her dig in.

"Doesn't your man feed you?" he asked, studying her with a wily squint.

"*Mullus barbatus*," said Kits, avoiding the question. "Good. Really good."

"They're *rouget*, caught this morning. Don't get fancy with Le Pic."

He refilled her glass with a sharp, dry wine. "Now, where was I?" he said.

"Where you've been for an hour. Talking about David Stone."

"I talk too much about everyone, everything. What else for a man my age to do, but eat, drink and talk." His smile wrinkled the corners of his eyes. "I tell you, it is not until a fish opens his mouth that he gets into trouble. A man should remember this."

"I've enjoyed it, Le Pic, truly. You don't know how much."

"The key to David, I think"—he paused, scratching at

his jaw while he found the words—"is patience. Not to ask things too quickly."

The three-legged dog hobbled over from the bar to nudge itself under Le Pic's feet. He pushed it away, but it came back tenaciously. The second time he reached down to scratch its neck.

"I didn't ask much of Stone," Kits protested, "not really."

"You must understand. David has lost his boat, with friends aboard. And now, when he is ready to set off in search of one thing—"

"Search for what? Stone is leaving?"

Le Pic heard something in her voice, but went on, "And now instead of his boat you tell him about this *traite des blanches* and your own missing daughter."

With measured calm, Kits put down her fork. "Because time is against me, that's why. I was hoping Stone would help."

She'd almost said *I need Stone to help*, but checked herself. She'd sensed a quality in David Stone, a determination others could feel. She'd seen it echoed in small, important ways by those in the Bar des Marines. It was one of Burt's Great Theories that there were only two places worth a damn for a woman to learn about a man: in bed, and in a room full of his friends. She'd discovered a few more subtle tests of her own, including a minimum three days alone without telephone or TV. She'd once passed such a weekend in Vermont with Mark in the middle of a snowstorm that had left them without electricity. What had evolved was a rather classic case of anxiety-depression she'd heretofore only witnessed in laboratory rats.

In the Bar des Marines she'd been aware of the way others reacted to Stone, the way the fishermen listened when he spoke, watched even when he said nothing. By nature, he was a focal point. Even silent, as he often was, Stone was catalytic, the kind of man who made things happen by whatever chemistry; it was a quality Mark was especially quick to recognize and value, and one which he tried to emulate without the true stuff of its substance.

Allied with Kits and Christian, Stone would make things happen.

Kits didn't want to dwell on the other discovery she had made about David Stone because she was still too surprised by it. But there'd come a moment when she'd found herself watching David Stone and wondering what he would be like in bed.

Moving in a largely male world, Kits was used to dealing with the ever-present appraisal and accompanying nonverbal messages that signal interest or indifference. She wasn't sure she'd ever consciously set out to bed Mark Tyler, but from the first she'd found something fascinating in his predatory calculation and self-assurance.

With Mark she'd known that every move would come at the right moment in the right way, and that she wouldn't be embarrassed by any stumbling uncertainty, or the excess verbiage and explanations most men mistakenly seemed to think would win them invitations into a woman's heart and bedroom. In bed, at least, Mark knew when to shut up and let his marvelous body speak for itself. A hard man was good to find, as Mae West once observed, and to wake up next to one smelling of Hermès instead of beer and Mexican cigars was, after Burt, a novelty. She often told herself that Mark was everything in bed that Burt was not: patient, sensitive to her rhythms and wants. She didn't really know why it peeved her to suspect that he rose secretly each night they slept together to bathe and scent himself in preparation for the energetic lovemaking that would come in the morning as predictably as orange juice and coffee.

*Predictable* was a word she would never apply to David Stone. The first moment in the Bar des Marines had proven that. He seemed to be a man ready to explode in any direction, barely under control. Was it a quality that carried over to his lovemaking? How controlled then?

She felt the heat flow upward from somewhere deep, hardening her nipples beneath her sweater. Her face flushed with an embarrassment that made Le Pic cock his head curiously. *He misses nothing, the old bastard.* Right there and then she vowed not to let her feelings get out of hand. Stone could help her find Polly, and she felt so raw and emotionally exposed that she might have been drawn to anyone who offered a possibility of help. That simple. Her redefining of the attraction to Stone made her feel instantly better.

Scratching a stubbled chin, Le Pic rocked back in his chair, regarding her with a faint smile.

"Let me tell you a little secret about David Stone. Why this morning he was very much like his name."

"I'd like to know."

The little something again beneath her words. Le Pic sighed inwardly. Why, when he was younger, had he never heard the things in a woman's voice, the true things she was saying. Always too busy talking to listen.

"David is afraid, I think. Afraid to care about something. Afraid that once he begins he risks the chance of being beaten again."

"Like the business with his first boat, the *Mary Anne*, trying to get the navy to admit guilt?"

"When a person gives everything and loses, it forces him down. So low it takes a long time to try again. When I first met David he was a crazy man, trying to wash the failure away. You know the ways a man has. This"—he held up the wineglass—"the wrong women, anything to prove he is still a man."

"I've seen it at work." She was thinking of Burt, his constant need to test himself. She tried to relate it to Stone.

"That's when he took a job he shouldn't have. He knew, but he took it anyway."

"And ended up in the prison you told me about?" Le Pic nodded.

Kits said, "And you think David is frightened of getting caught up in something that will beat him again?"

"I think David is already caught up. More than he realizes."

Le Pic squinted into his wineglass, avoiding Kits's questioning look.

"Ah, here comes Basso with something to fatten you up a bit. Why do women these days all want to look like little boys?"

"I want Stone's help, Le Pic. How do I get it?"

Basso put a steaming bowl of dark meat in front of them. A spicy smell filled the air. Le Pic regarded it suspiciously, then glanced up at Basso's stern countenance.

"One day, *mon petit*, you will make someone a fine *sous chef*. If I survive your experiments."

She thought she saw a flicker of a smile before Basso turned away, leaving them to the most delicious braised lamb she'd ever tasted.

She looked up to find Le Pic studying her, his food untouched.

"You can't ask David Stone for help. You must prove to him, beyond a doubt, that *he* desperately needs *your* help."

# Chapter 14
## Gambit

"Hello, anyone aboard?"

Kits waited a moment, then summoned her courage and knocked on the hull. She didn't intend giving Stone the narrowest excuse to deny her what she wanted; stepping aboard uninvited was no way to begin.

A moment later Stone's head appeared above the transom. "I should have guessed."

"Le Pic told me where to find you."

"Le Pic is a softy," he replied slowly. "I'm not. I am getting ready for a voyage, Mrs. Maitland." His face glistened with sweat. Shirtless, his chest and shoulders were well muscled but lean, too lean. "There are provisions to catalogue . . . things to do."

"I know something about boats, Captain."

"Then you will understand why I don't have time for you. I've already talked with Christian. If I find out anything that has a bearing on the disappearance of your daughter Polly, you'll hear about it."

The girl appeared then, coming up from below. As beautiful a girl as Kits Maitland had ever seen. Deeply browned, hair and face distinctively Polynesian, but with almond-shaped Oriental eyes. Twenty at most, padding around comfortably in a clinging *pareu*.

Stone followed Kits's eyes. "She doesn't speak English."

"She doesn't need to," said Kits, instantly regretting the cattiness in her voice. It was Stone's own business if he had a Tahitian playmate. Kits wasn't there to compete in a beauty contest, and she reminded herself again of Le Pic's advice. Damn it, she had something he needed; and, she told herself again, he'd be a fool not to see it. Whatever David Stone may or may not have been, fool wasn't on the list.

Stone nodded a goodbye and began his retreat down the stairwell.

"Captain, why bother with the boat at all, if time is so important?"

When Stone looked out at her, he found she hadn't budged an inch. Her moss-green eyes were steady on him, and something in the set of her mouth said she wasn't about to be lightly dismissed. Le Pic's warning, *Beware*; he understood it now.

"Because the place I came ashore is a long way from an airport. And because I'd rather cover that coastline afloat than barefoot."

"Christian said you think the *Pegasus* was sunk."

"Le Pic and Christian seem to have said a great deal."

He was watching her, peculiarly. Knows something is coming, she thought.

"Sunk along that coast?"

"Which is precisely why I am sailing in that direction. Now . . ." And again he began down the stairwell.

Evenly, not raising her voice in the slightest, Kits said, "What are you going to use to find it, a water witch?"

Slowly the head appeared again, Stone's jaws working uncertainly.

"I've scuba gear aboard."

"How many tanks? Two, four?"

After a long moment, Stone said, "Four."

"And a compressor for recharging them, naturally." When Stone didn't answer, Kits shook her head. "Captain, by all evidence you're a stubborn man, but I don't think you're a stupid one."

"You're working pretty hard to prove otherwise."

"Because you're venturing into something you think you understand but don't. You know that saying about a little knowledge being a dangerous thing? Well, when it comes to diving, you've very little knowledge, Captain Stone."

"What do you suggest?"

"Inviting me aboard, for openers, so I don't have to keep shouting at you from here. You need me. If not me, someone who knows as much as I do about working undersea. If I'm wrong, forgive the intrusion and bon voyage."

She knew better than to try a bluff unless willing to pay the price of losing. She couldn't afford to lose this one, to lose her one shot at David Stone. Still, she broke her own rule and turned, walking angrily away.

"Mrs. Maitland!"

As he called her name again she realized she was truly angry, angry at herself for letting the presence of the lovely Tahitian girl rattle her. She had no claims, barely knew the man. It was less a case of good old-fashioned jealousy, she told herself, than the fact that she was a competitive woman who didn't like to be bettered in any circumstance. The girl was aboard and she was not.

Kits turned and waited. Stone was standing on the afterdeck, hands on his hips. "Why not come aboard," he said, "so I don't have to keep standing here shouting at you."

* * *

They sat facing each other over the small galley table.

"Even with half a dozen divers," said Kits, "all well equipped, you can't just go down at random, hoping to find your boat."

"I have a rough idea where it is," said Stone. "Very rough."

"Then let's talk equipment."

Stone held up his hand. "Mrs. Maitland—"

"Make it Kits . . . please."

"Mrs. Maitland," Stone persisted. Le Pic was right, she surmised. Stone's gruff exterior was there in part to keep people from getting too close. An emotional appeal would get her nowhere. Bless Le Pic. She had to make Stone see how much her talent was worth.

Observing them silently, the Tahitian girl curled catlike on a narrow bunk nearby. Those dark almond eyes never left Kits's face.

"Mrs. Maitland, I appreciate your intent," said Stone.

"And I your optimism, Captain. Running a boat across the Med single-handed for openers. Attempting to be your own chief diver and tender."

Kits paused, trying to determine whether she was having any impact on Stone at all. Finally he nodded, reluctantly.

"You've the sound of experience, all right."

He found a bottle of calvados and a pair of glasses. He poured them each a drink.

"That's one word for it," said Kits, the sardonic tone clear in her voice. "Cheers," she said, and took the calvados down in a shot.

Experience all right. Filed under the category of the things you were glad you'd done but wouldn't necessarily want to go through again.

She'd married Burt Maitland at the age of seventeen,

common enough in the small California beach town where they'd grown up. They honeymooned in Hawaii and decided to stay on—a lazy year of North Shore surfing, diving the clear waters off Waianae, snorkeling in Haunama Bay.

When Polly was born, Burt had made a try at settling into the role of responsible husband. He landed a job with Maui Divers, who in those days were pioneering the commercial use of small submersibles, using them to mine the weedy branches of pink coral for local jewelry-makers from depths no one had ever worked before.

It was a good couple of years, but by the end of it they could feel the islands changing—and not to their liking. The clutter of Waikiki, the condominiums spreading cheek by jowl along Kaanapali, the most beautiful beach Kits had ever seen, before or since. The mass tourist hucksterism that filled local pockets, yet took away the thing that had once made the islands very nearly the paradise they advertised themselves to be.

Even then she was accumulating the mental images that would later focus her scientific work. Always, she'd been aware of the contact points between man and nature. What ideally should have been a harmonious larger view of life on the planet giving each its due, more often became a battleground. Technology had given man momentary dominance, but ultimately was taking its toll; unbridled it would destroy the planet and thus man himself.

It was the underlying theme of her scientific work—to show the contact points between man and his environment, what could be done to benefit each. She'd often meant to explain to Polly that there wasn't really a basis for feeling that mother and daughter were in competition, not when it came to anything that mattered. So much of life was finding the things within oneself that were deeper than fad or fashionable pursuit. She had been lucky to find her own niche, but Polly would have to search out one for herself. Kits had had the time to explain, but hadn't taken it.

After Hawaii, she, Burt, and infant Polly had tried Santa Barbara, a sleepy little city one hundred miles up the coast from Los Angeles. For a while Burt found work diving for abalone, the sponge-sized mollusk with an incredible taste that existed only along a few hundred miles of North American coast. But progress caught up with them there, too, in the form of overfishing the abalone and the death of what remained in water newly polluted by the surge of offshore oil drilling.

The abalone was the beginning of Kits as scientist. She remembered once ranting at Burt, "Whole tribes of Indians once lived off shellfish, whole societies, and now you can't find a pink abalone north of Baja California."

"What are you so sore about?"

"Greed, that's what. Greed, and mismanagement, and people like us just sitting around while the oil companies carve into the ecocycle without any understanding of what the impact will be."

Burt had stared at Kits as though she were speaking another language. And a few weeks later he took a job diving for one of the oil companies.

Most of his former abalone diving pals were doing the same, and one night over beers they decided to form a company of their own to give them leverage. Much against her will, when the papers were drawn up, Kits found herself company secretary, with Burt president and general manager. A year later she was virtually running the operation.

"I was doing everything," she told Stone. "Scheduling the work of a dozen divers: pulling them out of bars, sobering them up, diving with them when their partners couldn't. I'd deliver them to their rigs in the company boat, ferry them to hospitals with collapsed muscles or the bends. Experience all right. I've run small craft in storms and fog, and in my sleep. Watched a couple of good men die, and their wives want to."

Diving was a rough, dangerous job that had little to do with running a business, and Burt hadn't much given a damn. Kits had thought she could do without any of it until the day Burt came home and told her he'd had it. They were moving to Scotland, something new called North Sea oil.

By then Polly was happily enrolled in a good school, and Kits found that running the company was something she needed. She wanted more than just to keep busy; she wanted to do something real, to use some of the talents she was beginning to uncover. Already she'd begun night courses in marine biology at the nearby university, hauling Polly along with her to class when Burt was out with the boys, or wherever.

She told him she wasn't going to Scotland. "It might be right for you, but it isn't for me." When the divorce came through, Burt was in the Persian Gulf, and Kits found herself with his shares of company stock. A year later the company was bought by one of the big oil-well servicing outfits, and she was left with a profit that was almost unimaginable to a twenty-eight-year-old woman used to spaghetti dinners.

Six months later she and Polly were living in La Jolla, Kits a full-time student in Marine Science at the nearby university. If there was a less complicated time in her life, she couldn't remember it.

Now she told Stone some of it, mainly about the divers and working afloat. She stopped when she sensed she was saying too much.

Stone poured himself another calvados, the lines

deepening around his eyes. She couldn't read this man worth a damn, and that bothered her.

"Afraid I'll get in the way?" she finally asked.

"That's part of it." He'd been thinking about the loss of the *Mary Anne*, and now the *Pegasus*. There were captains in port who said he was jinxed.

"And the other part?"

"I don't want more problems than I have."

"Meaning men—husbands and such?"

Stone was silent.

"Burt Maitland is dead, over a year ago."

"Sorry."

"Don't be. Burt lived the life he wanted, which was pretty damn good. He died in a diving accident. We'd been divorced a long time. But yes, there *is* a man. We go our separate ways. Often." It was enough to say.

Stone was quiet, then replied, "The truth is, even if we find *Pegasus*, it may not put you any closer to your daughter. It may be a waste of time."

"I've thought about that."

"And came up with what?"

"I've treated it as a research problem, trying to leave Polly out of it. Let's say I've defined the problem. Look here." She took paper and pencil from the map rack and sketched out a single straight line. This she divided into three parts.

She explained, "Graphically, we're dealing with a linear process."

"Keep it simple, now."

She went on, fighting to hold down her enthusiasm. "If Christian is right, the boat you boarded is the middle stage of a pipeline. That is, moving the girls from a collection point—"

"Hold on," interrupted Stone. "What's this about a collection point?"

"Call it a deduction," said Kits. "I hope I'm not penalized for using my brain. Look, the *Sea Fox* wasn't cruising along the coast scooping little lost girls from beaches and bars. Christian made inquiries of the police and customs. Sooner or later a boat that size would have been boarded, papers checked."

"Le Pic believed the same thing."

"The first step in the pipeline has to be more subtle." She thought of Polly's note, the other missing girls drifting toward the port cities of the south. "Something to do with boats maybe. What exactly, I don't know. However it happens, the girls are taken to a collection point, then run by boatload to the coast of Africa—our pipeline's middle sector."

"Go on," Stone said, nodding intently.

"Now somewhere, we don't know where yet, the girls are off-loaded. Then—"

She stopped suddenly. She had an image of Polly crammed into the back of some truck, or hauled like cattle to be left in some filthy city, turned into an addict to keep her close to home, and killed if she proved intractable. The thought of her daughter ending up in some tropical brothel ran wild in her usually disciplined mind.

"Take it easy," said Stone, sensing her thoughts. "You've a right to worry."

"But it stops the brain from thinking. Stone, if we find the place where they land the girls, we put ourselves straight across the pipeline." She made a slash with her pencil between sectors two and three. "Maybe dead in their path."

"She's very lovely, David," said the Tahitian girl, Nani, when Kits was gone.

"I suppose she is."

"When will you sleep with her?"

"Ah, dear Nani. Would that I had a Tahitian view of life. No hangover, no complications."

"But it is very good with us."

Very good indeed. Nani offering comfort without a price of any kind. No emotional holds asked or offered. No midnight promises tested in the morning light. Nani exploring his sensitive regions with a child's curiosity but the knowing mouth and hands of a woman, laughing unselfconsciously when she discovered new ways to give pleasure.

Gone, she would leave a soft memory of time filled without pain and the thin aroma of coconut oil in his bunk that wouldn't last the day. It was enough, Stone told himself.

"It would be different with her," said Stone.

"Not good?"

"Not simple."

"Not worth the trouble then," the girl said.

"No," replied Stone. "Not worth the trouble."

# Chapter 15
## Odyssey

By ten the next morning a series of delivery vans began finding their way to the *Marie-Hélène:* Air tanks, a small gasoline-powered compressor, shallow-water gear. From all evidence, Kits Maitland was making a wide sweep through the city's dive shops and marine suppliers.

"What the hell," murmured Stone, and began hauling the gear aboard.

The *Marie-Hélène* was only thirty-four feet. Wrecked some years before off Cap Rouge, she'd been rebuilt by Le Pic himself, plank by plank. The design was local with something of the graceful lines of a fishing *pointu*, but more beam, and sloop-rigged as a motor sailor. A 70hp Mercedes diesel with large fuel tanks gave her plenty of range, with or without sail.

If the *Marie-Hélène* lacked anything, it was storage space for an underwater expedition in the fashion Kits Maitland anticipated.

Stone was still stowing gear when Le Pic and Basso came aboard.

"I hear you've taken on crew," hummed Le Pic.

"Thanks to you, you pirate."

"Ah, but the nights at sea are lonely, my friend." Basso lowered a case of wine, Armagnac, and Le Pic's standard ration of calvados, a half-dozen bottles.

"We're not throwing a party," protested Stone.

"Sometimes a bottle in the hands of the right official . . ." He beckoned Stone below. "Truthfully, David, you might find much trouble, eh?"

"I don't know, Le Pic. I don't know what I'll find."

"A man owes it to himself to be prepared. Shh." His voice lowered conspiratorially. "Something I want you to know about."

He nodded to Basso, who climbed partway up the stairs to the deck. Le Pic pushed up the face of the top stair where it had been skillfully grooved into the molding on either side, and withdrew something wrapped in oily muslin. He let the cloth fall away.

It was an old but well-cared-for Bren light machine gun, complete with bipod mount.

"For someone a nice surprise, eh?"

"For me," said Stone, "if a customs man finds that stash."

Basso dug out a clip, snapped it expertly into the receiver, and swung the weapon easily, braced against his hip.

Le Pic nodded approvingly. Le Pic Vert, the green bird of the Maquis, retired, but itching for a proxy battle.

"Worth the risk, David," Le Pic said gravely. "When a man needs a gun, he needs one."

Kits came aboard a little after six, bringing several wetsuits still in boxes.

"That does it," she said, taking a slow look around the boat. "Where's your Tahitian deckhand?"

"Like the tide, she comes and goes."

"I've left a few things at the hotel, not enough to worry about. When are we off?"

Stone wondered now if he hadn't been caught up by the woman's sureness, her confidence in an area Stone admittedly knew little about.

She stood, waiting for him to answer.

"We'll clear port before first light. Four hundred hours latest."

"You're the skipper. The sooner the better," she added, but her gaze drifted away. What caught her eye bent her mouth down at the corners.

Stone turned to see a sleek Alfa coupe slide to a stop at the foot of the quay. The man behind the wheel waved when he saw them. He approached in easy, controlled strides, the broad smile on his face too fixed to be genuine.

Kits gave a small sigh. "The man in my life I told you about. Making his entrance in the firm, decisive mode."


"I didn't want you to make a fool out of either of us," said Mark.

Less than thirty minutes after he'd arrived at the *Marie-Hélène* they were in Mark's Alfa speeding back along the *bord de mer* toward Kits's hotel.

"You know, Mark, saving people from themselves is such a boring way to spend your time."

"As with most of my clients, you included, saving them from themselves is the name of the game."

"In my case unnecessary," said Kits.

"Don't kid yourself," he countered severely. "You are talented, beautiful, and I love you, but none of the above have endowed you with the thing at which I excel—the ability to extract people from the lousy deals they walk into."

"There is nothing wrong with Stone's idea."

"I'm sure there isn't. I'm also sure that at this moment David Stone is a man much relieved."

*Damn, Stone. Damn him to hell.* If only he'd offered her one hint to indicate that, yes, her presence on this voyage was something he wanted and needed badly.

Instead he'd watched Mark with a blank expression that revealed absolutely nothing, Poker face. *Stone face.* In customary style, Mark had dominated their encounter.

*Permission to come aboard?* That's it, carefully remove the Guccis before you do. The handshake? Firm no doubt, the tone in his voice respectful and "just between us boys."

"Kits, would you mind if Captain Stone and I had a little talk, just the two of us?"

"Since the talk is about me, I most certainly would mind."

With an icy smile, Mark had addressed himself to Stone. "I wanted to ask the captain how important your presence is on this, ah, expedition."

"I'll manage," replied Stone, "one way or the other."

Mark had to swallow his crow of easy victory.

"Kits, we've people working on Polly's disappearance from several angles now. Captain Stone has his own problem. We ought to let him get on with it."

"The problems are related, Mark."

"I'm sure Stone here will let us know if anything turns up about Polly." An eyebrow raised toward Stone in question.

"Of course," said Stone, his voice dead flat.

Mark had risked a smile then. "You've commitments, Kits—speaking dates in Boston and Chicago."

Holding in her anger, anger at the two of them, she'd looked toward Stone. "Sailing at four hundred hours?"

"On the button."

"I'll be here."

"We'll discuss it," said Mark, smiling diplomatically.

"We'll discuss it elsewhere," said Kits, stepping onto the quay. "I'd rather not hang our dirty laundry on Captain Stone's boat."

Pulling away in the Alfa, she'd missed seeing Stone's steady gaze follow their departure. Missed seeing him pour a drink from the bottle of calvados, then hammer in the cork with the hard palm of his hand.

# Chapter 16
## Risk

"My friend is dead," said Dolph Hess. "Von Richert is dead. I can't believe it."

Stone remembered Dolph's drinking buddy who had served on the German Naval Command Staff in the Mediterranean. Stone had hoped he might provide a lead to the identity of the man in German uniform aboard the *Sea Fox*, a long shot at best.

Dolph stared disconsolately at Stone from behind the chart table in his spacious cabin aboard the *Wunderkind*. Curled on a daybed nearby, the Tahitian girl, Nani, was applying bright red polish to her toenails.

"I drove to his place above San Remo. His wife said he died four months ago. Four months and I never knew."

Dolph's large fist came down heavily on the table. "That war is still killing people, I tell you. Automobiles crash into the pillboxes near the highway at La Naupoule. People find bombs in their backyard, and poof! Ach!"

Dolph had been drinking plenty.

"Always a gentleman, Max," said Dolph thoughtfully, "even in his suicide. Oh yes, he killed himself. His wife said she awoke one morning to find he wasn't in bed. No arguments, she said; happy, she thought. Until she walked into the garden and found him hanging from a trellis of vine leaves. Thoughtful, eh? Nothing to clean up. Just cut down the old man's body and put him in the ground. I brought those back with me."

He indicated a wine case in one corner of the cabin. "His wife said I could look through his things. Like sifting through my own coffin."

"What sort of things?"

"Papers, some diaries. I haven't had the courage yet. By the time you return, I promise." He managed a thin smile. "You have enough to worry about where you're going. Here."

He handed Stone two books bound in bright blue, the Mediterranean volumes of the Admiralty *Sailing Directions*, and several rolled charts.

"They say damn little beyond the usual: 'North facing anchorages beware storms from the north.' And not much of that." His voice took on an ominous tone of warning. "Whole sections of that coast are still unchartered, David. People on the moon and not yet a decent set of coastal pilots for the busiest ocean on earth."

"I'll go easy."

"A graveyard," said Dolph distantly. "A bloody great graveyard." His watery blue eyes cleared for a moment. "We used to wait along that coast for the British convoys out of Gibraltar, the escorts from Force K seeing the freighters through to Malta. A graveyard, I tell you. For them. For us." Dolph looked away. "A lot of good men."

Stone agreed and left him to what would doubtless be a night of schnapps and Schopenhauer and Dolph's zither recording of "Lili Marlene."

The Tahitian girl followed him out on deck.

"I'll come with you, if you like."

"Not tonight, Nani."

"You are sleeping with the woman tonight. The one with the green eyes."

"No, not the woman."

"But you are thinking about her, yes?"

"No."

*Yes, the woman, under his skin.*

"Then I'll stay with Dolph. Later he will be very lonely, I think."

"Yes, I think," Stone agreed. He took the long way around to the *Marie-Hélène*, needing the cool night air.

He knew it wasn't right the moment he stepped aboard.

Every boat has its own smell. Aboard the *Marie-Hélène* it was diesel fuel and wet dog hair, and some distilled essence of Le Pic: Gauloise, garlic, and calvados.

Stepping down into the cabin, Stone caught the smell of something foreign and musky. He moved quickly sidewise to keep from being framed in the hatchway.

"Easy, Mr. Stone," a voice said from the darkness. "No need of anything rash." A woman's voice, controlled and unpanicked.

He risked the cabin light and found her sitting at the chart table, both hands in view and empty. Her skin was milk pale, the kind that so often went with red hair. This time there was no scarf over her head. The hair was close-cropped, almost boyish; the face square, eyes steady. The woman who'd followed him in London.

"I know it's bad manners," she said, "but I just wanted to look around while you were gone."

"Find anything?"

"What is there to find?"

"Then you can climb right up the stairs and go home."

"I wanted to be sure about you. Make sure you weren't in on it."

"In on what?" asked Stone. The girl's "it" had the sound of dark conspiracy.

"The disappearance of the Gabrieles with your boat."

"You're a friend?"

"That's a word we'll use. My name is Sophie."

"A name we're using, or the real one?"

"Does it matter?"

"It all matters. You following me around London, then showing up here to snoop. I'm sorry about the Gabrieles, glad they have a concerned friend. Now get the hell off this boat."

She didn't move, and when she spoke she was hesitant. Stone had noticed the slight accent. Perfect English, but something in it he couldn't place—like the Gabrieles.

"I want to help."

"Help what?"

"Find the people responsible. I'm not alone, Mr. Stone. Hanna . . . Alec, had friends, you understand?"

"I wish the hell I did." He tried to remember what he knew about the Gabrieles. No more, no less than he did about most charters. You learned a lot about anyone you lived with for a week or two on a boat the size of *Pegasus*, but usually not what their lives were like the other fifty weeks a year. That suited Stone fine.

The Gabrieles had been what Aggie called the "nonesuch trade." There were cycles in the Mediterranean charter business. When Stone began, it was fat, though not happy, with the petro-dollar boom of rich Arabs buying half the boats on the Côte d'Azur and leasing those they couldn't buy. They'd moved on to Spain now, looking for new fields to mow over, and in their place had come a new brand of quiet money.

People like Sophie, who spoke accented English, along with accented French, or accented German, or any of a dozen languages they might have spoken fluently. Arrangements made by phone from New York, or London, or Rio. Payments from Swiss banks. If there were no landfalls, passports stayed tucked away. Nice people, some young, some old. People without histories they felt obliged to talk about, and with money they talked about even less. Although the Gabrieles had come aboard the *Pegasus* as nonesuches, two surprising facts about them had come to light during the Board of Inquiry: their lives were heavily insured through a Swiss company; and they carried Israeli passports.

"Powerful friends," Sophie said, "who would like to help."

Sophie stood and handed him a card with a telephone number on it. She had square muscular shoulders, and up close he could see the small hairline scar in one eyebrow.

"If you find the people you're after," she said, "if you need help—"

"Bertrand," said Stone.

She stared at him, wrestling to figure out the significance of that name.

Hell, he hadn't a thing to lose. Let these powerful concerned people show their stuff or get out of his life.

"Bertrand," Stone repeated. "A Swiss lawyer, with an office in Geneva,. The boat I boarded the night *Pegasus* was hijacked was a special type. We've tracked down all but one. The one bought by this lawyer Bertrand from a Belgian industrialist."

Sophie wrote it down.

"I want to know who is behind Bertrand," said Stone.

It was a strange moment for the realization. No longer was it only a question of *Pegasus*, finding her afloat or underwater. Maybe it was the influence of Kits, her persuasive determination to find her daughter, take on anyone and everyone responsible. Whatever, he only knew he'd follow it to the end. Beyond *Pegasus*, whatever it was a part of.

Sophie thought a moment, then silently moved past him to the stairs leading topside. "When I know something, we'll meet again," she said at last. It had the sound of a promise. "Bon voyage, Mr. Stone. And remember, when fired, a Bren gun climbs hard, high and left. Don't hurt yourself."

A little before 0400 hours, he mounted the stairs into the cockpit of the *Marie-Hélène*. At the other end of the city, trucks loaded with fresh produce were rolling into the market. If the fishing was bad, the Bar des Marines would already be filled with fishermen taking extra *marc* in their coffee.

He hadn't slept worth a damn. Somewhere about 2:00 a.m. he'd written a note to Christian, asking him to find out what he could about the Gabrieles, telling him of the redhead's visit. He left the note with Le Pic for delivery.

He made coffee now and stared out at the empty quay. At five minutes to four he reached over and hit the starter button for *Marie-Hélène*'s diesel.

He was gambling in four directions: with Christian; the lady Sophie; Dolph Hess; and the scant possibility of his finding a name to match the face of the U-boat skipper aboard the *Sea Fox*.

But most of all he was chancing it with Kits.

He needn't really have given the powerful engine the extra minutes to warm up, but he did.

Finally, without looking at his watch, for he knew the time exactly, he threw off the moorings and eased the *Marie-Hélène* into gear.

Three minutes later he cleared the Cannes light. He watched its triple-wink slide astern, then tossed overboard what was left in his cup, wondering if he'd always made such rotten coffee.

# Part II

## The Spoiler

# Chapter 17
## Far Shores

The inescapable truth came to Robert Christian in a one-star hotel near Paris's St. Lazare station.

His room was unique only in the revelation experienced there. A small room, not space enough for a decent worried pace. Two windows with flowered curtains, big leafy patterns gone slightly mad like Van Gogh paintings.

On the floor, four pieces of unequal-sized carpet, laid askew. The armoir was of plastic simulated wood. A Chinese peasant's hat, the pointed kind, hung upside down from the ceiling to shield a dim globe. The lampshade at bedside was brittle, its yellow parchment-like covering marked with a dark brown burn. All of it had a familiar seediness, comforting in the way familiar things always are.

His only objection was to the black fingermarks around the door the maid was too lazy to wash off. That, and the five-franc charge they'd added to his bill for the privilege of taking a bath along the hall, as though it were a luxury anyone who stayed there would not require.

In partial retribution, he urinated in the washbasin, not fully trusting his legs to descend the flight of stairs to the toilet. His own hollowed face stared back at him from the mirror, his eyes pinched with a fear he'd seen often enough in the eyes of others.

He was going to die. And not at all in the fashion he had anticipated. He'd always imagined the likely instrument of death to be a bullet or bludgeon in the hands of someone he had put in prison or deprived of a fortune. In his desk was a thick envelope of threats collected over the years, promising him enough harm of varying descriptions to have mutilated an army. It was the way a policeman should be prepared to die, just as a man who raced automobiles should be ready to expire in the wreckage of his machine.

Christian certainly hadn't expected to go from some degenerative disease. If the test reports he'd received only twenty-four hours ago had been presented him as evidence in a court of law, his judgment would have been quick and dispassionate: death. They'd cut him open tomorrow if he let them—the esophagus first, out through a J-incision. He knew there was worse to find.

The thought of his own imminent death had settled in his mind the moment the church bells awakened him. St. Augustine chiming 4:00 a.m. The before-dawn images that had always haunted him were truly terrifying now. He felt like a child discovering that the demons waiting in the night were real. Death was everywhere, in the faces of missing girls pulled from police files. The others he'd looked at in the past days, staring up opaquely from cold morgue tiles. The eighteen-year-old Spanish girl, who had murdered her *ponce* and escaped only to cut her own throat in a Salvation Army home the day her parents were cabled of her whereabouts. Murder, drug overdose, suicide, the end of innumerable stories that all began as *disparition*. Young girls, life itself.

The latest was a pretty French teenager named Camille Chabaud. *Disparition*, the newspaper said, as though it were an end and not a beginning.

He found himself remembering what must have been his own starting point, buried away and festering. He could still recall every detail of that night, the pale figures and their grotesque, suggestive beckoning, calling him and the others to dance naked with them in the yellow light from oil lanterns. Later the shrill laughter of Arab merchants as one by one they made their selection from among the young girls, fondling their pubescent mounds, stroking their pointed breasts as they drew them away into the darkness.

In February of '44 Christian heard about the Allied landings at Anzio in a British Army rest camp on the Bay of Algiers. Even then his body had begun its betrayal. A mild case of jaundice had kept him from landing with his platoon, and while his friends were being killed and wounded in the frightful German counterattack, Christian drank tea and sipped cheap *mousseaux* at the Aletti bar and the Bosphore, and generally tried to keep from going mad.

That night, in his weakened condition, a half-bottle of wine had turned him mean drunk. He had sobered to find himself in a Land Rover with two other young officers, absolute strangers, and an Arab boy named Hafid. They were heading into the low ranges of the Atlas Minor for a spectacle, something very special, Hafid promised. "Not for soldiers, but I arrange everything."

The dance, and later the brothel of children. It sickened Christian now to think of it. How totally he had lost himself in the arms of two small girls whose age between them hadn't equaled his own worldly twenty years.

He dressed now, avoiding his wasted reflection in the mirror, and took coffee in a brasserie on the street. As an afterthought, he ordered brandy. Rigid self-discipline had never allowed him brandy before lunch. But the warmth made him feel better, helped clear his mind. He had to find strength from whatever source.

He reread Stone's note about the couple that had disappeared with the *Pegasus*, Alec and Hanna Gabriele, and the woman Sophie who claimed to be their friend.

Then he put in a call to Israel Katz at home. He wanted to catch the detective before he reached his office at Interpol. As the telephone rang, Christian wondered which among the unsavory items he carried in his private mental file he was going to trade Katz for the information he wanted.

In the still heat of midafternoon Stone climbed the narrow street that led from the port to the main square of the village. To any veiled face that might have ventured a look from behind a shuttered window, his gait was that of a drunken man, sea legs wobbly from the passage aboard the *Marie-Hélène*.

Dizzying heat. Flies. The only sign he understood: COCA-COLA. Goat smell in the air, none in sight; God-knows-what running in open gutters. *The sea anytime*. But he walked on.

The prefecture of police occupied half the ground floor of the village's city hall. The building was two-storied, built in 1924, A. Fernandez, architect, according to the cornerstone: a monument to the grandeur of Empire in what was then a distant corner of a sleepy district. Little had altered, except that independence had changed banners on the flagpole.

A half-century of unrelenting sun had blistered the plaster on the south-facing wall, cracking the molding around the door Stone pushed open to enter.

He remembered the outer office, unchanged from two months before when he'd been brought here after being found ashore. In these two offices and the customs house resided the force of law on this desolate, arid coast, and they were welcome to it. A gray-uniformed officer sat at his desk, head resting on his arms in the local equivalent of siesta. The only sound in the room came from an electric fan, cranking around on a squeaky bearing.

Stone knocked on the counter. When the startled officer oriented himself, Stone asked to see Labatt. The man had a full row of colored BIC pens in his breast pocket, Africa's true badge of self-importance.

Half an hour later Stone sat in the inner office, the thickly built chief of police facing him across a desk.

"Yes," said Labatt, without warmth. "I was told of your arrival."

Stone had left the *Marie-Hélène* at the customs wharf, and after paying the required official visits he was stamped into port.

"You are in good health?" inquired the policeman. Labatt had all the shrugs and grimaces of a native Frenchman. Yet before independence the European influence along this coast had been Spanish, giving cultural ground each year to the Arab and the tackier elements of Western consumerism. What had brought and kept Labatt here, Stone couldn't guess.

"Better than the last time we met," Stone said.

"And why, pray, have you returned? To this of all wonderful places." Labatt's hand waved vaguely beyond the window.

"To talk with the boy who found me. See the place again."

Labatt's head tilted uncomfortably. "But he is only a shepherd boy. It is the hot season now and the flocks are in the sierra. He may be ten kilometers from here, or a hundred. Who knows?"

He gave a good Frenchman's shrug that indicated it wasn't worth the pain to all concerned. "I take it you are still looking for your boat, the . . . ?" A finger pointed toward the ceiling, searching its name.

"*Pegasus.*"

"If it will help you, Monsieur Stone, I myself will take you where you were found. It isn't far."

"I don't want to waste your time."

Labatt looked uncomfortably around the room. "My day is filled with time. Life here is a game to fill time. We will go in late afternoon. Cooler then."


For several miles west of the village the road was roughly paved; then it gave way to a single tire track that snaked along near the sea. Several miles inland, sharp truncated mountains, purple now in the slanting afternoon sunlight, here and there reached down almost to the water. Between were low dunes, an occasional dark valley filled with palm and a low, thick scrub.

At a spot that looked like any other, Labatt pulled his ancient Peugeot from the track and stopped.

He got out, pointing toward a wide, empty stretch of beach. "You were found there," he said, waving in a loose circle and shrugging again. Clearly he saw nothing in the exercise. Stone wasn't sure he did either, but it was a starting point. He noted the sharp ridge of jagged rocks that rose from the sea at the far end of the beach. He wanted to find it again aboard the *Marie-Hélène*.

"Enough, Monsieur Stone?"

Stone nodded.

Back in Labatt's office, the policeman offered him a

*pastis* with a single cube of ice and made one for himself. Swirling the milky liquid around in his glass, he perfunctorily said, "If I may be of further service, let me know." Labatt's fingers began drumming the desktop.

"One thing."

A sigh, not quite imperceptible. "Yes, Monsieur Stone?"

"The customs patrol. It's a lot of coast for one boat."

"But little enough work. This is not a prosperous region. Perhaps with that great hope of every poor country, tourism."

"I'd like to know where the customs boat was the night I was found. That night, and a few nights before."

"A phone call, and I will know by tomorrow. Or perhaps the day after. And how long do you plan to stay?" Labatt smiled with the question.

"Not long," said Stone.

As Stone rose to leave, the telephone on the policeman's desk rang twice. He picked it up, listened, grunted, and rang off.

He spun to face Stone. "You might have told me about the woman."

"What woman?"

"The one aboard your boat," said Labatt.

She was sitting in a deck chair, shoes off, feet propped up. Her dress was white, doubtless some miracle fabric. She looked fresh and clean, and totally content with the tall, ice-filled drink she sipped.

"No captain around to ask permission, so I just came aboard," said Kits Maitland. "You were right. We are a long way from where airplanes land."

"Not a moment for questions, I suppose."

Her head shook from side to side. "*Finito*," she said. "Let's just leave it there."

# Chapter 18
## Neptune's Fork

Blistering heat enveloped them the instant the sun broke the horizon. They'd set off before dawn, running westward along the coast. When Stone recognized the beach he'd visited with Labatt, he pointed:

"The place I was found two months ago."

"Rustic," said Kits, eyes darting from the rocky beach itself, to the sweep of current closer in.

"A shepherd boy stumbled upon me just about this time of morning. I remember waking up with a headache worse than an elephant's hangover. Before that, lots of blur."

"No recollection of being in the water?"

"Nothing. The last thing before waking up on that beach was a girl's face pressing close to mine in the darkness."

"Aboard *Pegasus*?"

"I'm almost sure."

Kits could hear the doubt, could see how much it bothered Stone. She took a moment to study the chart of the coast before asking, "David, go over it again. What you think happened that night, step by step." When she

138

saw his reluctance, she said quickly, "Please . . . I've a reason."

He looked off toward the beach. "Step one, after *Pegasus*'s captain is unceremoniously knocked on the head, *Sea Fox* transfers its cargo in mid-ocean."

"Girl or girls," said Kits, "from *Sea Fox* to *Pegasus*."

"Correct," said Stone. "*Pegasus* had a master cabin forward, two small double cabins, plus a crew's quarters aft. Room enough."

"Where did they tie you?"

"Aft. The crew's cabin . . . I think."

"Then what?"

"*Pegasus* makes the run *Sea Fox* was supposed to make to somewhere along this coast."

"A place with a shallow approach, or an anchorage sheltered enough to let them off-load the girls by inflatable boat."

"Exactly," Stone replied slowly, his gaze on her narrowing just the slightest.

"Which means we can eliminate stretches of coastline unapproachable for whatever reason—bars, reefs, cliffs."

"We might."

*Hard bastard*. "I said I had a reason for this," she repeated. "I am trying to find some limits. If neither vessel could get in close enough to land a boat, all I am suggesting is that we drop the place off our search list. Make sense or not, Captain?"

The smile now, thin enough to shave with. "Agreed."

"All right, the girls are put ashore," said Kits. "What then?"

"I think they ran *Pegasus* out to deep water and sank her."

"With you still aboard."

"With me, Devlin, and the Gabrieles."

"They'd kill four innocent people and sink a valuable boat?"

"They would," said Stone. "They were smugglers with valuable cargo, not boat thieves. Getting rid of a hot boat is a specialized business. You don't just hang out a For Sale sign. The risk wouldn't be worth their time or money."

"But four lives . . ."

"Worth damn little to those people," said Stone. "I can see you don't want to accept that."

"You see correctly, Captain. Is caring about human life so extraordinary in this part of the world?"

"People care about their daughters. Slightly less than their sons. But they care."

"You don't have to be that personal," she said angrily.

"But about strangers not at all, and enemies worse than that. Do you really give a damn about the safety and rehabilitation of the people who took Polly, if they are caught?" When she was silent, he said, "Or would you vote for the kind of justice that is still dealt out, in this part of the world as you call it, quickly and with a sharp blade?"

"You go straight to it, don't you?"

"Just making a small point. To those smugglers, Devlin and I, the lot of us, were nothing but trouble. Better to get rid of us and the *Pegasus* and get on with their work."

"I guess I wanted to hear something else. The detective Jobert said the same thing about the girls. The ones that don't bend, or become too troublesome. They just disappear. Taken out into the bush I suppose and . . ."

She was quiet a moment, struggling with the thought of it. Visibly she gathered herself, then looked at Stone.

"After *Pegasus* went down, you remember nothing about being in the water."

"I'm told a concussion can do that," said Stone. "Wipe out portions of recent memory."

"You couldn't have been in the water too long," she said. When he frowned in question, she added, "Hypothermia would have set in. And then shock and death in close order."

"Hypothermia?"

"The loss of deep body heat. But if you weren't in the water long enough to suffer hypothermia, then we might have another of our limits."

"I don't get it," said Stone. He was watching the chart on the echo sounder peck out a steady fifteen fathoms, deep enough for either *Pegasus* or the *Sea Fox*. Then he thought of something else, something about *Sea Fox*'s malfunctioning engines. A clue that wouldn't quite come to him.

Kits was saying, "You see, given a known water temperature, it's fairly easy to predict how long anyone will last before the onset of hypothermia."

"But these waters are warm," Stone argued. "At least seventy degrees Fahrenheit."

"Closer to sixty-eight." When he looked at her oddly, she said, "All right, I'm splitting fine hairs, but for a reason. Even in water well into the nineties, hypothermia will get you, given enough time. Two months ago the water along this coast was a good six degrees colder than it is now. I checked."

Stone turned to look at her. "A point for the scientist. Which adds up to . . . ?"

"A limit of eight hours in the water, maybe a little more."

"I couldn't have kept swimming for eight hours.

Maybe with one of the flotation cushions from the *Pegasus*."

"I don't think you would have lasted that long," she remarked evenly, "with or without a cushion."

"Well, thanks a helluva lot."

"Don't take it personally. You were semiconscious, bleeding from a wound on your forehead that later needed twelve stitches, and sending out all manner of long-wave vibrations."

"You mean I was shark bait."

"Eight hours in the water is a long time."

"But sharks in the Med aren't known for jaws that snap in the night."

"There are dangerous sharks in every ocean, given the right or wrong circumstances—that I promise you. True, most of the species common in the Med are harmless to man. Except for the hammerhead. Of course, in eight hours you could have drowned."

"Sorry I asked."

Kits was quiet a moment. "David, we're wasting our time here." She saw his argument form, but went on before he could begin: "I mean right here, this spot. Come, take a look."

Instinctively, she reached for his arm, to pull him near the chart. Innocent contact, but they were both instantly aware, and she drew away.

"The *Sailing Directions* indicates a fairly steady two-mile-an-hour drift along the whole stretch of coast east from Cabo Très Forcas. If you were in the water a maximum of eight hours, moving with the current because you were in no shape to do otherwise . . ."

He understood it now. "Then the point where I started—the place they sank *Pegasus*—may have been fifteen or sixteen miles farther along the coast."

"Figure twenty at the outside. That's our limit. I say

sail west and work our way back, checking out every approachable bay or beach. Still a gamble, but it narrows it some."

To a haystack twenty miles long, thought Stone.

They passed the morning motoring westward to their projected limit point.

Kits didn't waste a minute of it, scanning the shoreline with the 8 × 50's. It was a low coastline of open, north-facing bays, scant shelter from the storms of winter. Here and there were low offshore islands, unpopulated except for sea birds. Where narrow rivers had cut through to the sea, flat bars made approach impossible, even for the shallow-drafted *Sea Fox*. "Seek local knowledge," the *Sailing Directions* offered in its conventional wisdom. From the birds, maybe. The shoreline was deserted.

"There's another element in the place we're looking for," said Kits. "I should have thought of it earlier."

"You're doing all right."

"Why Captain, you sound like I've just done a snazzy job of waxing your car." Kits laughed, a little too brittlely. "You don't have an easy time of it, do you? Saying what you feel."

"What I feel doesn't matter," he answered levelly. That was precisely it, reckoned Stone. He was trying to keep his feelings out of it. The hurt that he still carried along with the thought of Devlin, likely dead from Stone's ill-placed sense of duty the night he boarded the *Sea Fox*. His paramount duty should have been to those who counted upon him. He'd thought often enough that if he hadn't taken his wife to sea long ago, taught her to love it as he did, against her basic nature, she would still be alive. Now there was another woman aboard. Aboard of her own free will, sharing his table, sharing the risk. He didn't want to feel responsible for her.

"This other thing you thought of," he prompted.

Kits didn't press it. "Only that the place we're looking for not only needs access from the sea; it needs a way out. So many of these beaches and valleys are walled in by mountains. I haven't seen a road in miles."

She looked off toward the mountains bleached white now by the dazzling midday sun.

"Doesn't anyone live up there?"

"Montagnards," said Stone, "people who like to be left alone."

"Well, they're good at it. I haven't seen a soul."

Stone's sudden grin peeled away ten years from his age. "Ah, but they've seen *you*," he said, "I guarantee."

When they reached the limit point, Stone turned the *Marie-Hélène* about and started back along their course more slowly.

By late afternoon they'd covered only four miles of coast, most of it barred by impassable reefs. At the occasional narrow passage, Kits would turn to give Stone a questioning look: Here, shall we try here?

Somewhere inside his brain things felt and seen that night in a semiconscious state were buried, but trying to surface—a sixth sense it wasn't in his nature to trust as much as the other five, but for once he gave into it. Still nothing.

"I'm beat," said Kits finally, looking wilted from heat and frustration. "Let's take a break."

She stripped off her blouse and tossed the floppy hat at Stone. A moment later she was over the side, circling the boat with smooth, powerful strokes.

She climbed back aboard and stood a moment, grinning at Stone in pure pleasure. "I've missed the water, I didn't know how much." Then her frown. "What are you looking at?"

Free of the baggy blouse, she had the lithe body of a gymnast, without the boyish flatness—the body of a mature woman—and with rather larger than average breasts which the bikini top tried unsuccessfully to flatten.

"I guess you might say I was staring." He seemed surprised by the frankness of his own admission.

"Captain."

"Aye."

"Why not see if you can put the *Marie-Hélène* near those rocks over there without running into them. You do that, and I'll find us dinner."

She dipped belowdecks and a moment later was back with mask and snorkel, fins, and a spear gun mounting a wicked trident tip.

"Take it easy down there," said Stone. She cocked her head at the sound of concern in his voice, but said nothing before disappearing over the side again.

Using the binoculars, he watched her swim easily toward the rocks, vanishing occasionally in free dives that Stone began to time—forty-five seconds, fifty, then two that exceeded a minute.

He decided she knew what she was doing, and scanned the coastline beyond.

Once, far to the east, he saw the glint of something that could have been late afternoon sunlight reflected from the windscreen of another boat.

The feeling was there, and this one he didn't ignore: they weren't as alone and unobserved on this ragged coast as he would have liked.

# Chapter 19
## Red Sky in Morning

That night they ate spiney lobster steamed in seawater, with the last of the fresh butter and a bottle of wine chilled on the ocean bottom.

"A lady of commendable talent," said Stone, "but from now on we dive together. Partners."

"Were you worried? About me diving alone, I mean?"

When Stone seemed a little too intent on his lobster, she realized she'd struck a nerve. "David, don't be. I'm not."

"Doesn't anything worry you out there?"

"I think about a lot of things, but I don't worry. The only time I'm really frightened is when I know that I'm pressing my own limits. But the thing is, I know where those limits are. One step beyond and a little something inside me goes *click* and then I'm out of the water fast."

Maybe it went beyond the water, she thought suddenly. Like that moment in bed with Mark the day after they'd left Stone aboard the *Marie-Hélène*. When the long-delayed click came she'd pulled herself from his arms, the decision to join Stone so strong she couldn't ignore it. She'd wasted enough time letting herself be flattered by the right words said by the wrong person. She'd begun packing, even while Mark trotted out his most tested verbal gambits to keep her from leaving.

Thoughtfully, she told Stone, "I'm only afraid that one day the click won't come. Or I'll think I'm better than I am and won't listen."

"So from now on we dive together," Stone insisted. "Deal?"

"Deal."

Late the third morning they found the bay.

A day of warnings.

Stone awoke before dawn, rising from the narrow bunk next to the galley table. He'd left Kits the cramped privacy of the forward cabin. But as he sat up, he saw the cabin door propped open for ventilation. In the mirror mounted on the door he caught Kits's reflection as she knelt naked on her bunk, slowly brushing out her shoulder-length hair.

Sunshine from the skylight overhead caught the ripple of her fine muscles, the smoothness of her skin interrupted only by the darkish fluff at the join of her thighs. He felt like a kid peering over the back fence at the neighbor lady, and started to turn away. But something held him, something more than the firm but mature curves of her body. It was the unguardedness that left her for a moment open and vulnerable; her sureness of self wasn't yet in place, and in a second Stone understood how thin and fragile it was.

Then her eyes lifted to meet his, a brief electric contact before he looked away, and Kits, without abruptness, toed shut the door.

Later she brought coffee into the cockpit. They were motoring slowly toward a bay Stone had circled on the chart, not quite sure why. And there was a new problem now: the diesel engine running hot and close to the danger line.

"I have something to say," Kits began, her moss-green eyes troubled.

"Sorry about this morning," Stone said.

"I'm not talking about that, not exactly. We're too damn wary, Stone, both of us. Too guarded and tight-lipped for our own good." She laughed suddenly. "See, sometimes I want to call you David. Other times it comes out Stone. And there are moments when only Captain will do, capital C."

"I wouldn't call that serious."

"The distance you put between us is, between you and me."

"And I can do without the psychoanalysis. If I'd wanted a shrink along, I'd have brought one."

"Then I'll put it another way. Stop treating me like glass. I'm in this too, all of it. My eyes are open and I'm well past twenty-one."

Sharply, Stone looked over. "I'm trying not to mix things up. I don't want anything in the way. Anything that might cause either of us to hesitate at the wrong moment. Or keep us from hearing that click you were talking about if we've pushed too far." Her eyes turned bright with anger when he asked, "Is that clear?"

"Very. Okay, Captain, nothing will get in the way. It's a promise."

She left him then and went below to ready their diving gear.

A little after 1100 hours, the *Marie-Hélène* rounded a promontory of jagged red rock. Ahead was a crescent-shaped bay a half-mile across, a second promontory at the far curve tapering out into the sea. On the chart the bay had the shape of a devil's horns.

Closer in, the murky water color provided little clue to the bottom, and Stone guessed that somewhere a stream emptied into the bay. Beyond the dark line of foliage behind the beach was a saddle-shaped ridge of hills.

"What do you think?" asked Kits.

"The same thing you do," Stone said. "A place to try."

Ten minutes later they pulled the inflatable boat up onto the sandy beach. Stone had run the *Marie-Hélène* in, keeping a cautious eye on the depth recorder. Satisfied, he wheeled the *Marie-Hélène* back out to anchor.

"What was that all about?"

"Just checking. Either *Sea Fox* or *Pegasus* could have come in close enough to just about drop anchor on the beach."

Ashore, Kits said, "David, listen. I'm sorry I got so steamed up back there."

Stone turned to look at her.

"I don't want to captain your boat," she said, "or even lead this expedition. I just want to know what we are doing and why, and not be expected to read your mind."

"Fair enough."

"Like now. I'm not sure what we're looking for."

Stone was listening. Kits thought she heard it too: the sound of an engine, distant, fading away. Hard to be sure.

"Signs," he said. "People signs, proving we're not the first to discover this place."

"Like Indians."

He nodded. "Like Indians. Want to split up?"

"The hell I do."

\* \* \*

The beach had been scoured clean by the tide and they went inland through occasional carob trees and a low, thorny scrub that pricked at Kits's legs. It took an hour before they found it—a clearing where the trees had been hacked away. There were remains of a cooking fire, and at one side, an overgrown but well-used tire track leading off toward the saddle-shaped hills.

Stone kicked at the charred embers and felt the earth cool beneath.

"Do you think this is the place?" asked Kits.

"I don't know. Something doesn't add up."

Kits cocked her head inquiringly.

Stone said, "First, you wouldn't need a shallow-draft boat to land a few girls in this bay."

"Maybe the shallow draft of the *Sea Fox* was incidental, something the craft just happened to have."

He considered it. "Then why here, this particular place on this particular coast?"

Kits pointed toward the road. "The route inland."

"Inland to where? The girls are supposedly destined for a market thousands of miles from here. Why not land them near an airfield, a major highway, something to make the transport easier? Christian saw it, too, the economics not adding up."

"Adding up to what?"

"Something more. Something directly related to where we are now, this place."

"Where we are now is the middle of nowhere," said Kits, looking around.

"Wait here," said Stone, "while I take a look along that road, see where it leads."

Inland the heat was oppressive. He wondered whether following the road would lead him anywhere. He'd gone a quarter of a mile at most when he heard Kits's distant cry from the clearing.

By the time he reached her, his sweat-soaked clothing was rubbing him raw in a dozen places. She stood in the direct center of the clearing, eyes fixed on the thick scrub to one side.

"What's wrong?"

"Something in there," she said, pointing. "Something moving."

Stone found himself smiling. In the water, things that made his skin crawl were part of her accepted environment—dangers calmly catalogued, given their priority, and mentally filed away. Here, the elements were foreign. A fish out of water.

"David!"

Then he heard it, too, something grunting its way through the undergrowth. Stone picked up a jagged rock and hurled it toward the sound.

A large *sanglier*, yellow-tusked and bristling, burst from the thicket. It skirted the clearing, cast them one challenging look, and then was gone.

"We missed a fine dinner."

"*You* missed a fine dinner," said Kits. "I wouldn't touch anything that ugly."

"Just a wild pig rooting around for food."

"Let's get out of here," said Kits. "There's something strange about this place. Something I can feel."

They'd almost reached the beach again when Stone halted. Kits saw his forehead ridge, his eyes sharp with discovery.

"What's wrong?"

"You go on. Wait for me on the beach."

"David?" she called, but he was already moving silently back the way they had come.

Kits was mystified.

Twenty minutes later he was back, pushing his way through the scrub to stride toward her across the beach.

He stopped, brushing the sweat from his forehead, and looking suddenly fatigued.

"We've found the place," he said.

"You're sure, aren't you? I can tell by your voice."

"I'm sure."

That night Stone dreamed again of the girl. Except it was Kits and he awoke in a bed damp with sweat, as frightened as he'd ever been in his life.

# Chapter 20
## The Depths

They began the search for *Pegasus* at first light. Using the scuba gear and working together, they zigzagged their way across the bay, just deep enough to see the bottom, but careful to stay above a depth of thirty feet. "Any deeper," Kits warned, "and nitrogen will begin to accumulate, which means time lost in decompression."

By noon they'd traversed the bay twice, each turn taking them into deeper water. Aboard the *Marie-Hélène*, the compressor was working full time, recharging their spare tanks.

By early afternoon Stone's legs felt like rubber, while Kits seemed inexhaustible. Her propulsion looked effortless, her trim figure and gliding movement giving her the appearance of some new form of sea life—part human, part creature perfectly at home here. Her glances of concern became more frequent as the afternoon wore on, forcing Stone to reluctantly admit he was holding her back.

"No diving alone," Stone insisted. "That was our deal."

He dragged on a fresh pair of tanks and once more

plunged in behind Kits. They made another traverse of the bay, then another. Toward late afternoon, Kits voiced the doubt that had been building for hours.

"It's more water than I'd calculated. We'll never cover this bay and the rest of the coast in anything short of months."

"The *Pegasus* is here," said Stone, determined.

"Then we'll find her," she said, wanting it for David's sake. He hadn't allowed himself the possibility of failure; she could hear his fear of it in his voice. But by the end of the next circuit, they both knew they'd reached their day's limit.

Stone dragged himself aboard the *Marie-Hélène* and lay a moment on the deck, thankful this once for the heat. Even in his wet suit, his body felt chilled to the core.

Exhausted, he watched as Kits unslung her tanks. She went below and came back with a single tank and regulator and the small spear gun.

"You're tough, lady."

"We've got to eat, whether you feel like it or not. Important to charge the batteries," she added, and went over the side with less grace than usual.

The *Marie-Hélène* was anchored about fifty yards off the rocky promontory that enclosed one extremity of the bay. She took the swim slowly, turning once to see Stone watching her from the deck. It gave her an odd sensation of contentment, to use her body to its limit, physically, to feel David Stone's unspoken concern. Her reserves were slight and she didn't push herself now. She employed conservation in every move, an old player's skill to make up for the raw energy a younger one has to burn.

She dived about ten yards from the rocks, going deep for a look: a lot of dull-colored fish, bland in comparison with their tropical reef cousins—soup fish. She was hoping for a *daurade* or turbot, something that would feed the two of them in one score.

When she saw the tiny rodlike appendage, like the bent stem of a flower above a gray rock, she had a target. The "rock" was a fair-sized angler fish, the ugly brute the French called *lotte*. The appendage lured curious smaller fish over the large, wide mouth beneath.

She circled and fired the spear gun, but too hastily. The tip struck the fish far along its narrow tail. Instantly the angler exploded from the bottom, and Kits damned her impatience. A sign of fatigue, mentally noted.

She let the fish play out the line knotted to the spear shank, and followed along, determined to take this one home for the pot.

The ugly fish was equally determined to shake the irritation. It dove into a rock hole, and Kits went with it, arching her body and gracefully clearing a space between two sharp rock pillars that hadn't looked wide enough for an eel.

When she cleared the other side she saw the fish clearly, the taut line, like a narrow ray of light, connecting them. She realized with a start that she must now be in the clearer water beyond the confines of the bay, and in confirmation she felt the surge of a strong current forcing her farther out. The first click of warning and again the mental assessment: strength, distance to the *Marie-Hélène*, the amount of fight left in the ugly broad-headed fish pulling on ahead of her.

Still on the safe side of the red line, she calculated. Just barely.

Time to quit playing and either take the fish or give him his victory. Using her powerful kick, she tried to slow its flight, drawing on the slender line with arms that quickly drained of their strength.

Intent on the contest, she almost missed it.

As she corkscrewed her body around to force the fish to expand itself dragging her weight behind it, she caught, on the periphery of vision, the barest hint of a shape foreign to the sea bottom.

Without a second's hesitation, she let go of the spear gun, line, and fish. There, in deeper water, she could make out the blue hull, the long sweep of keel painted a deep red. Fifty yards below her, Kits had discovered the sunken *Pegasus*.

"She must be in a hundred and fifty feet," said Kits, "maybe more. Can you handle that depth?"

"Never tried," said Stone, continuing to load 35mm film into the Nickonos. In the light of the kerosene lantern, Stone's jaw was set and determined.

"Out past the rocks the currents are strong; the less swimming horizontally, the better," Kits said.

"I'll put the *Marie-Hélène* on top of her."

"David, how did you know? It's been troubling me."

"I found something ashore," he said, not looking up from the camera.

"When you went back to the clearing?"

"Yes."

*He doesn't want this*. Odd.

"Something to do with the pig?"

When, after the longest time, he nodded, she felt her guts heave as she remembered his words: *Rooting around for food*.

"Oh, God no!"

She started past him for the Zodiac. Stone leaped in front of her, grabbing her wrists and trying to wrestle her arms to her sides. The muscles in her thighs drove against him like coiled springs.

"A body, wasn't it?" Kits said, accusing him.

"Listen to me."

"It was Polly!"

Her head thrashed sidewise, something hooded and animal behind her eyes.

"It wasn't Polly."

"You're lying. Liar!"

"It wasn't Polly. A girl, yes. But . . . she'd been dead longer. Before Polly even disappeared."

"How do you know?"

"It was the girl from the boat. The one who untied me. The hair . . . I could tell. Do you want me to spell it out?"

Her fists unclenched and she went limp in his grip.

"You believe me?"

"But why was she killed?"

"I don't know. Maybe they found out she'd freed me, or maybe she fought them."

"You were right," said Kits. "I'd like to face those people. Hurt them, somehow."

"You and Christian."

"What about you? Is finding your boat it? The place you draw the line?"

Stone didn't answer her, not then.

Later, on deck, she stood silently next to him and looked out toward the point in the ocean beneath which was the *Pegasus*. A moment later she was in his arms, her face pressed close to his chest. She could hear the slow thump of his heart deepen its beat. They didn't kiss, although she knew it would be all right between them now. They stood in silence, content to hold each other, to let their bodies say whatever needed to be said.

They dove at first light.

Stone took the camera, Kits a short alloy prying bar. Both carried lights.

She worked out the timing of the dive, calculating the air in their tanks and the time needed to ascend and descend.

"Counting in decompression time we'll have a maximum of ten minutes working below a hundred and fifty feet. No horsing around either," she told Stone. "When I point, we go up."

Stone offered a grin, a little less rare these days. "Aye, aye, Captain."

The water was brilliantly clear. Kits saw the *Pegasus* almost the moment they oriented themselves and began the descent. She could sense Stone's impatience and reached out to hold him back. Finally he nodded; let her guide this part of it.

The boat rested nearly upright, supported by a gray finger of rock. Stone's first photo was made as they approached and would show the craft's line and paintwork. The antifouling was still holding out against the sea, and at a distance *Pegasus* looked almost fit enough to sail away—except that the main and mizzen masts had been sawn through and left to hang by their rigging. Stone took photos of both.

Circling the boat, he found the angry tear in the hull where the interior plumbing exited the hull via a demand valve. Smart. A small explosive charge there would have profited from the inherent weakness where the fitting passed through the hull.

As he moved toward the small crew's cabin aft of the cockpit, he felt Kits next to him. The door latch had been tied shut, but a crawlspace from the cabin along the inside of the hull led to the engine compartment; it was large enough so someone could get in or out. He cut loose the door, and shined in the light.

The cords were still there, at all four corners of the bunk where he'd been tied.

So much for question one.

He looked at Kits and pointed back toward the cockpit.

She started to precede him, but it was his turn to restrain her. He pointed to himself. It had to be that way, and not only because he knew the boat's interior layout. She nodded and gave him an after-you-sir gesture.

Through the cockpit, then down into the companion-way that led to the main cabin and two smaller ones forward. He hadn't remembered it being so narrow. The interior of a small boat can be claustrophobic in even ideal conditions; now with 150 feet of water above them and darkness all around, he had to concentrate to keep his self-control, to breathe smoothly against the slight back pressure of the regulator clamped in his mouth.

He felt Kits's hand touch the center of his back, fingers splayed and caressing. Not pushing him ahead, but assuring him she knew and was there.

Stone played the light over the door that led to the main cabin. He pulled in a slow breath and turned the latch. It moved easily enough, but the door was jammed, either from the explosion or the subsequent battering of the vessel by the sea.

He exchanged the camera with Kits for the pry bar.

While she held the light, he worked the bar around the frame, levering the door free. He took back the light, held it ready, and pulled the cabin door toward him.

The eye was open—a beady, black gem set in a wrinkled socket. It seemed to peer out at him from a blanket of mottled brown tossed carelessly over the bed.

Then the blanket moved, the bulbous head taking shape around the eye. As Kits grabbed his weighted belt, the entire room came alive with moving legs and the sudden inky jet that billowed from beneath the large octopus. Stone felt himself pulled forcefully back and down upon Kits as the creature propelled itself past him, the touch deadly cold against his flesh. The mouthpiece of his regulator tore from his lips, life snatched away in a hissing stream of air bubbles.

He took in a mouthful of putrid water, gagging. The light dropped away as he grabbed for the mouthpiece. For a tight instant he knew his lungs were filling with water, but then Kits was there, calmly using the light to show the transfer of her own mouthpiece to his mouth.

He had the presence of mind to clear the water from it before taking in a slow, delicious suck of air that was sweeter than any he'd ever tasted in his life. Another and another, and by then Kits had retrieved his own mouthpiece. She presented it to him like a gift, which indeed it was.

The interior cabin was filled with impenetrable ink, and Stone gestured her topside. She didn't precisely understand, but led them out of the confinement of *Pegasus*'s hull.

From the top of the cockpit he pointed to a pair of hatchways forward, the largest the skylight to the main cabin. Stone didn't need the pry bar. It was closed but unlatched, and somehow, with instincts sharpened over millions of evolutionary years, the octopus had used it to gain entrance.

Stone pulled open the hatch, and waited until the ink cleared. Kits tapped him on the shoulder, pointed to her watch, and held up two fingers: two minutes. No putting it off. He swam to the edge of the hatchway and shined in the light.

When Kits approached, he reached out to hold her away. But she made an angry hum or protest loud enough for Stone to hear. He moved aside to give her a good look.

It wasn't one to forget.

There were three of them, laid out on the master bunk, bonds still in place. Their bones were a bit of a jumble, but she had no trouble recognizing the three skulls greenish with algae and decay. They looked up from empty dark sockets, through the open hatchway toward the sky far above them.

In his bedroom, the policeman Labatt lay awake, listening to the metallic rattle inside the air conditioner; louder tonight than the night before, he was certain. The woman next to him continued snoring.

Less than a year old and already the apparatus threatened to fail him. At his age, a man owed himself a few comforts. It was painful to think of once again enduring a night on this hellish coast to awake in a sweat-soaked bed. Or of his wife moving away in the darkness, complaining it was too hot for love. When was it not too hot for love in this country?

He sat up, wondering if he could hear the telephone in the next room above the infernal rattling.

The child was awake, too, standing in his crib. He watched Labatt with the same large black eyes of his mother. The face of a Hamitic angel, round with almond skin, the hair coarse and dark. Labatt often wondered what truly had been his own contribution in the creation of the child who called him Father. Long ago he admitted that his genes had taken the recessive path. Still, it would be his hands that would shape the child into a proper representative of civilization, the chief agent of which would be a school in France.

Which meant money.

Fatima scarcely understood what he had done for her and the child, was prepared to do. Fatima, the common lower-class name of his wife; he detested it. Granted she had other appealing attributes, excessive in almost every regard.

Four years ago she had been a small, sensuous delight. A body of curves and fullness with pointed breasts the color of chocolate and a pliancy in her young limbs that wrung a pleasure from his sagging physique that he had never before experienced.

Occasionally he thought of his previous life, his French wife. Still his wife legally, for they had never divorced. Even ten years ago, when he'd fled, she'd been sinking comfortably into middle-age. A life that centered on the dinner table—buying food, preparing food, endless meals, often in silence except for the clatter of silverware against her favorite Limoges. Twice a day, every day of their marriage. In his clearest memory of her she was seated at a dinner table.

Of Fatima, the memory was a figure beneath him in bed, using her body to urge more from him, to give him pleasure.

Yet, at scarcely past twenty, the curves of her body already showed the striations of pregnancy and child-birth, and the added weight promised by her bloodlines. In ten years she, too, would be old; but then so would he. What would they talk about? What did they talk about now? The child. If only she understood the chances he had taken to separate their lives from the sterile privation of the village. They had a TV set and two radios (one forever turned to the atonal jibberish of Arabic pop music), the trips to Tangier, and a year ago the air conditioner.

And what if she were to understand his risk? What more could she give him?

In the other room, the telephone was ringing.

# Chapter 21
## Pierre

Labatt held the phone to his ear and checked the time: a little past 5:00 a.m.

From the bedroom, Fatima called, "Chéri."

Labatt covered the mouthpiece. "I'm here. I haven't left you."

At the wrong moments she had the temperament of a demanding child. He needed a few seconds' peace to calculate what must be done.

Experience as a policeman had taught him there were times when it was best to do nothing. Put off a decision long enough and it would make itself; ignore the discomforting question until it was forgotten. But failure to make a decision now would put initiative in the hands of others, a dangerous business.

Two hours later he made a call from a public phone in the post office of a nearby village. The number he dialed from memory was in Tangier.

When he heard a familiar voice, he said, "A word from Pierre."

In the silence, Labatt thought his contact had forgotten the call words.

But then: "Go ahead."

Labatt knew this man only as a telephone number and voice. His accent, though neither of Paris nor the Midi, was French, a singular item of rapport.

"The landing place and boat have been discovered," Labatt told him. "And something more."

"Yes?"

"The remains of a body."

"You are sure?"

"The people I sent to watch are very sure. Did you know?"

"It's not our concern," the man answered evasively. "Where is our visitor?"

"At sea. I've ordered the customs boat to intercept him under the pretense of irregularities. It is never difficult to find a few."

"Things will not be left in this fashion," the voice said. "We must protect ourselves."

Labatt shut his eyes. Vague, but clear enough.

The voice told him, "Call again in one hour."

Labatt waited in a café. He always did as directed. His part was a small one, a single hand out among many. Hands reaching, he had little doubt, from the very center of the government. And how many others spread across Europe?

When he called a second time, the voice delivered his instructions.

By ten o'clock that morning, freshly shaved and in uniform, Labatt sat waiting behind his desk.

A little before noon Stone sighted the sleek gray hull of the French-built customs boat a few miles astern.

Kits shaded her eyes. "What could they want?"

Stone had been trying for the twelve-mile limit before first light, but the *Marie-Hélène*'s diesel failed to cooperate, running dangerously hot. He'd been forced to shut it down and set sail. He wanted to get the roll of film he'd taken of the *Pegasus* to Christian for starters; so far, it was his only item of tangible evidence.

"Routine, maybe," he answered.

"You're a lousy liar, David Stone."

He thought about radioing a Mayday, but it was hardly the gesture of an innocent sailing craft, still within territorial jurisdiction.

There was always the Bren, hidden just forward of the wheel. Its 30-caliber bullets would do a neat job chewing up the customs boat's plywood hull, but he dismissed the thought instantly, uncomfortable to have even considered it.

As the boat drew near, a uniformed officer hailed them over a bullhorn, requesting they return to port.

"What's the problem?" Stone called out.

Again the officer requested they return to port, and when a sailor appeared on deck with a machine pistol held loosely in the crook of his arm, Stone offered a salute and brought the *Marie-Hélène* around.

Labatt was waiting for them on the customs wharf.


"Nothing serious, Captain Stone. Irregularities, I am told, in the manner you cleared port." Labatt gestured off toward the vacant customs shed. "Tomorrow the *douane* will wish to inspect your boat more closely."

Labatt shrugged sadly. "I have reserved rooms for you in the hotel. Come."

"We'd prefer to stay aboard," said Kits, "if it's all the same."

"Come," said Labatt, his smile of invitation oddly frozen.

\* \* \*

The "hotel" was four rooms on the second floor of a bar and small restaurant. The building was of white plastered brick on a dusty square near the dirt highway that led toward the mountains. Stunted olive trees lined the square; behind the building was a grove of date palms.

When they entered, the mixed aromas of strong disinfectant and roasting goat rolled over them. "Lovely," said Kits without enthusiasm.

They were greeted by a hard-faced Muslim woman in her sixties, who exited the kitchen long enough to pour two glasses of red wine for Labatt and his police driver. She produced a pair of large brass keys, took one unsmiling look at her guests, and left them without a word.

The driver drank his wine down in a gulp, and pulled up a chair by the door. A birthmark in the shape of a clover leaf splotched one cheek, and he scratched at it irritably, watching them with empty black eyes.

"Are we under arrest?" asked Stone.

"Not precisely," said Labatt. "Shall we say he is for our mutual protection. There are sometimes robberies, an occasional kidnapping." He shrugged. "The woman will feed you, and tomorrow, if all goes well, you will be on your way. *Bon appétit!*"

He bowed to Kits, saluted Stone, and left them with a glance toward the policeman near the door.

"In French or English, it still means we've been had," said Kits. "I just wish I knew how."

In the front seat of his parked auto, Labatt sat waiting. He could feel the sweat rolling down his stomach inside his shirt, and he promised himself his next automobile would have air conditioning. Even dirty business could be conducted in comfort, and he sipped again at a flask of cognac.

A dust-covered Renault 16 with Tangier plates arrived a quarter of an hour later. The vehicle was doubtless stolen—in this circumstance, hardly his concern.

The two men who stepped from the car fitted the type: twenty, if that; dark, slim-hipped Arab boys in tight trousers and high-heeled boots.

Without exchanging courtesies, Labatt told them where to find the hotel.

"Rooms one and two, second floor. During the half-hour before midnight the hotel will be empty."

"A man and a woman," one of the boys confirmed.

"Isn't that what you were told?" Labatt snapped. "They're alone in the hotel."

Labatt wondered how much they were being paid. He was curious to know what a human life was worth these days.

"One thing," Labatt added. "It would be better if the bodies were never found."

In the narrow hotel room, Kits looked at the bed and bowed mattress.

"It's only for a night," said Stone. "We're not buying the place."

"That doesn't mean I have to like it."

Kits caught the complaining tone in her own voice and tried to smile. "Sorry, I've been thinking again about Polly. Worrying about where she might be sleeping tonight."

"If she saw this place, she'd be worrying about you."

"David, we're not too late, are we? Could she already have passed this point in the pipeline?"

Stone tried to buoy her up. "I'm not a great reader of

trail, but that clearing we explored hadn't any signs of recent use."

"Maybe they have other landing places."

"Possible. But they aren't moving the girls one at a time. It must take some time before they have enough to make a run worthwhile."

It was the disturbing question of economics again. To Stone it still didn't add up. Boats, more than one. And a bloody lot of scheming to scoop girls off the Riviera and transport them thousands of miles before the payoff. Le Pic had told him about the East African slave market that still existed in Zanzibar. There, a few ounces of gold would buy a Nordic blond or a young village maiden.

The picture of a human auction wasn't the one he wanted Kits to sleep on. He needn't have worried; exhausted, she had already put her head down and drifted off.

Stone extinguished the lights and stepped to the window. Her room faced the square, empty, and dimly lit by a single bare globe.

He tiptoed from the room, crossed the hall, and left his door open a crack. He lay down on the bed, not bothering to undress.

He'd considered telling Labatt about their discovery of the *Pegasus*, but decided firmly against it. The rules here were different. Let Christian take heart in boards of inquiry and due process of law. Here it was friends, bribery, and quiet money that bought favorable judgments, licenses, or customs clearance. All to be settled in the morning, Stone had no doubt, with the *duoane* and Labatt each getting his slice.

How well would Christian have functioned here, or the mysterious Sophie and her supposedly influential friends? He thought about the Swiss lawyer Bertrand, the people he'd fronted for in the purchase of the *Sea Fox*.

All a long way from a narrow bed in a fly-stained hotel room on the margin of Africa. Still they kept turning over in his mind.

A quarter of an hour later, he heard the sound of metal scrape against plaster below his window. Then a rough female voice swearing in Arabic. He rose and crossed to the window.

Below, the hard-faced woman from the restaurant was righting her ancient bicycle. He watched her move off in the darkness, her body bobbing machinelike as she gained speed. What task was so calling in the middle of the night? Stone dismissed the thought. But not quite.

He started again for the bed, his limbs heavy with fatigue but his mind racing. Instead, he went to the partially open door and listened.

Below music continued on the radio, strident and nasal. He walked softly to the top of the stairs, paused, then descended partway.

In the bar, the lamps were still on, bathing the room in a yellowish glare. Labatt's policeman was nowhere in sight. No one. Not a soul. Only music and bright lights, like a beacon.

And across the square, a dusty black Renault parked without headlights. When he'd looked out at the square from Kits's room, it had been empty.

When two men stepped from the car and started across the square, Stone eased himself back up the stairs. When he could no longer be seen, he began to run.

# Chapter 22
## Escape

"David!"

"Get up."

"So early?"

He pulled her upright and shook her.

Kits's eyes went wide. "What's wrong?"

"Trouble. Come on." He whirled her toward the door.

"But my things. My purse."

"Leave it."

"I will not."

Pushing her ahead, he stopped long enough to lock the door to her room. It might buy a few seconds' time, something.

"Inside my room, fast." When Kits eyed him strangely, he said, "Move, woman! We've no time."

He shut and locked the door, then went straight to the window and swung it open.

"Out."

"The window? You're mad and I'm still asleep."

"Out, or I'll throw you out."

She looked down, judging it eleven or twelve feet to the ground.

170

"Granted, it's a rotten hotel . . ."

"Here, grab my arm." He swept her legs from under her and sat her on the window frame. "Run for the trees, and don't look back."

He eased her down as far as he could. She hit with a grunt, mouthed something rude, but began to run.

As Stone legged himself over the sill, he could hear footsteps on the stairwell.

They'd nearly reached the dark wall of date trees when a shot rang out behind him. He saw Kits falter, start to go down.

"You're hit?"

"No," she breathed. "Big feet."

He jerked her upright, forced her ahead as a second shot came, and a third snapped through the palms overhead. Then they were among the trees, moving deeper into the grove.

He risked a glance back toward the hotel, saw a figure framed in the lighted window. A second man was already running toward the date trees, thirty yards behind them.

"That way," he said, pointing off to the left. They ran low for another twenty yards before Stone caught the back of her jeans and pulled her down behind the thick trunk of a palm.

He laid a finger across his lips. Behind them, close to the point they'd just left; someone swore; they heard the crush of dry foliage as the footfalls continued deeper into the grove, following a direct line. One pursuer, estimated Stone, no more a woodsman than himself.

"I hope it's a bad dream I'll soon wake up from," whispered Kits. But she immediately sensed that the new tactic was stealth, and set off in a half-crouch. They continued for what seemed like an hour, but when Stone put his watch close to his face, he calculated a maximum of five minutes.

Again they crouched and listened. In the distance a dog began to bark.

"Now what," she breathed, "or dare I ask?"

"Sorry for the hasty exit."

"Don't be. I'm sure I wouldn't have liked what they had in mind. But why?"

"We'll ask Labatt."

Stone was trying to remember the lay of the land. An exercise in futility, but he didn't want to tell Kits. Hiding in a date grove from gunmen trying to kill them. Escape, and what came next?

Labatt's setup. Once the two gunmen reported a slight delay in schedule, the policeman would cover the boat and wait. The chance of two foreigners escaping on foot from this lonely corner of the earth was nil, especially with Labatt's police behind them.

The boat was their only chance. The boat, and a hiding place along the coast until they could run for the open sea.

Opposite the hotel, a road led back toward the village, but to reach it they'd have to skirt the square.

"Come on," said Stone, "we've got to take a chance."

"David, is this the way you live?"

"Exciting, isn't it?" When they reached the edge of the date grove, Stone knelt to survey the darkness ahead of them. To the left, perhaps a hundred yards distant, was the hotel. Beyond it the square, with the gunmen's automobile on the far side.

Tempting.

But what chance that the keys were in the ignition? The French locked everything; the Arabs locked and chained it down. Not so much out of distrust, one was told, as a kindness to spare a fellow man temptation.

Far behind them a pair of shots. Then immediately the

deeper sound of a shotgun firing once. A woman started to yell, a high-pitched rattle in Arabic joined by a chorus of barking dogs.

"Let's cross," said Stone.

But as he rose, he heard a voice not sixty feet ahead of him speaking loudly in Arabic.

He froze, tensed instinctively for the gunshot that would follow. Instead, there came the sudden flare of a lighted match.

The face that bent to light a cigarette wore a blue and gold kepi. A raw, clover-shaped birthmark splotched his cheek.

Labatt's policeman.

Not moving an inch, Stone watched as the man took a deep drag on his cigarette, then began a slow unsteady circle while engaged in a spirited conversation with himself.

"Drunk?" whispered Kits.

"Drunk enough," said Stone.


Above the metallic rattle of the air conditioner, Labatt wasn't even sure he heard it.

He sat in the darkened room, sipping from a large balloon of cognac. A Browning automatic rested in his lap.

The second time the *tap*, *tap*, *tap* on his outer door was louder.

"Idiot," murmured Labatt softly. His policeman was to have called when it was finished. He didn't want the man here, bringing this filthy business into his home.

From the other room, his wife Fatima sleepily called to him.

Labatt sighed. The God he whispered to that night had abandoned him.

"It's all right," he soothed. But something told him

that wasn't true. He went to the door, taking the Browning with him.

Peeking through the Judas hole, he saw it was his man all right, the bloodred cloverleaf on his cheek blending into a raw gash across his upper lip.

"Fool," said Labatt through the closed door. "What do you want?"

"Something's happened."

"*Chéri*," called Fatima, her voice whining in a special way that told him her favors were waiting.

Angrily, Labatt pulled open the door.

"Be quick, man. I told you to stay away from here."

"Not much choice," came the voice of David Stone. Standing to one side, Stone aimed the small service automatic levelly at Labatt's head. The Maitland woman was with him. "Now, we'll all step inside. Unless you want me to start shooting here."

As Stone closed the door behind him, Labatt fought to maintain his composure. So much of his authority resided in his official uniform, worn in the proper environment.

Now, facing an armed man in his own home, his words had the false bluster of a private citizen suffering an invasion of his narrow kingdom.

"What do you want?"

Stone took Labatt's heavy Browning and pocketed the smaller pistol. "Handcuff your flunky to the couch before he passes out on it."

Labatt did so, the man averting his eyes. *He would pay.*

"Please, this is my home." Labatt cast an anxious glance toward the bedroom. "My wife and child."

"Then mark how it feels. We need the keys to your car."

When Labatt hesitated, Stone spoke to the woman. "Get his kid."

"Wait." Labatt went to the desk and held up the car keys. "Take it. There's enough petrol to reach Tangier."

"Is there a guard on the boat?"

"No guard," Labatt assured him. But with Stone's question, the policeman realized that he might not only survive this ordeal, but solve the whole problem. "For such a routine matter, why should there be a guard?"

Stone walked to the telephone and tore the cord from the wall. When he blocked the door to the bedroom with a straight-backed chair, a child began to cry inside.

"You drive."

"I never argue with a gun," said Labatt, managing a narrow smile. "It's not too late. No one has to know about this. Among ourselves we can make an arrangement."

Stone looked inquiringly at the woman, who shrugged. His resolve beginning to fade? Labatt would give him things to think about, promises.

"We'll talk in the car," said Stone.

The drive wasn't far, the narrow streets of the village poorly lit and empty.

"Why are you doing this?" asked Labatt, hoping he sounded properly mystified.

While Stone told him what had happened at the hotel, the woman watched Labatt steadily.

"A robbery attempt, perhaps. Nothing more," Labatt said lightly.

"Whatever it was, everyone helped make it easy. Including your cop taking a hike."

"Am I to blame for such a blending of circumstances?"

Stone and the woman exchanged another look. Uncertain? Yes, he was sure now. But Stone still held the gun.

If he couldn't convince Stone to surrender the weapon, then the guns of the customs boat would finish him at sea. Crude, but ultimately the same result: Stone and the woman dead, thus silent.

As the wharf came into view, Labatt said, "Give me the gun, before it's too late."

Stone gestured for Labatt to park near the *Marie-Hélène* and told the woman, "Go start the engine."

So be it, thought Labatt. He had given Stone the final unknowing choice in the manner of his own demise.

"Leave now and the consequences will be grave," Labatt warned, without conviction. "If you stay and give me the gun . . ."

"What then?"

"An arrangement, between you and me."

"We saw one at work tonight. I'll chance the boat."

"I am sorry, Monsieur Stone."

"So am I. You don't look in shape for a trip."

It dawned on Labatt slowly, as Stone smiled, all signs of vacillation gone. It was Stone who had been toying with him, to keep his mind occupied.

"You're taking me?" Labatt's voice broke, incredulous.

"Not very far."

"I don't understand."

"You will."

# Chapter 23
## Hammerhead

"What are you doing?" asked Labatt. An idiot's question. He was going to die, here and now.

They were running parallel with the coast in the *Marie-Hélène* when Stone eased back the throttle and asked Kits to take the wheel. He dug a skein of nylon line from a locker and threw it at Labatt's feet.

"I want to know what you know."

"I know nothing. From the beginning, you've been mistaken."

"I want to know what happens in that bay up ahead, and what happened to my boat."

The woman watched them; Labatt directed his plea toward her. "A mistake," he cried. "Please." She looked away.

"And I want to know who sent the gunmen," said Stone. "Who is behind this whole rotten business."

A brief, horrifying vision flashed through Labatt's mind. He imagined the exchange taking place in the prefecture with he himself the interrogator. The pleading suspect, feeble explanations in the face of obvious guilt, a defense dependent upon mercy. He would have squeezed the suspect to a dry husk.

Stone said, "Labatt, I am out of patience." He nudged the nylon line with his foot. "Tie it around your feet. Do a good job because your life will depend on it."

"I don't understand," he said, but complied quickly.

Silently Stone checked the knots; then he pointed the pistol and thumbed back the hammer.

"You won't shoot," said Labatt. "Not in cold blood."

"Right now my blood isn't that cold."

"Not an execution."

Stone called over his shoulder. "Kits, what were you telling me about hammerheads?"

Kits caught on, relieved that Stone intended only to scare Labatt; his manner had frightened her. "You mean about their being night feeders?"

"Hammerheads?" questioned Labatt, failing to understand.

Stone put it into French: "*Requins marteau.* Sharks, Labatt, the big ugly ones with eyes out to here so they get a good look before they bite."

Labatt blinked, the mouth firming a little too bravely.

Kits said, "Or did you mean about their ability to sense a creature in distress at great distances—it's called lateral line sense."

Labatt shook his head defiantly. "Words, Monsieur Stone. Only words."

"Ah hell, Labatt," he said, crestfallen. "I knew I couldn't fool you."

At the Frenchman's cry, Kits turned in time to see Stone lift him over the rail and drop him into the sea.

"They're around," Stone called after him. Labatt's scream pierced the darkness astern.

"David, you bastard!"

But already Stone had looped the fast-playing-out line

around a stanchion. As it zinged tight, he leapt to the wheel. "I'll take it."

Immediately he eased the throttle forward, the pulse of the diesel engine taking on a new sound.

"You'll drown him," Kits shouted.

"Or loosen his mouth."

Kits moved to the rail now, trying to pick out the policeman. A sliver of moon cast a pale light on the water, and she could see his wake as he plowed along behind them, glimmers of phosphorescence marking his path. A face, a hand, and she realized Labatt had grabbed the line and pulled himself around, only to take a mouthful of seawater with each cry.

Then for the barest instant, the boat, Labatt, and a moonlit ocean were in perfect alignment.

Stone saw Kits strain forward.

"Oh my God," she whispered.

Her tone sent a jolt of alarm through Stone.

"What's wrong?"

"Something is out there."

"What do you mean *something*?"

"Out beyond Labatt. I saw something break the surface."

"You mean he really has drawn a shark?"

She looked around. "I think so."

Immediately Stone backed off the throttle and spun the wheel hard to port, steering the *Marie-Hélène* in a tight circle back toward the policeman.

"Watch Labatt," he shouted.

"There, David, look," Kits said, pointing.

In the dying wake of the boat, Stone thought he saw the large dorsal fin veering away a hundred yards beyond Labatt.

"I've lost him," Kits cried. "Him *and* the shark."

Easy enough to lose someone in the water even in full daylight. "Labatt!" Stone yelled.

In reply he heard the policeman's feeble call.

"Start hauling in slack line," Stone ordered, ducking down into the companionway. He reappeared with the Bren, working a curved magazine into its receiver.

"There!" said Kits, marking the direction of Labatt's cry. The boat's *Marie-Hélène*'s momentum had kept him moving on the surface. But now, with the boat motionless and his feet tied together, Labatt was frantically slapping his arms at the water to keep himself from going under.

"Don't, Labatt, it's the worst thing you can do!"

But caught in panic, the policeman only flailed more wildly.

Stone aimed the heavy Bren at the point beyond Labatt where he'd seen the dorsal fin. He nudged the trigger, loosing off a burst that sent small plumes of water toward the horizon. Hard, high, and left; Sophie had been right.

He fired again, two short bursts that exploded closer to the policeman than he intended. He saw Labatt's head duck under.

When the Frenchman reappeared, he called out, "Please, no more. I will tell everything."

It took Stone a long second to understand. Labatt thought he intended his execution.

"Everything?" asked Stone and waited.

Next to him Kits whispered, "You're a horrible man."

And from the water: "Yes, everything."

When they brought Labatt aboard, he fell forward, resting his cheek against the deck.

For a moment Kits searched the dark water. "Nothing. I must have been wrong."

"Funny about the ocean at night," said Stone. He was looking directly at Labatt.

"I knew it would end," Labatt explained. Stone poured him an Armagnac, which the policeman savored deeply. "I knew it when I heard you'd come back."

"So you tried to have us killed."

"I was, as they say, following orders."

He pushed the glass toward Stone for a refill before going on:

"My part in it was small."

"How small?" asked Stone.

"Assigning the customs boat to pursue cigarette smugglers along the coast in the opposite direction. A little money passed . . . here and there."

"But you knew they were running in girls."

"I was told," Labatt acknowledged slowly.

Kits asked, "How often did they make their trips?"

"About two months apart."

"And the last time?" she pursued.

"Only once since they used Captain Stone's boat. A few weeks after."

"And when next?" she asked.

"Soon," Labatt said. "But since they know of your discoveries, they'll choose another place."

Kits slid a forlorn glance toward Stone.

"Where does the *Sea Fox* come from?" asked Stone.

"It wasn't a thing they'd tell me."

"Who'd tell you?"

"My contact," Labatt replied. "A man I knew only as a voice on the telephone."

"And none of it bothered you?" questioned Kits. "You never thought about those poor girls, what became of them?"

Labatt sighed wearily.

"Conscience, madame, is a luxury of people who have never faced temptation. The money brought me comfort. My wife is young, she needs things. You must understand."

He searched her face. Kits said nothing, but there was a hardness in her expression Stone hadn't seen before. Labatt shrugged, beaten.

"What became of the girls after they were landed?" Kits asked.

Labatt frowned at her persistence. "Taken by truck into the mountains. The exchange was made there. The Montagnards profited greatly from the arrangement."

Stone took a moment to react. "You mean the girls were items of trade?"

"More precisely, items of barter," answered Labatt. "The girls only became worth the effort when delivered at some distant market. It was their transport with great difficulty that made them valuable."

"Why, you pig!" said Kits.

"Madame, I am merely explaining how the trade functioned."

Stone nodded, finally understanding. "And the item the Montagnards bartered in exchange for the girls. Likewise, on a lonely bay on the coast of Africa, worth little more than coffee or tea."

"Less at times," said Labatt. "But a fortune in the markets of Europe and North America. The profit goes to the shipper."

"Because the risk was in getting the goods to market. I knew it," said Stone, sadly triumphant. "The whole setup was too big, too organized."

"To do what?" said Kits, still mystified. "You mean the girls weren't the point of the whole business?"

"An item of trade in a complex arrangement," said Labatt, "but, no, not the essential element."

"Trade for what?" asked Kits.

"Hashish, my good lady. Bricks of it, bags full, truckloads."

"And boatloads," added Stone.

"Tons," said Labatt. "So much hashish I can't even imagine."

Twenty minutes later Stone put Labatt ashore in the Zodiac.

"Where are we?" asked the policeman, looking toward the dark line of trees, the ridge of hills beyond.

"The bay where they landed the girls and loaded the dope. Out there they sunk the *Pegasus* with three people aboard."

"*Mon Dieu*," groaned Labatt.

"You didn't know?"

"Not about that, I swear."

"Get out of here, Labatt."

The policeman took a moment to comprehend.

"I'm not going to shoot you," Stone said. "You're right, I'd probably do something stupid like worry. By the time you reach the village, we'll be safe."

"Safe?" His laugh was bitter. "For how long? We'll both be punished. Me for failing to have you disappear, you for becoming the spoiler. I know these people. You've seen what they will do."

"If you believe that, then you'd better run for it."

"Where does a man like me run? To France? With an ignorant country girl and a half-caste child. Where to start again?"

"People start again all the time."

"I've always run, from one thing or another. Through the eyes of a policeman the entire world appears to be running. Never toward anything, always in flight. I don't suppose you think of such things."

"Not more than a couple of times a day." Stone unloaded the pistol and held it out. "Take the goddamn thing."

Labatt stared at it. Then he accepted the weapon and a moment later was lost in the darkness.

# Chapter 24
## Vessel Down

*The Gods smile . . .*

But not today, thought Stone. He lay on his side in several inches of foul-smelling bilge water, arms outstretched and aching from exertion.

A grunt of muscular force escaped his clenched teeth, as he pulled at the wrench and felt the final bolt come free.

Kits peered into *Marie-Hélène*'s engine well to find Stone wrapped unnaturally around the large Mercedes diesel.

"You look like you're giving birth."

"I am planning the demise of the so-called designer of this ill-conceived—"

"You told me all boats were trouble," she broke in.

"Which is why so many are named after women."

"Ah, but the pleasures."

Fifty nautical miles south of Majorca the temperature of the engine had suddenly red-lined during the daily charging of the batteries.

Setting sail and leaving Kits to the wheel, Stone had

begun checking out the cooling system, hoping that whatever was wrong would not require major surgery.

Proudly, he held up the large bolt he'd just extracted and grinned.

"A lot of work for such a little thing," said Kits. "And don't look for any double meanings."

"You're the one smiling, lady."

"Thinking of last night. Of you, and my own silliness. All those emotional lines people draw when they know they're about to lose themselves to something."

Or someone.

Close to midnight she'd poured Stone coffee, but found herself standing back a moment to watch him at the wheel.

Through all of it he'd been so steady. But now the strain of decision had settled upon him; the line of his neck and shoulders spoke of a fatigue beyond tiredness. She'd wanted Stone in one way from the beginning, she no longer argued that. But now the components of her desire had changed and she wasn't sure why. Because of the danger shared, perhaps, or the test of wills that had left neither of them victorious. Whatever the reason, she wanted David Stone, wanted more than his body. Wanted to share some of the burden for which Kits herself was so responsible.

As if touched by something telepathic, Stone turned, a look in his eyes she'd never seen before. She felt the heat rise again to her breasts, her nipples already hard and erect. Little betrayers.

The *Marie-Hélène* veered suddenly off course as Stone released the wheel and stepped toward her. There was no doubt at all about his intent, or what her response would be. "It's time," he said, and was there against her, their bodies pressing hungrily together, demanding more than mere tactile stimulation. A pressure that seemed generated from within. She was aware of motion but could no longer tell if it was the moving of their own bodies, the pitch of the *Marie-Hélène*, or some combination of the two intensified by a swirling of feelings within her own brain, a special reality of the moment she would be incapable of reconstructing even seconds later.

She had no idea what became of their clothing, could not recall having removed anything. She only knew that David's hands and mouth were suddenly on bare skin, seeking her out, moving as surely as if the body he touched were his own, for in that moment he must have known that it was. And then he was in her hands, swollen, an extension of her own desire, communicated through her mouth and fingertips. She wanted two mouths, needed two mouths and four hands to reach all parts of him at once, to tell him in a way that words could never convey how truthful this moment was, destined from the first contact of their eyes.

"Here. I want you here."

"Yes . . ."

There on the deck he entered her, a long, deep thrust that seemed to carry upward to her breastbone. Then another lifting her, his motion driving her pelvis away only to be drawn back around him by the strength in her own legs locked over his. *Oh, David* she might have said, or maybe it caught in her throat as she felt him begin to swell, swell then burst as she herself was just beginning to ride the waves, like the *jacaré*, like the dolphins rising so effortlessly from the depths, as his rumbling orgasm erupted. Still inside her, he hardened again, and this time, a dozen light years later, she *did* yell his name. A yell that was loud enough to reach the horizon, a yell that for the first time in her life was unconstrained by convention and the need to make love unheard by neighbors beyond plaster walls, a yell of peace and pleasure and ecstasy that must have sounded like a call from the core of her soul as she fell off the end of the earth.

Later she awoke to silence. The *Marie-Hélène* was adrift, and she was alone in the bed.

She sat up just as Stone, naked, stepped down into the cabin.

"What's the mat—?" she started to ask, but he answered before she finished.

"Just making sure we're alone on an empty sea."

They made love again, slowly this time, knowing the night had served its purpose well. Gone were all inhibitions, and the hasty defenses they'd both thrown up to protect themselves. All things worth saying they said, and when the final rising came from within them, Kits's rolling upon her like a storm wave, becoming more fierce as it reached its destination, they called out together and she felt the heat of tears falling wet upon her arms and realized they were David Stone's.

Now in the midday heat, she watched him wipe sweat from his forehead. Where they were going together she didn't know; but the past had left two very different people behind.

The Gods smile, indeed.

Again Stone bent down to the engine.

"David, why are we heading for Majorca?"

"To put you on a plane. Take our story and the roll of film to Christian." He tapped loose a rust-colored something the size of her fist.

"Is that the end of it?" He shot her a hard glance, very much the old David Stone, and Kits said, "I mean, you proved what you set out to prove: that your boat was pirated and sunk. I want to know if that's where it stops. You don't owe me for our time in bed together. I needed it more than you did."

"Did you ever think it might be too much for you and me. What comes next, I mean. Fine, we have Christian looking in closets, and Le Pic and Dolph and Aggie for moral support."

"Do you believe that?"

"I believe all we know is that the *Sea Fox* was running girls in and taking hashish out. Where to?—that's a question mark. Who's behind it all?—another question mark."

He spared her Labbat's opinion that whoever it was had a long, dangerous reach.

"But you've always come up with something to keep us going," she persisted.

Stone said, "The only thing I've come up with now is a frozen thermostat in the engine."

He held up the rusty part.

The worry crossed her eyes. "Does that mean more time lost?" She was thinking again of Polly.

"Not much. We can pick one up in Palma or have one air-freighted in overnight."

When he looked again at the rusted part, some small thing changed in his face.

Stubbornly, Kits said, "If you want me to catch a plane without you, you'll have to take back a lot of things you said last night."

"Possible."

"You creep!"

"Just possible," said Stone.

With a flush of relief she understood: he wasn't talking to her at all.


In a noisy surgery near the Place de la Madeleine, the doctor signed the prescription and held it out to Christian.

"Powerful," he warned. "*Très fort.*"

*Quit feigning reluctance, you quack.* Wasn't Christian paying him double the official price for a few minutes' consultation, and the pills?

"And try to stop drinking," the man advised sternly.

Try it yourself, thought Christian. The doctor was overweight with dry skin and fingers yellowed from too many cigarettes.

"The drinking only aggravates things."

*And keeps me going.* Christian paid the man, and was glad to be on the street again.

He walked into the nearest bar, ordered a *pastis*, and removed the two telegrams he'd received that morning from David Stone.

The first read:

> PEGASUS DISCOVERED IN THIRTY FATHOMS. HAVE PHOTOS.

Seven words that would likely mean Stone's vindication.

The second telegram gave Christian two new things to ponder. He read it again.

> CHECK DESTINATION ALL AIR-FREIGHT SHIPMENT RE-PAIR PARTS FOR PACKMAN DIESELS. TIME PERIOD COVERING DISAPPEARANCE *PEGASUS*.

Christian quickly grasped what Stone was getting at. If the *Sea Fox* had lost its engines at sea, there was a good chance new parts had been needed for their repair. The parts-replacement business for both aircraft and marine engines used air freight to fill "aircraft or vessel down" orders. Tracing the parts sent about the time the *Sea Fox* had its trouble might give them some clue to the mysterious vessel's home port.

He ordered another *pastis*, noting how difficult it was becoming to swallow even liquids. Time was running against him, against his body.

He'd drawn a blank in his attempt to find out who owned the *Sea Fox*. The secret remained locked away in the office of a Swiss lawyer.

Christian's connection with Israel Katz at Interpol had provided him with a few facts about the two passengers missing aboard the *Pegasus*, Hanna and Alec Gabriele, and more importantly, the organization they'd worked with. The massive German computer complex at Weisbaden had additionally spewed forth some delicious items on the woman Sophie, seeking vengeance on their behalf. Both stories were juicy enough, but unconnected to anything else he had.

As Christian hailed a cab, he smiled privately. Between the lines of the second telegram was a message Stone hadn't intended. Whatever had transpired on the quest with the Maitland woman, Stone was now firmly in the game, despite his earlier protests against involvement.

The Gods smile, all right.

But the devil laughs.

# Chapter 25
## Soldiers in the Night

Thirty-six hours after returning aboard the *Marie-Hélène*, Stone met Christian at the Nice–Côte d'Azur airport. Christian had taken the first early afternoon flight down from Paris.

"If the information you have is any good," he said, "I'm catching the next plane back. It's coming together. Fast."

He fell into stride with Stone. They took the elevator to the bar on the top floor, and found a table on the terrace.

In the harsh afternoon sunlight Christian's skin was waxy and pale except for the fine pattern of broken blood vessels that colored his cheekbones like rouge.

Smiling, he said, "It would amuse me no end if so small a thing as a few diesel parts were to bring our quarry down." That cadaverous grin on his gaunt, bony face. Christian wore a death mask.

"What did you turn up?" asked Stone.

"A vendor in Greenwich who air-freighted a cylinder assembly with a set of injectors the same week the *Pegasus* disappeared."

"Air-freighted where?"

Again the skeletal smile. "To Sardinia. Someone named Enzo care of Agenza Oliva at Di Fertilia airport. Of course we can't be certain they were for the *Sea Fox* . . ."

Stone was reviewing his earlier calculations about the *Sea Fox*'s possible home, based on Labatt's revelations.

"What we badly need," said Christian, "is a couple of separate lines of evidence to cross." He ordered a large whiskey.

"Try this," said Stone, holding out a thick, brown envelope filled with Xeroxed pages. "A gift from Bertrand."

"The Swiss lawyer?"

"Not a gift exactly. Information about a company called Opteros."

"Opteros?" Christian's high forehead ridged, puzzled.

"They own real estate," said Stone. "And a hundred-foot Ham-class minesweeper."

"Good Lord, you've found it! But how?" Christian's eyes flashed doubt.

"The lady Sophie bagged it from Bertrand's office in Geneva or had it done. Walked in, found the Opteros file, used the office's Xerox machine, and walked out again with no one the wiser."

Within hours of Stone's putting into port, Sophie had appeared with the file, in the exact fashion of their first meeting: she'd been waiting for him in the dark cabin of the *Marie-Hélène*. She seemed to know his every move in Cannes, and he was reasonably sure she had waited until Kits had packed herself off to Juan-les-Pins, explaining vaguely that she had loose ends to tidy up, before she'd made her approach.

"You still don't know with whom you're dealing, do you?" asked Christian.

"I know Sophie isn't your average bear," said Stone, ignoring Christian's tone of censure. "The Gabrieles carried Israeli passports. Sophie and her friends have unusual talents, and my first guess is they have something to do with Israeli intelligence. And whatever that is, it isn't official—I'd bet on it."

"What makes you say that?"

"Because Sophie didn't know what to make of the Opteros file once she had it. That's why she's tagging after you and me. If she had entrée to Israeli intelligence, they'd have access to the same sources you have, wouldn't they?"

"All but a French detective. The computer data, most certainly."

"So Sophie assembles a few old friends of the Gabrieles, or maybe not."

"Meaning what?"

"Meaning maybe she's working alone, waiting for us to do our job. Alone or with a team, it doesn't matter. Sophie delivered."

"Oh, she'd deliver, all right. Results, abundant and bloody."

"What's eating you?"

"The way things are done is important, Stone. A dirty operation doesn't suddenly cleanse itself because it settles a score. Sophie and her friends, the press dubbed them 'the Hit Team.' Ring a bell?"

"Something about the Israelis hunting down terrorists, six, eight years ago. It made the papers."

"Indeed," said Christian, gulping his drink. "When Israeli athletes were murdered by Black September terrorists during the '72 Olympics, the Israelis secretly formed a special assassination unit drawn from the Mossad and the army. Revenge, pure and simple. Of course, the man they wanted most was the planner of the

Munich massacre—a young Palestinian named Abu Hassan, whose father was murdered by the Israelis years before. Noble causes on both sides, don't you see? Which leaves a just God rather in a pickle."

"How do you know all this?"

"Most of it came out later in the papers. The names of the people involved who are still alive remain in police computers, to which I have access."

"Sophie?"

"Quite prominently."

"Go on," said Stone, sitting back, but only partly listening. He was thinking of Kits. What exactly had she meant by "loose ends to tie up in Juan-les-Pins." She was under his skin and digging deeper.

"So now the hit team began tracking down the Black September leadership and assassinating them. Cyprus, Paris, Rome. Superb organization," said Christian, without admiration. "Support groups called *heths* would enter a city days ahead of the planned assassination. Work out escape routes, rent cars, hotel rooms, whatever was needed. Then came the *beths*, the first of the operational groups, small teams that would directly support the assassination—drivers, back-up guns, that sort of thing. Then, when the proper time came, the *alephs* arrived."

"The guns," said Stone.

"The guns," Christian confirmed. "Teams of two or three, armed with whatever special weapons the killing required. Their favored weapon was an unsilenced .22 automatic, with underpowered loads but large-capacity magazines. It was not unusual to find one of the hit team's victims with a dozen bullets in the head. Pop-pop-pop."

"The lead would tend to add up."

"Quick, if not clean, and out of the city within minutes of the assassination. Oh, they were good."

"If they were that good, how did the press get on to them?"

"Because they hit the wrong man and got caught. You see, all the while they'd been searching in vain for Abu Hassan. They thought they'd tracked him to a small Norwegian town and found him working as a waiter. They set up the hit using some inexperienced people because, you see, the whole operation was taking its toll. Mental breakdowns, an array of problems the planners hadn't taken into account."

"They missed him."

"They hit the waiter all right, but he turned out to be just that—an Arab waiter. Then the team stumbled trying to get across the border, and several were caught by the police. In court most of it came out, and lo and behold, the Israelis ended up looking just as murderous as the Palestinians. Terribly bad press."

"So that ended the hit team."

"Not at all." Christian smiled narrowly. "Oh, certain more prominent members disappeared, but the organization searching for Abu Hassan continued its work, if anything more secretively than before. Until they found him. In 1979 in Beirut. Finally got him, along with a carload of bodyguards and a half-dozen innocent people who just happened to be around when they blew up his automobile. An operational hazard, of course. Quite acceptable, given the result."

Christian sat back, fingered his drink, then took the last of it in a single swallow.

"The Gabrieles?" asked Stone.

"They were *heths*, members of the support group. Which no doubt included people with the talents needed to black-bag a safe in the office of a Swiss lawyer."

"Dare I ask about Sophie?"

"An *aleph*," said Christian. "A killer, Stone. The woman suspected of pushing the button in Beirut that blew Abu Hassan and nine others to pieces."

After a moment, Stone held out the Opteros file.

"Do you want it, or don't you?"

Christian sighed. "Maybe it's the times—one has no choice against an amoral enemy except to employ equal amorality. Of course I want it."

As Christian thumbed through the file, Stone told him, "Opteros appears to be a holding company for investments in real estate. Five separate deals, each with a different set of investors. I'm not sure why Opteros was used to buy the *Sea Fox*."

"Obviously it was thought to be a safe umbrella. I expect Bertrand was acting on behalf of one of those investors." Christian closed the file. "There is more here than either of us know. But I'll dig it out. All of it."

"I'll tell you what isn't there," said Stone. "Names. The investors in each of those deals are identified by initials only."

Christian sighed. "I hate the Swiss. They're so bloody . . . smart."

"But one set of initials appears in all five deals," said Stone. "The initials A.M."

"I think we can assume the purpose of Opteros is to shield certain people with money to invest." Looking away, Christian made a hum of discovery deep in his throat.

"No secrets," prompted Stone.

"I was thinking of the Five Dragons—the ex–Hong Kong police sergeants who were so involved in the Asian heroin trade a few years back. Rumor has it that half the new office buildings in downtown Vancouver were built with their money. Prime real estate is the dope trade's favored investment.''

"Two of Opteros's investments might qualify as prime: an office building in New York City and a hotel in Aspen.''

"And the other three?'' Christian was watching him, waiting.

"Undeveloped parcels of land. Hawaii, the gulf coast of Florida, and—you fill in the blank.''

"Sardinia? Damn, I knew it!'' A bony fist rapped the table for emphasis. It was the closest thing to a display of joy Stone had seen in Christian.

"Maybe we should take a look?'' Stone offered slowly.

"Most definitely.'' Christian tucked the Opteros file beneath his arm, clutching it with an elbow. "But I'm not through with this. The initials A.M. might mean something to one of my contacts.'' Christian was thinking of Israel Katz at Interpol; the file itself would be a tempting bargaining chip. "In the meantime, beware of Sophie. We don't want her muddying our play, and she's dangerous.''

"Given her present state of mind, you can add unpredictable.''

Again Christian frowned. Motionless, he waited for Stone to continue.

"You see, there's a little something more to Sophie's story. It took a half-bottle of calvados to shake it loose. The story beneath the story.''

"There always is one, isn't there, Stone? If you look deep enough.'' Christian was watching him.

"Sophie's story is right on her sleeve. She thinks the people who pirated *Pegasus* are responsible for the death of her one true love, and Sophie wants to get even.''

"Alec Gabriele?" mused Christian. "After all, they did work together."

"You missed it by half. Not Alec," said Stone. "His wife, Hanna."

# Chapter 26
## The Gun and the Fist

"Tonight," said Le Pic gravely, "the action committee will give this careful attention."

"The action committee?" Stone couldn't be sure if Le Pic was serious or not.

They were in Le Pic's single room behind the kitchen of the Bar des Marines, a cramped place, carelessly arranged, the corners littered with miscellaneous junk, from anchors to rusted *petanque* balls. On the walls were several Bellini prints of a Côte d'Azur that would never again exist. One framed photograph: a younger, smiling Le Pic standing with a U.S. army captain and a British corporal, his OSS Jedburg unit from World War II.

Le Pic stared a moment at the photo, then rummaged through a sagging armoir and produced an ancient Lebel revolver. He blew lint from the empty chambers, and sighted, one-eyed, at his nameless dog as it circled the room growling at shadows.

"We'll need Basso, of course; he understands these things. And I've asked Conacci—a *poulet*, but family and an ex-para."

Stone interrupted before Le Pic could raise a batallion.

"Le Pic, listen . . ."

The old man reacted indignantly. "How can you be angry? Basso said eighteen rounds were fired from the Bren. I was right about trouble."

"Not trouble. Target practice."

"Practice, my short hairs." Le Pic sighted the revolver at one of the wall prints and squeezed off a click that would have put a hole through the stately old casino, gone now to the wrecking ball. "When trouble comes, you need warriors," he said with finality.

"All I want is the *Marie-Hélène* for one week."

"So you can make a voyage to Sardinia." He waved the revolver toward an imaginary horizon. "A land of bandits and thieves, and your pirates, yes?"

"Maybe."

"Maybe, maybe. Commit yourself to something, David. Something crazy, a wild idea, but give your whole self to something for once in your life. Learn what it is to live."

"Le Pic, you're trying to turn a quiet look at a piece of Sardinia seacoast into a military expedition. I don't want an action committee. And I don't need warriors."

"I've experience in these things, and you may need more than you think," argued Le Pic.

"When I do, I'll let you know," Stone said gruffly. Later he realized he could have softened it. Told Le Pic how much he loved him, in some way the old man would have accepted; the kind of thing remembered too late.

He left Le Pic, silent for once, staring at his dog as it continued to hobble around the room in search of demons.

Exiting through the bar, Stone noted among the familiar grizzled regulars, a cheery, smiling man, drinking alone. With his red button nose and flushed cheeks, he had the look of a nautical Santa Claus.

But as Stone passed by, the man turned away to stare thoughtfully into his glass.

It was after midnight by the time Stone found Dolph Hess, staggering drunk, in a bar near the old port.

They needed the whole long walk back around to the *Wunderkind* before Dolph's legs were steady enough to climb the gangway.

"It's love, David," he mumbled, as he pushed into the plush master cabin. "And it's going to be my early death." He went directly to the bar and poured two chilled glasses of Williamsbirne, then glanced forlornly at the king-sized bed. "Ach, an empty bed."

"Nani?"

"A race apart, the Tahitians. A little breath of summer into old Dolph's life, but it's like trying to keep smoke in a barrel. I know, you told me." He shrugged it off, and rose, leading the way into the navigation room.

He snapped some Corelli into the tape deck and dug out a half-dozen large-scale maps of Sardinia. This was business, and Stone had seen the phenomenon before: Dolph Hess willing himself sober.

"A big island, David. Sardinia, Sicily, the two biggest in the Med." He touched the northeast coast. "Real money here. The Costa Esmeralda, the Aga Khan's dream. Estates and hotels as grand as any in Bermuda; they make a few rich men richer. But does a haven for the rich make the island less poor? Not in this world, my friend."

"And this stretch here?" Stone traced a section of northwest coastline, on it the property owned by Opteros.

"A rough coast. Rocky bays, steep cliffs, a few marine caves. There are grottoes all over the island."

"What I'm looking for is a place isolated so that a boat could come and go without attracting a crowd."

"A funny thing about the Sards," said Dolph. "An island people who hate the sea. Too many centuries of plundering pirates, maybe. Or the malaria. Until the war much of the coast was uninhabitable, good only for animals and soldiers." He laughed and filled their glasses. "Whole stretches of that coast are still empty as the moon."

"You were based where?"

"On the north coast, here at Maddalena." He touched the map. "An Italian base we used when Hitler ordered our boats into the Med in September '41. Later, when the Allied bombing became too fierce, we went to the south of France, to Toulon. The wine was better there."

"Any luck with our U-boat commander, the one aboard the *Sea Fox*?"

"I've been trying, David. Von Richert's diaries helped stir this, you know." He tapped the side of his head. "Sad. Even then he thought only of death: 'Today we lost the U-21, today the U-658.' But I made a list of all the captains and first officers I knew. There were never more than thirty or thirty-five German boats operating in the Med. Then I concentrated on your description, this tall man with the dueling scar."

"Who might have operated off the North African coast, and maybe around Sardinia."

"North Africa, almost all of us. Sniping at the Malta convoys. Sardinia . . ." He shook his head.

"Damn," Stone whispered.

Dolph's gaze had lost its sharp focus. "A U-boat commander with a dueling scar." Again, he shook his head. "David, I'm sorry."

Stone found himself thinking of something Kits had said earlier. About making the mistake of linking the shallow draft of the *Sea Fox* to the place where they landed the girls ashore in North Africa. A shallow draught didn't necessarily mean a shallow landing. And a scar on the face . . .

"Dolph, what if it's not a dueling scar?"

"But that's what you said."

"I know. It looked like a dueling scar, I knew they weren't uncommon, and you jumped in before we thought it out."

"Not a dueling scar?"

"A scar he got later. Suppose when you knew our man he had no scar. Would that make a difference?"

Dolph turned to his chart table and drew out the list. "North Africa . . . Sardinia." He thought a moment, then murmured, "The milch-cow."

"Milch-cow?"

"The U-66. an old Deutsche Werk ocean-going sub, of eight hundred tons. Listen, David," he said, his voice rising excitedly. "In mid-'43, German intelligence recovered some documents that indicated the Allied invasion of Italy—which everyone knew was coming—would hit first at Sardinia."

"Instead of Sicily, where it actually did happen?"

"Yes, but Hitler thought the documents were genuine and ordered Sardinia reinforced, mainly by cruiser and submarine. Until then, Bunnerman's craft had been used for training and courier work—a milch-cow. Bunnerman was crazy for a combat command."

"Would this Bunnerman have known the North African coast?"

"Of course. And I don't know how many supply runs the U-66 made into Sardinia, but plenty. Along that coast you asked about. Volunteering for every dangerous mission, when the U-66 should never have left sight of shore. Too bad."

"In what way, too bad?"

"Always out of step with the war, Bunnerman was. Got his command all right—in July of '44."

"You remember him that clearly?"

"For a special reason. He was given a beautiful combat vessel, one of the new fleet-type U-boats. Then came the invasion of the south of France, the bombing of Toulon. The end."

"What happened to Bunnerman?"

"He was ordered to destroy his boat. He scuttled her at the wharf in Toulon." Dolph shrugged. "As far as I know, Horst Bunnerman finished the war without firing a shot."

Walking slowly back to the *Marie-Hélène*, Stone became his own devil's advocate, questioning all of it. Still he came to the same conclusion. A third line of evidence had crossed the previous two: the land holdings of Opteros, the shipment of diesel parts traced by Christian—and now the name Horst Bunnerman.

And all evidence led to a lonely stretch of Sardinian coast.

Stone was trying to calculate what came next, each careful step, when a flash of orange lighted the night sky in the direction of the Bar des Marines. A fraction of a second later the earth seemed to rip apart around him.

Stone saw the flash an instant before he felt the explosion. He was running by the time the concussion pounded his ears, shattering window glass for a city block.

He reached the Bar des Marines in less than a minute. Already the ever-present crowd had gathered. A nation of watchers, wondering at their own fortune, or the injured's folly. He'd never been able to decide which.

Even as he pushed through them, Stone could see there was nothing to be done. The explosion had ripped a great raw hole through the bar's roof, and already a tongue of flame was leaping thirty feet into the air.

Thick walls had channeled the explosion, blowing out the building front in a gust and crushing the apartment behind the kitchen, and with it, Le Pic.

Stone pressed nearer, until the heat forced him to halt. He stood helpless while the prescribed government services arrived, went about their jobs, clucked misfortune, and, toward dawn, went their separate ways. Only the police remained, with their blue vans and notepads.

When finally Stone turned to leave, he found the ex-para, Basso, standing nearby. Dry-eyed, mouth set beneath his pencil-thin moustache, Basso lifted his gaze to meet Stone's. "For this someone will pay," he said softly.

A quiet vow—the first words Stone had ever heard Basso utter.

# Chapter 27
## Bogeyman

It wasn't the kind of place Christian would have expected Interpol's Israel Katz to choose. Stepping from a taxi near a hamburger shop on the Boulevard. St.-Germain, Christian sighed.

Once upon a time, eating had been the single sensual pleasure he allowed himself. And once there was no city like Paris to satisfy that desire. But now, after years of siege, the battle was lost against the tour buses, those chrome-and-glass monstrosities hauling in their cargo of Brughians and Genoese pinching their centimes and lira. Travelers searched for adventure however it fell; tourists required bargains, and thus had come the true *nouvelle cuisine* of the times—the hamburger and the pizza. Christian had lived too long.

He found the detective waiting in a booth of molded yellow fiberglass. He was seated against the wall, facing the door like a modern-day gunfighter.

Nothing else about Katz furthered the gunfighter image. Christian always visualized him in shades of brown: brown suit, brown hair indifferently combed, flat brown eyes. In an era when the police of all Europe worshipped their super computers, Katz still looked upon paper-shuffling as his given craft.

Christian knew that Katz would mine things from the Opteros file that he'd never dreamed of. Add bits and pieces to a dozen mental files gathered over decades, accretions around a grain of irritant that would eventually produce its manner of pearl.

Not disappointing him, Katz now said, "I have a name for the initials A.M. in the Opteros file." He produced a photograph.

A man in his fifties, well conserved. The heavy good looks of the Mediterranean, along with an immaculate attention to detail in his dress that hinted French. An attractive man, as the hungry look of the young woman with him attested. But the eyes betrayed him, dead and black, and arrogant.

"His name?" asked Christian.

"Antoine Michaelis."

"The woman?"

"Of no consequence. A chorus girl from the Lido."

"Michaelis."

"Born in Cyprus—Greek father, French mother. Raised in Athens and Paris. By the age of twenty he knew a dozen major cities equally well, and doubtless a fair share of dark alleys."

"Really," said Christian absently. *Michaelis.*

"His father dealt in money—precious metals, currency; moving it, converting it, hiding it." Katz spoke from memory.

"All legally of course."

"Never proven otherwise. No police record, although the father did die in peculiar circumstances. An ice pick penetrating a sensitive area."

When Katz smiled even his smile, somehow, was brown.

"And the son?"

"A small infraction. Caught smuggling lira into Switzerland twenty years ago. Confiscation, a fine, since then not a spot."

"Except now it's kidnapping, the sex trade, and drugs."

"Gold, money, drugs, women. All commodities," said Katz blandly. "Little different in principle."

For a moment the detective's eyes held on a young couple entering the restaurant. The man was muscular, with broad shoulders tapering to a narrow waist, fine black hair matted on a chest exposed nearly to his navel. Christian recognized the type, even to the cigarette dangling carelessly from his lip. The girl was thin, with a pouty mouth, and in good Parisienne fashion she paid her escort no attention. They chose a table nearby and ordered coffee.

When the man opened his newspaper, the girl looked away, bored.

"The problem with Michaelis," said Katz, "is not information but evidence. There is no definite proof that the initials A.M. are his at all."

"But you were so sure."

"My dear Robert, let me tell you something. Since the arrest of Francis Giraud—*le blond* as he was known—the European drug trade has moved out of the Corsican and Sicilian networks' control. They ran it for three decades. Now there are half a dozen organizations: Yugoslav, Lebanese—"

"And a French-Greek?"

"I can give you names of the top men, where their wives and mistresses spend their money. But . . ." Katz shrugged and let Christian reach his own conclusion.

"But you can't hang them."

"Because people like Michaelis don't dirty their hands. They never see drugs; they don't use them. They never receive or handle the money. People once-removed from Michaelis in the chain of command don't even know his name. If the system breaks down, the weak link merely disappears."

"Then how do you catch them?"

"We don't," said Katz. "Unless they make a mistake. The Americans would be most interested in the Opteros file. They are working on things like this. Trying to find out where the money goes—bank accounts, investments. The other tactic is to hurt the big importers at the source. Interdiction as they say. Cutting the stuff off where it's grown, the lines of transport."

Nearby the girl with the pouty mouth spoke reluctantly to her escort. He passed her an ashtray without looking up from the newspaper. If that was love, thought Christian, he was glad he'd lived his life without it.

"The Americans," Katz was saying, "try to pressure the countries directly—Mexico, Thailand—to cut it off where it grows."

"With not much luck."

"Because someone like Michaelis can buy anyone willing to be bought. You need a club, Robert. Imagine the French trying to lean on Iraq or Libya. By demanding what? Stop your poor farmers from raising their poisonous flowers, or we'll stop buying your oil? Hah!"

"I'm not fighting an industry," said Christian. "One evil man. The ruination seen with my own eyes."

"And in the eyes of the law, Michaelis is clean. A losing battle, Robert."

"My battle." He extended his hand toward Katz. "You owe me."

Katz took an envelope from his pocket and pushed it across the table.

"Everything I kow about Michaelis. Addresses, hang-outs, contacts, sexual habits. And one more thing . . ." His eyes flicked to the muscular man with the girl. "Him."

They left and found a place more to their liking. A noisy wine bar behind Notre Dame.

"That was Andre Rico," said Katz, feeding a grainy piece of brown bread into his mouth. Christian ordered wine; the sight of solid food now made him nauseous.

Katz added, "Stay near Rico, and you'll always find Michaelis."

"Bodyguard?"

"Self-styled. I don't know how good. Driver, pimp, and arranger. People are always asking for Rico."

"I'll remember."

"Rico isn't so clean." Katz washed down the bread with wine. He glanced at Christian's untouched glass, but said nothing. "A little item three years ago. In Brussels. Two girls missing from a *très snob* dancing school. Turned up later in a Kinshasa brothel, both addicts by then."

"Was Rico involved?"

"He worked at the dancing school as an instructor," said Katz. "But no connection was proven. His presence a coincidence I'm sure."

"Amazing how many there are."

Katz told him about the Ibiza ring. "The rich, the artists bought their chemical pleasures. Then came the followers, chasing their spirals upward, and downward. As girls here and there ran out of money, they became desperate. One syndicate began recruiting them, promis-ing exciting jobs in the Middle East. Cash was offered so they could buy drugs. Then off the girls went, to find themselves employed in a fashion they'd never expected."

"It's that story, you know," said Christian. "The one French fathers tell their daughters, to frighten them."

"Except the bogeyman is real and worse than they think."

"One bogeyman," said Christian. "To break one man, that's all." It sounded like a vow.

"A useless crusade, Robert." Katz leaned toward him, his voice lowering. "If you want Michaelis, you should rent a large car from Hertz and run him over with it."

# Chapter 28
## The Team

They were five.

Once, Stone would have thought them an unlikely lot: Kits; Christian; silent Basso; and the newcomer, Le Pic's nephew, a policeman named Conacci.

They sat bunched around the *Marie-Hélène*'s galley table, studying the single 1:25,000 ordinance map spread out before them.

"It's clear enough," said Stone. "Find *Sea Fox* and the place where the girls are held. Find them, and take them."

Le Pic had won out after all: a military expedition.

Stone looked from face to face, wondering at their differing reasons for being here.

*Kits.*

On the surface, Kit's motive was the most clear-cut: to find Polly. She'd returned to Stone and the *Marie-Hélène* the day after Le Pic's murder. By then the police had extracted his battered body from the wreckage of the bar. His and two others: a dog missing one hind leg, and a young woman with brightly painted toenails—the Tahitian girl, Nani.

When Kits had left Stone a day earlier he hadn't asked why, but he hadn't liked it either. He felt better with her back aboard.

"I talked again with the police. I think they were embarrassed that I was still around. I'd expected too much, David, too much of everyone except myself. No more."

Then she told him she'd seen Mark.

"He flew down from London talking forgive-and-forget. But I'm not willing to do either. He told me to grow up, to learn to make commitments. Et cetera."

She made a bored face. "I finally understand Mark. The words were the important thing, maybe the only thing. Not action, feeling, caring about something. He preferred the words. *Finito*, darling. Truly, *finito*. The rest, I'm seeing through."

"Rest of what?"

"Polly. And you."


*Christian*.

Paler, even more tightly wound than he'd been the last time Stone had met him. He told them what he'd learned in Paris:

"It's almost certain that Opteros is a company created to launder drug money. The power behind it is a man named Antoine Michaelis. Supposedly unreachable. But as responsible for these deaths as if he'd pushed the button himself."

Later he told Stone every detail of his meeting with Israel Katz. Everything Katz knew about Michaelis and his driver, Andre Rico.

"I want them, Stone. Because they're smug and safe, convinced the police can't touch them. But guilty."

To Christian, Michaelis had become something more than a man trying to enrich his pockets, uncaring of human life. He'd become a symbol of some greater evil. Christian's name suddenly seemed entirely appropriate. Facing Stone, energy charging every gesture, he was a rural preacher stumping fire and brimstone and promising the anti-Christ would take them all down if he weren't acknowledged, and then destroyed, in the exact manner of Christian's private vision.

Stone didn't know what to make of that vision, but it fueled Christian in a way nothing physical could.

*Basso*, the sad hound.

It was Stone who had sought out Basso; found him alone in his stuffy little room in the heart of the city. The room smelled of sweat and cheap wine.

"His death was my fault," Stone said. "They were out to punish me, and got Le Pic instead."

The policeman, Labatt, had warned him. He'd listened, without really hearing. Punishment. By people with a long reach. Stone's was a confession of guilt, and Basso listened silently before denying it with a shake of his head.

"They could have taken you. Or tried," he reasoned deliberately. "They picked a thing that would mark you inside. They deserve a proper killing. We will do that, David. You and I."

Even in death, Le Pic had given Basso a reason to live.

*Conacci*.

A younger version of Le Pic in build and gesture, with a fringe of ginger-colored beard. He owed nothing to Stone. "Something I must do," he said simply.

The night before, a black police car had arrived with Conacci alone behind the wheel.

The three large suitcases he carried aboard the *Marie-Hélène* were heavy for good reason. Two machine pistols and three hundred rounds of 9mm ammunition, three automatic pistols of the same caliber, and a half-dozen hand grenades, painted gray with yellow bands—tear gas. With them were three two-way radios, looking like metal lunch boxes: the type used by the local police.

"Le Pic had many friends," Conacci offered and was gone.


*And you Stone?*

The *Pegasus* disappearance was solved. Devlin and Le Pic were gone, whatever he chose to do, or not do. Was it the fear in the lady's moss-green eyes, the fear that they were already too late to save Polly? Or, had he, like Christian, seen the corruption that spread outward from Antoine Michaelis as a mark of something larger, a paramount example of man drowning himself in his own greed. No need of justification for Basso. Revenge for the loss of a friend, an eye for an eye.

Stone had taken something from all of them, more than enough.

"The odds are long," said Stone. "Understand that going in."

"Everyone understands," said Kits. "If we fail, we fail."

"We're not going to fail," blustered Christian. A thin finger stabbed the chart. "The boat is there someplace, and the girls nearby. Too many things tell me so."

Stone envied Christian his certainty.

Christian flicked a glance toward the others. "Mrs. Maitland and I have two leads, and we'll get cracking soonest."

They were leaving that night aboard a ferry out of Toulon. By morning they'd be on the island. Stone,

Basso, and Conacci were bringing the *Marie-Hélène*, plus their armory.

"First," continued Christian, "we've this lovely piece of real estate to explore."

"The parcel owned by Opteros," said Kits, "with almost two miles of coastline."

"Second, we've the name Enzo from the shipment of spare diesel parts sent to repair the *Sea Fox*. We'll find something."

The boat, thought Stone. Nothing would follow unless they could find the boat: a hundred-foot former mine-sweeper, hidden somewhere by a former U-boat skipper named Bunnerman.

"But no move until we're all together," Stone warned. "Nothing to make them put up defenses."

They all agreed, but he wondered if Christian really heard him.

"In two days we'll know," Christian said, his fiery gaze returned by a dark steady look from Conacci and Basso. They already knew, thought Stone: somehow, someday, their time would come.

# Chapter 29
## Prisoners

For a time Polly Maitland thought she was the victim of a conventional kidnapping.

The European newspapers were full of them. Kidnappers these days didn't pick only the rich. The children of postmen were taken and held for ransoms. It was business. Some criminals robbed banks or snatched purses; others kidnapped people's children and didn't give them back until they were paid.

One case she remembered was especially frightening. In Italy an obscure film producer was kidnapped, and negotiations for his release dragged on for more than a year. She could never last a year like this. Not without word or hope. Or something more to eat besides flat crackly bread and dry roasted meat. She'd lost twenty pounds at least, and she felt crawly underneath her filthy clothing.

By the sixteenth day Polly understood: this kidnapping was different. That was the day Mrs. Hawk brought in the girl, Camille.

Mrs. Hawk wasn't her real name. If Polly ever learned it, the name would be added to Pino's on her private list marked "Revenge Only." She was a thick-shouldered woman, forty or so, with high, flat cheekbones beneath mean black eyes, and a large chicken-hawk nose. She always wore the same dark brown dress beneath a thick tunic. She came twice a day: once in the morning with a bucket of water and some bitter coffee; once in the evening with a plate of food.

Polly had tried to engage her in conversation, first trying English and French and then the little German and Italian she knew. The mean black eyes would look through her as the warden backed out of the cell without a word.

A cell with a dirt floor, and damp walls of loaf-sized stones; the curved outer wall gave the room the shape of a pie slice. The stones were covered by slimy moss, and Polly discovered that the heavy stones, granite she thought, were fitted together without mortar. A hole in one corner served the purpose of sanitation; through it a watery sound reached her from far below—not a river, more like the surge of tides and waves.

Granite rock, tides, Mrs. Hawk's strange costume—they were clues, but Polly could make nothing of them.

The high slit of a window at least allowed her to gauge night and day, and from the moment she had stopped feeling so nauseous she'd started marking their passage with scratches on the wall, just like the Man in the Iron Mask, or Jean ValJean. Someone.

The day Mrs. Hawk brought in Camille, Polly knew there was more to it. There had been no notes, no word from her mother, no posing for photos or speaking into a tape recorder, none of the things she'd heard of kidnappers doing to prove their victims were still alive. For days she was sure nobody cared, but finally she told herself to stop being childish. People cared. Kits cared, if only she knew. Once, just the day before, she'd awakened from a shallow sleep in the heat of the afternoon with the strangest feeling: that someone was close, someone who cared.

Camille was unconscious when Mrs. Hawk brought her in. The two men, one of whom was always with Mrs. Hawk when she visited, dropped a blanket on the floor and left her. The men were older than Mrs. Hawk, muscular with fair hair and sort of broken faces. She heard them speak German as the door locked again.

The new arrival was a little pup of a girl, younger than Polly, with a plain flowered skirt she'd thrown up on a couple of times. A French look about her, judging from the cut of her hair, her unshaven armpits. Polly tried to clean her up while she slept, with water from the bucket, and in doing so found the blotchy needle marks on the girl's bare buttocks and thighs.

*Bastards.*

*Pino.*

When Camille began to surface—it seemed like hours before she stopped trying to empty her already wrung-out stomach—her first words were in French. When the tears stopped, the questions began. When she asked what happened, where they were, Polly could tell her nothing.

"We're at the end of the earth, waiting."

"Waiting for what?"

"Just waiting, that's all."

For the pilot, Gian Carlo Peroni, the key to understanding was so often a matter of context. One had to view a thing in its setting.

Waiting in the fine, modern, boxlike office of Aerotax Air Service, a hundred yards from di Fertilia's passenger terminal, he knew this to be so. Watching the arrival of an Alitalia 707 from Milan, debarking 140 Germans for their island vacations, Gian Carlo felt, in contrast to the new arrivals, the smug superiority of belonging.

No tourist outsider, he, but a man with honest work to do; a man with purpose, given the chance. His clients, a man and woman, were late.

But if, for example, he were to encounter a tourist, German or American say, at the bar in one of the Costa Esmeralda hotels, there was a point he made immediately. No, he was not local, not Sardo, not one of those poor *ignoranti* who preferred their mountains and bullocks. He was Italian, a pilot, a modern man who flew a sleek aircraft.

Of course if the tourist himself was Italian, Gian Carlo Peroni would coldly deny his allegiance to Italy—that country of poor *ignoranti* who grew grapes and made large families to leave their stamp on the earth. In that context Gian Carlo would confirm that he was not Italian but Roman, and let the weight of that speak for itself.

The trouble was that in the context of the Aerotax office the man and woman who presented themselves looked very much what they claimed to be: tourists, interested in a little sightseeing by air. Once in the air, it was quite another matter.

"Ah, you are American."

The man nodded, and ignored the invitation to make conversation. At one time an American tourist was a tourist with money. These days who could tell, with their checked pants and credit cards; they all looked the same, spoke in those same sharp voices, like members of a large family who borrowed each other's clothing. A Roman with only one suit of clothes would at least make sure its material was the best he could afford, and the tailoring flattering to the human form.

Granted the woman was tanned and lovely with dark hair worn in a thick braid and soft green eyes. Given the context of her and Gian Carlo alone she might have been worth the time. But her jeans did nothing to display her figure to advantage, an opportunity no Roman woman would allow to pass. Her cheap rope-soled espadrilles could have been bought for a few thousand lira.

"You like them?" she asked suddenly, as Gian Carlo was helping her into the aircraft. "I saw you looking at them."

"They are very nice," Gian Carlo said, grinning quickly in defense.

The man, he thought, held back a smile. The kind of face that hid more than it revealed. No Latin blood in that one. But like the woman, well tanned; not the shallow boiled color of the two-week vacationer. A rich yachtsman, Gian Carlo might have said, except the man's hands were scarred and calloused from too much work. He noticed them when the man held out a map with a line of flight penciled in.

"Ah, yes, the coast is lovely," said Gian Carlo amiably. "I'll take you over the most beautiful coasts."

"We're speliologists," said the woman. "Interested in caves and things," she added.

They needed to hit a bull's-eye.

For two days they'd been on target; Kits could feel it. But its center—the location of the *Sea Fox* and, she had to believe, Polly—eluded them.

It was Christian who found the Enzo farm. "I promise you, the same Enzo who picked up the parts for the Packman diesels from the freight forwarders." He gave her a wolfish grin, eyes gleaming.

"How can you be sure?"

"It's my business to be sure."

"You know what David said about making no contact."

"I do not plan a frontal assault, dear lady. Only a little careful reconnaissance. I am under the impression you feel time is rather valuable."

So Kits had put on a pair of culottes, tied a scarf over her head, and rented a bicycle. "It would be better if you were English," said Christian. "I assure you, every hill and country road in Italy has its allotment of English schoolteachers who have lost their way."

Turning from the narrow, two-laned, *strada bianca*, the highway running parallel with the coast, she caught sight of the low farm building a hundred yards distant. From beyond came the sound of a gasoline engine. But she didn't have the chance to advance any farther, for in the same moment she saw two dogs, great hulking animals, appear from behind the farmhouse.

As they bounded toward her in eerie silence, she wheeled the bicycle around, trying to reclimb the track to the main road. She'd gone scarcely a few yards when the dogs sprang, the first one butting her in the side with his head, and she went tumbling from the bicycle. When she tried to stand, both dogs bared their teeth.

She decided to stay motionless, and they backed away, watching her every move. Each of the lead-gray mastiffs weighed easily as much as she did, and their small piggy ears pressed tightly against their skulls indicated what she assumed was their particular attack behavior.

*I'll stay put, if you will.*

She saw the woman then, walking out from behind the farmhouse.

"Hello there," Kits called out. The squarely built woman came on without a greeting. She wore a quilted tunic over a drab brown dress.

"*Privado*," said the woman. "*Privado*. Go away."

"I'd love to," Kits breathed, then shouted, "I'm sorry, I didn't know. I'm lost."

"*Privado*," the woman repeated, beckoning to the dogs, and pointing her back toward the road.

There was nothing to do but retreat, smiling, and with as much speed as she could muster. One quick glance took in the surrounding land. Here they were at least a half-mile from the sea. Past the farmhouse Kits noted one of the ancient stone fortresses that were everywhere on the island. A wall of rough stone surrounded an interior column, overlooking the ocean from the edge of steep sea cliffs.

Later, when Kits told Stone about the incident, he became as visibly angry as she'd ever seen him.

"What do I have to do? Lock you and Christian up? How did he find the place?"

"I don't know," she said, trying to calm him, "but I think he's right. There's something strange going on at the Enzo farm. Just before I was cornered by their nasty pets, I heard an engine running in the distance. Running, then fading, like the one for the compressor on the *Marie-Hélène*."

Stone's expression didn't soften in the slightest.

"Well, it could mean something," said Kits dispiritedly. "I thought it might be a generator to light that ancient fortress. Even an underground cave."

"Possible."

"I'll tell you this. When I left I didn't hear the engine anymore. And another thing. I was followed by a man with a gun."

"And you wonder why I'm sore?"

"A shotgun. Following along the track behind me to make sure I reached the main road. They didn't want me snooping around, don't you see?"

"Which is precisely the same reaction you'd get from any other farmer on this island."

"David, that wasn't any farm. I looked on the map. It

adjoins the property owned by Opteros. And that stone fortress is dead on it."

Stone shook his head. "But we've covered that coast in the *Marie-Hélène* and come up blank."

They'd worked the water slowly, with fishing gear out, while Basso, Conacci, and Stone himself alternated with the binoculars.

A jagged coast of undercut cliffs, shoals, and a few narrow bays used by local coral fishermen. On the clifftops they'd picked out the stone pillars mentioned in the *Sailing Directions*—three of them marking the ancient house-fortresses built before the time of Christ and carrying the unpronounceable local name of *nuraghe*.

"One of them must be the same one I saw," said Kits, her enthusiasm undampened.

"But it doesn't lead us to a thing," said Stone. He told her about the profusion of marine caves. On parts of the island, underground rivers had carved huge grottoes that sometimes extended for miles and weren't fully explored. Any one of them could have hidden a flotilla of Ham-class minesweepers *or* German U-boats.

"I picked out at least a half-dozen caves on that length of coast, but the only two we could reach were too small to hold anything but nesting gulls. The approach to the others is barred either by a fringing reef or impassable shoals."

"Even with *Sea Fox*'s shallow draft?"

"Even at high tide," said Stone.

So now they were taking their final go at the coast, airborne, listening to the Italian pilot's canned patter.

"On this coast are many seals," he said.

"Where did they come from?" An idle question while Stone's attention remained on the shoals and reef below.

The pilot shrugged, baffled. "They have always been here."

"Since the last Ice Age," said Kits, "if you really want to know. The only seals left in the Med, a species existing nowhere else on earth."

"Like the people," said the pilot with a grin. A gold tooth glittered brightly in his mouth. "Thick, here." He pointed to his head. "Real *ignoranti*."

Kits nudged Stone's leg and nodded below.

At fifteen hundred feet they could make out the Enzo farm, and closer to the sea the *nuraghe* with its circular watch tower.

Twenty minutes later they reached Capo Falcone— land's end. When the pilot banked the aircraft for the return, Kits looked over at Stone in despair.

Stone tapped the pilot's shoulder. "Can you take her lower. Along the water, just outside the edge of the reef."

"Sure," said the pilot obligingly. "Beautiful, eh?" The late afternoon sun struck the water obliquely, clearly illuminating the brownish reef edge and the dark blue of deeper water.

Later, Stone said, "Beautiful all right."

From the air, he could see it clearly. In the *Marie-Hélène* they'd passed within a hundred yards of it. Below, etched bright green against muddy blue, he could make out a narrow channel blasted through the reef. The channel lost itself in the dark shark's mouth of a cave entrance.

"Just beautiful," he said.

# Chapter 30
## Sailors' Delight

The hotel was low, boxy, and modern. It fitted the narrow, graceful promontory at the extreme end of a sweeping bay like a wart on Sophia Loren's shoulder. Mass tourism had found even this lonely corner of a lonely island, and the lobby, when Stone passed through, resounded with Swedish, French, and German.

But the protective coloring, as Christian called it, suited their purpose. Stone met Kits and Christian a little after seven in the evening behind the closed doors of Christian's hotel room. He'd left Basso and Conacci the unpleasant task of unstepping and lashing down the *Marie-Hélène*'s twenty-eight-foot mast.

Christian greeted him, tall drink in hand, his complexion pasty and pale.

"So you've found a channel through the reef?"

Stone caught the unsteadiness in Christian's gait as he stepped away. He flicked a questioning look toward Kits, who moved her shoulders in a slight shrug.

"A simple dog leg about a half-dozen yards wide," said Stone.

"Wide enough for the *Sea Fox*?"

"With a couple of reference points, a good man at the wheel, and the right tide."

"Well then, what next?" Christian tried a confident smile that was a little off.

"We have a look," said Stone.

"Like a blind man down a one-way street," said Kits, ready for the hard glance Stone snapped in her direction. She really was coming to know the man. "You spend an entire afternoon making me feel stupid for taking a look at the Enzo farm, and now you want to tip the whole game by driving a boat into their front yard."

Christian's head moved slowly from Kits to Stone. "I detect something less than agreement."

"You're damn right you do." Her eyes drilled hotly into Stone. "All right, so maybe the *Sea Fox* is using that grotto as a base. You still don't know what you'll find inside. The boat might be gone or it might be there, guarded and armed to the teeth."

Something amusing softened Stone's expression, but he said nothing.

Kits pointed at him with an accusing finger. "You don't know where Polly is. Or what will happen when you and those mercenaries of yours raid the place, guns blazing, no doubt."

"She's right, you know," Christian chimed in.

Watching her steadily, Stone remarked, "She often is. But not about what comes next."

Christian's mouth puckered as he tried to follow Stone's meaning.

"You're so damn sure of yourself, Captain Stone." Kits made no attempt to keep a check on her temper.

"About this I am."

"About what?" asked Christian, feeling as though he might have been in a separate room.

"What's wrong with the idea?" said Kits. "Tell me."

"For heaven's sake, what idea?" howled Christian, stepping between them.

"Tell him," said Stone.

"That I take a look first," she said. "Go in with a single air tank. Check out the channel, then the cave."

Open-mouthed, Christian glanced to Stone, who was at the window now, looking out. In the gathering darkness, the coastline was a jagged shadow against the sea. The last deep reds of sunset, and not a trace of wind against his face. Red sky at night.

He took a piece of paper from his pocket, studied it, and spoke without looking up.

"We'd stand a better chance trying the channel at high tide. There's one tomorrow at 7:40 hours, another at 16:20."

"I'll go in at first light and be back in plenty of time," said Kits. "What about the local police?" Her question was to Christian. "Bringing them in for help?"

"Out of the question," Christian replied without a moment's hesitation. "An operation of this kind doesn't work without some local sanction. We might just as well advertise our intention by newspaper."

"Don't forget Labatt," Stone reminded Kits. "So sure the grease was applied right up to the central government."

"I'm afraid we've no one but ourselves," said Christian.

Outside in the hotel gardens, Christian swallowed two painkillers with whiskey out of a small silver flask. From somewhere in the hotel the sound of rock music reached him. The conventional pleasures of even his own generation had always felt alien, and as the first sensation of drug warmth washed over him, he decided there was no place he would rather be, nothing that would legitimize his passage through life more than putting a few of the bastards of this earth behind bars. Not a do-gooder out to benefit his fellow man, but narrow, and totally selfish.

He took another pill for good measure, gulping it down painfully. He'd discovered that alcohol potentiated the drugs and for a few moments, as the warmth reached his every extremity, his mind would be as lucid as he could ever remember.

Then, the morass of depression, and a pain so numbing he could scarcely put two consecutive thoughts together. He'd felt his composure coming apart in the hotel room and had left Stone and the Maitland woman, claiming a touch of tourist tummy and the need for fresh air.

Feeling better, he turned to find Stone standing a few feet away.

"What's wrong with you? I can see that you're a sick man, but what exactly is it?"

Stone was at the far end of a telescope, every stern feature etched unnaturally, but distant. The music was louder now, pounding inside his skull.

"It matters not the slightest. Stone, we've made all of the lines cross, don't you see? Now we must move quickly and with skill."

The words, the rhythm of the phrases seemed to glide from his lips. Why was Stone looking at him so oddly?

"I want to know how you found Enzo?"

Pleased, Christian smiled. "A bit of inspiration, that. I cabled the firm that handled the shipment of spare diesel parts. Asked them to reship the same order. When Enzo showed at the forwarders, I shadowed him to the farm. He never suspected a thing."

"Not even that no one had ordered any parts?"

"He's no engineer, man; he's a farmer. How would he know what was ordered, and what wasn't?"

"Someone will."

"I considered the risk."

"Who the hell are you?" said Stone, his voice cutting. "Willing to let Kits wander alone into that cave betting on some risk you considered?"

"An error in processing the original order. A dozen logical reasons that would explain a reshipment." Christian's confidence was unshaken. The doubt would come later, alone in his hotel room.

"Including the idea that someone reshipped those parts to find out where they were delivered. Get some sleep, Christian. Your end of this is finished."

When Stone's meaning finally filtered through, Christian's voice rose, anguished. "You can't edge me out, not now. Stone, listen. That girl I told you about. The one cut apart on film. My daughter. I swear.

"Was she?"

"You owe me this."

"Go home, Christian. Before you do something that gets us all killed."

"You think I am lying?"

"Go home."

Watching Stone turn away, Christian damned the man's prescience. Yes, a lie. Not even a good one. The whole story had been false, even to the detail of it happening to a fellow policeman. A lurid tale he'd read once in the *Sun*. A brand of lie he'd never thought himself capable of. Honor eroding, honor gone. Dreams indeed might have been the first illusions to abandon man. But in the end, it mattered little whether they were first or last—dreams, honor, all the elements upon which he'd built a careful self-satisfied self image. As soon as he was faced with something that touched to the core, they crumbled like pillars of sand.

"Stone," he called out, but his voice lacked the strength to rise above the twang of electric guitars and the thump of percussion.

Christian tried to sleep and couldn't. He took two more pills and finished the last of the whiskey in his flask. None of it worked. He'd spent so many nights in third-rate hotels. Ones with windows that shook as nearby trains rumbled past. Listening to faucets drip and floorboards groan overhead as neighbors paced their nights away; to lovers who cried out behind paper-thin walls. With it all, sleep would always come. But no longer.

He dressed, found that the hotel bar was closed, and walked out into the heavy night air. He followed the promenade along the oceanfront, past great, ancient arches he scarcely noticed.

Finally he found an open bar, a place lit brightly enough to make him wince. One drink, to help him sleep. He entered and edged through a crowd of androgynous youths, most with 1950s haircuts and tattoos. He took a table as two of them playing an electronic game nearby began executing tiny ranks of creatures marching in from outer space.

He doubted one drink would be enough.

He was sitting over a second carafe of sweetish local wine when his glance fell on a man and woman seated across from him. Something caught in his mind, but it slipped away before he could separate it from the blur.

Christian was halfway back to the hotel before he made the connection.

He'd seen the man and his sulky girl friend before, in Paris. Pointed out by Israel Katz: Michaelis's driver and bodyguard, Andre Rico. He spun around and painfully wended his way back to the café, but it was closed.

Christian made a mental note to tell the others, but when he woke up the next morning he recalled nothing of the night except the vague memory of a late-night wander past great ancient arches along the oceanfront.

In the yellowish glow of a kerosene lamp, Horst Bunnerman irritably took another sip of bitter coffee. Being pulled from his bunk to be led through the dark night to an unexpected rendezvous had put him in foul spirits.

"I'm telling you it's over," said Yank, nothing at all jolly in his manner, "that's what I'm telling you."

The farmer Enzo had lit a wood fire, but for Yank the chill penetrated clear through; his mood was as acid as Bunnerman's.

Pacing, he slapped violently at his arms, trying to stimulate some warmth. "It's starting to come down on all sides."

"I do not understand," said Bunnerman stubbornly.

"You don't want to understand, that's all." Yank stopped pacing and ticked the items off on his fingers: "First this Stone finds that sunken boat of his, which he wasn't supposed to do."

"Ach," began Bunnerman, but Yank cut him short.

"What's done is done," said Yank. "Then that cop Labatt blows a nice simple removal. The people on that end don't want to do business for a while, that simple."

"But why does the insurance investigator come here? How does he know?" Bunnerman was thinking of the duplicate shipment of diesel parts two days before. His was an orderly mind, each item in place, and there was no place for a second shipment of parts.

"That's what I'm telling you. No one is sure about anything. Except it's over. That's an order."

Bunnerman stiffened.

To hell with him, Yank thought. "Yeah, an order. We close it down, get rid of everything."

"My boat?" said Bunnerman.

"Your boat. My boat. Maybe in a year . . ." From the other room came a sound it took Yank a moment to recognize. The farmer Enzo had picked this hour of the night to put an edge on his knife, long singing strokes with a sharpening steel. "Tell him to knock it off."

"Don't be nervous, my friend."

Yank flicked his head. "He gives me the shivers. Him and that woman of his."

Yank had them figured for brother and sister. A pair of throwbacks to the Middle Ages. Those same square skulls, heavy ridged brows.

Bunnerman said something in Sardo and the sound stopped. Yank began to pace again.

"When is the soonest you can get out?"

Bunnerman sighed and looked at his watch. "We'll need a few hours. There is a morning high tide, one later in the afternoon."

"The second one," said Yank. "Safer to run at night. You tell me where, and I'll pick up you and your people and we'll get rid of the boat."

"They want the boat destroyed?"

Yank stopped and looked at him. "You're not listening, Horst. You've had a standing order from day one about what to do if it fell apart. Well, it's falling."

"But a good boat—"

"It's a throwaway."

"I'm sorry."

"From the beginning, a write-off. You got no idea the money involved in this deal. A boat's nothing." He stopped. Explaining to Bunnerman was like driving nails into granite. "Horst, listen to me. I am not number one. I don't dream up these things to make life tough for you. I have my own problems."

Bunnerman stood wearily and nodded. "Jah, always good reasons."

"Nothing lasts."

The pale eyes darted toward Yank, looking for some mockery. The American shrugged.

"It was the boat, the *Pegasus*," said Bunnerman. "From that time on, bad luck."

"If you want to call it luck, yeah, I guess that's when it turned bad."

Bunnerman made an apologetic shrug of his shoulders. "What could I do? Wait for daylight with a holdful of drugged girls and false papers?"

"You did the right thing. Just like you'll do the right thing now."

"What about the girls?" the captain asked. "There are five girls."

He's just figured it out, thought Yank. "They go down with the boat. Unless you want to take them back to Mom and Pop. With the boat," Yank repeated slowly, to make sure he was understood. *"Capische?"*

# Chapter 31
## Dawn

It was still dark when Basso hauled in *Marie-Hélène*'s anchor. Stone eased the throttle forward, leaving behind the rock-studded cove they'd shared that night with a solitary coral fisherman. He wanted to reach the channel through the reef before first light.

From the deck of his small, worn boat, the fisherman watched them pass, motionless, before he raised his coffee mug in a toast for luck.

"It's as if he knows," said Kits, zipping herself into a dark blue wet suit.

Basso nodded toward the small boat. "A free man, David. A good life, eh?"

"It comes in all shapes and sizes."

"And yours, my friend?"

"I've never thought about it."

A smile twitched beneath Basso's thin moustache. "Ah, yes. Love, death. Better not to waste a man's thoughts on these small things of the spirit." His glance slid to Kits as she finished snapping a waterproof light onto her weight belt.

236

"I'll try to be out of the cave before high tide," she told them.

"We're still partners," said Stone. "I'm going in with you."

"Not this time," she replied firmly.

"Once we've put Conacci ashore, Basso can handle the boat solo until we're back on board."

They'd decided upon a two-pronged reconnaissance. Stone reasoned that if Kits was correct and power lines had been run into the cave from a generator on the Enzo property, then there had to be a land entrance somewhere. Taking one of the radios, Conacci would have two hours ashore for a search of the cliffs above the cave.

"I can't risk having you along," Kits insisted.

"And I can't risk sending you alone."

"But that's just the point. There will be tidal surge going in, coral to watch, maybe something extra Bunnerman has rigged by way of surprise. You're not good enough for this, David, and I won't have time to worry you through."

She belted a heavy knife to the inside of her left calf, adding, "Given the situation reversed, you'd turn me down without a blink."

Conacci came on deck, wearing a dark sweater and trousers. Basso handed him one of the machine pistols and observed like an inspector general while Conacci tested the action, then loaded the weapon and locked it.

"See, you don't need to do everything yourself." Kits grinned toward Stone. "What are friends for?"

"I'm beginning to wonder."

Twenty minutes later they put Conacci ashore, but not before Basso drew him aside. "Do nothing stupid. And cover the part of you that doesn't have eyes."

"Like old Le Pic, eh, through the Maquis like a shadow."

"Don't forget a pair of dogs out there in the Maquis."

Conacci held up a plastic bag filled with powder. "If they come for a sniff, pepper from the galley. You worry like an old woman."

"Because old women know there is much to worry about."

Stone pulled out the map of the coastline, pointing for Conacci's benefit. "Here's where we are now, and here is the pickup point. In between, the stone fortress on top of the cliffs. Two hours, Conacci, that's the limit."

As Conacci waded ashore, Basso called out "*Merde*" for good luck. But it wasn't loud enough to be heard.

*Il soldato va alla guerra.*

Fifteen minutes later it was Kits's turn.

"Quit stalling, David."

"This stalling is a lousy pilot's attempt to find that channel mouth in the middle of the night. Unless you prefer crawling across the reef."

"My, you are a salty captain."

When Stone nodded a few seconds later, her lips briefly brushed his cheek, and then she was gone over the side.

Basso scratched tenderly at the back of his neck and turned to look at Stone. Just the two of them now, them and the *Marie-Hélène*.

*Il soldato va alla guerra.*

*Mangia male, dorme en terra.*

Stone checked his watch.


Alone on the bridge of the *Sea Fox*, Horst Bunnerman cradled a glass of rough *grappa* in his long fingers.

More than once he'd tried mentally to chart the decline of his aging vessel. From its proud launching, with banners flying and the cheers of workmen. How long after a bottle of champagne sent her on her way full of expectation had the luck begun to turn? Stripped first of her weaponry and armor plate, the paravanes that had never been tested against an enemy's cunning. Then a forged registry, mercenaries for a crew. A decent vessel scuttled in spirit long before the fact.

He drained his glass, poured another, and called in his three crewmen: the young straw-haired, self-styled adventurer, Manfred, two years old when the *Sea Fox* was launched. To Manfred, Bunnerman's war was the distant, myth-filled crusade of the history books. A different breed were the two former German naval ratings, Shreck and Schrammel. Hard, tough men, still willing to serve and fight, but old. With a shock Bunnerman realized that he was their senior by a half-dozen years.

He didn't feel old. God's rude joke was that one aged from the outside inward, as his sagging jowls made clear each morning in the shaving mirror. On the inside his will was firm, his skills as sharp as ever, even if he had too often allowed them to be squandered by the men who gave orders from their comfortable chairs, distant and safe.

He repeated to the three of them what the American, Yank, had told him. "It's finished. Shreck, go to the farm. Find that hag of a woman and bring the girls down to the boat."

Shreck offered him a smart salute and was gone. To Schrammel he said, "Rig enough explosives in the engine room to sink her cleanly." At least a neat ending. "We'll be going out with the afternoon tide. A rendezvous later tonight and then we'll sink her in deep water."

"What about the girls?" asked Manfred, curious but uncaring. A cold one, Bunnerman had concluded long ago. The same coldness he saw in so many of the young these days. Perhaps it was always so. It was Manfred who'd learned about the freeing of *Pegasus*'s captain from the young English girl, methodically beating her to death in the process. Yet a captain was ultimately responsible for his crew.

"They are not to talk," said Bunnerman, feeling suddenly drained. What was the exact point in his life when the scuttling began; the small decisions, made or avoided, that had brought him to accept smuggling, murder, and the sinking of decent vessels? "They must not talk," he said louder, as though there were still something left to fear.

Polly awoke when the wind began. A sudden pulsing gust that shook the oak door of their stone cell. *Couldn't see your hand in front of your face.* Darkness, deep and absolute, wrapped around her like cold velvet.

She sat upright, listening.

Next to her, Camille whispered, "What's wrong?" The girl was curled up close, a small creature in need of Polly's warmth and strength.

"Nothing," said Polly. "Just the wind."

"No, there's something more."

Polly was still awake when the door bolt slid back, and the beam of an electric lantern was shined in her eyes.

"Up," said a gruff male voice. "We go."

Her first thought was, no, not the drugs again.

While the man held the light, Mrs. Hawk tied a rough blindfold around the two girls' eyes and led them from the cell.

The wind came as a sudden, sharp blow. Like the mistral, thought Conacci—the *maestrale* they called it here, except this wasn't from the valley of the Rhone. A wind, fetid and hot, blowing from the south, a wind from an Africa that had taken his youth and given him nothing in the bargain.

Before the wind struck he'd been moving through the scrubby *macchia*, skirting the cliff edge toward the stone fortress somewhere in the blackness ahead. The wind was a spoiler filling the night with unfamiliar sounds. Despite its warmth, a sudden chill of apprehension rippled through his body. The foreignness of everything, the reminders of the African *bled* and its long-ago dangers. Fighting was a game for young men—before they grew wise enough to know better. Basso was right to worry.

Conacci turned his back to the wind, checked the time, and made his first radio call to the *Marie-Hélène*.

Standing motionless in the dark, the farmer, Enzo, took a long draw on his pipe as the two great mastiffs nervously circled their pen. They'd stirred when the wind began, and Enzo watched them now arching their thick necks to sniff the air, then butting their rawboned snouts in mock contest. He knew his animals, knew the wind.

Enzo tapped out his pipe and reentered the farmhouse. A moment later he reemerged, wearing dark, tight-fitting trousers pinched at the knee, soft leather boots, and a rough wool sweater. He was armed with a shotgun and a long-bladed knife in a scabbard.

He went to the door of the pen and released the latch. Immediately the pair of dogs bolted silently into the darkness. Ready, and moving as noiselessly as his animals, the farmer followed them into the night.

# Chapter 32
## Labyrinth

A tidal surge, perilous and swift, pushed Kits through the shallow water of the narrow channel toward the dark cave mouth ahead. As she neared the surface, her dive vest partially inflated, the bulky air tank made her feel like some aquatic beast of burden. Already her hands were cut and bruised from the rough rock.

Then came the wind.

When it struck, the water around her erupted with foamy whitecaps. Friction on the surface swept the water across the reef like some bedeviling new current, demanding a counter-force with her fins that drew more energy than she could afford.

She took a single spray-blurred glance back toward the *Marie-Hélène*. Already its dim outline was farther along the coast, obscured by the boiling cauldron of white water pounding the reef's outer edge. For a fleeting instant she contemplated her own foolishness. This task she'd painted to the others as simplicity itself, now demanded everything she had to give. With an even more powerful kick, she directed herself toward the cave entrance, which seemed to be receding in the distance.

Still, in ten minutes she'd drawn measurably closer. As she came under the lee of the cliffs above, the wind lessened and she found herself moving more easily.

She had almost reached the cave mouth when she felt something at her back. A light touch, then turbulence as it moved away, a thing alive.

She whirled, hand clawing at the knife on her leg. At arm's distance she saw the head, the bulbous feminine eyes and cone-shaped snout. She smiled and swallowed a mouthful of seawater in payment.

A seal, the first she'd encountered, citizen of the local *noyeau* of marine life that shared the region. The deep interior of the caves sheltered the seals' young from traditional enemies—eagles from above, sharks from below.

She could see others moving easily with her toward the cave. A few seconds later she felt a sudden drop in temperature, as cold water from the underground river that had carved the grotto's interior over millions of years mixed here with the sea. With the seals she entered the wide mouth of the cave.

Immediately she found herself in a high-ceilinged vestibule. The structure of most marine caves was similar, thanks to the processes that had formed them. She knew that beyond, in the darkness, was a gallery that might stretch for miles. Bracing herself against a rock, she listened. When she was sure there were no human sounds in the rush of wind, she risked the light.

As she played it over the cave walls ahead, a feeling of powerlessness spread through Kits. She'd told herself to be ready for any wrinkle Bunnerman might have prepared to snag the unwary. But now, facing it, she was totally at a loss. Ahead, where the channel narrowed at the beginning of a deep gallery, a mesh of steel cable blocked the way.

She dove and followed it down to its base, a good twenty feet below the surface. A cable as thick as her wrist threaded across the entire span. Bracing her feet, she gripped and pulled. It wouldn't budge. Frantically, she worked her way around the edges and found the mesh tightly fitted and unyielding. Tears of frustration welled in her eyes as she clung to the mesh. She swore angrily, knowing that Bunnerman had beaten her even before she'd begun.

Three hundred feet above, the bearded policeman Conacci hunkered down close to the cliff edge and swore at a different adversary: the angry wind swirling about him.

He spit, and wiped dust from his eyes. Reasoning that he would only be ashore two hours, he'd neglected to bring any fresh water along. But now the wind was parching his throat raw, and he was plagued by a gnawing thirst he hadn't experienced in years. Too many things forgotten.

Ahead he could make out the stone walls of the fortress. The stumpy column in its center rose like a water tower, which he wished it truly was.

He had just made his third call to the *Marie-Hélène* to report his slow progress when he saw it: a light near the fortress walls, there and gone.

Immediately he angled away from the cliff edge. Off to his right the sky was a shade lighter now. He gave himself another quarter of an hour before he'd have to head for the pickup point or risk being caught exposed in the light of day. He had used only three minutes of his self-allotted time when he saw the long snake of a creature undulating its way between the fortress and the cliff edge—a creature being guided by someone with a lamp.

Then he recognized the undulations as the stumbling movements of separate people, each clinging to the one preceding by a hand on a shoulder. He counted five slender figures, each blindfolded. A man with a light in the lead, a woman following.

Staying low, he began walking parallel to the moving column, and a moment later saw their destination: stone steps descending the cliff face and, somewhere below, an entrance to the cave, he'd bet on it.

He was never sure if it was the wind or his preoccupation with the procession before him. In any case, he heard nothing. Not until the first dog was on him, a great snarling beast that took him down with a weight nearly equal his own.

He swung the radio at the thick skull, but the second animal was already there, its teeth sinking into his arm and grinding bone. They shook him like a plaything. God, how they stank, how everything on this worn-out piece of earth smelled of death and foul decay.

He went for one of the dog's small bright eyes, even as he heard a familiar sound, steel against steel, a blade withdrawn from a scabbard. Then he knew it no longer mattered.

The figure that bent over him, pushing the dogs aside, was death itself.

Kits wasn't sure how much time passed before the thought came to her. Clinging to the cable mesh across the grotto passage, she remembered a favorite professor quoting the words of Louis Pasteur: "chance favors the prepared mind, a mind ready to see."

For long minutes she'd stared blindly in the growing light of pre-dawn. She could hear the bark of seals deeper in the grotto, catch the wink of light refracted from their dark eyes. Lost in self-pity and blocked by her own emotions, she hadn't seen the obvious.

Seals. Inside, beyond the mesh barrier. A barrier with openings too narrow to admit even a single seal.

Somewhere was another entrance into the grotto.

She turned and swam back toward the cave mouth until she found a place to grasp the rock wall. Observing the seals, she noted that none of them approached the mesh; their sleek heads dipped below the surface a full thirty feet short of it.

She clamped down firmly on her mouthpiece, touched the regulator's purge valve, and a moment later let herself glide into the surging depths. Here the only sound of man was the metallic, rhythmic beat of her own breath. She let herself move among the seals who were now taking this slightly larger breed of sea creature if not for granted, at least without fear.

She found their private entrance in less than five minutes—a ragged fissure in the wall of rock, about the width of a half-closed door. Through it the seals came and went effortlessly. Using the light, she saw that this "doorway" led to a tube-shaped "hallway" several yards long. It quickly narrowed to a second vertical crack about four feet high and a foot or so in width. She hoped it was larger, for each inch would count if she tried to squeeze through.

She'd read plenty of accounts by cave divers who had explored the dark, wet interior of the earth, using mountaineers' skills, but dragging tanks and regulators with them.

Just the thought of it was enough to tighten her chest with incipient claustrophobia; make her long for a free dive in the open sea with clear vision all around and bright sunshine filtering down through a watery skylight overhead. Here there was no space, no freedom or light. A narrow crack in a rock wall leading where?

Easy enough to give up. Tell David the risk was too great. He understood risk, knew the danger in overestimating your own skill.

But she was thinking, too, that once in the grotto there had to be a way of lifting the mesh across its entrance. How else did the *Sea Fox* come and go? Raise it enough to allow her own exit, and reentrance again ahead of the *Marie-Hélène*.

Swimming through the narrow rock tube, she approached the second fissure, and shined her light in. A bend. Enough space for a human body if the body was small and the breathing controlled. A feet-first entrance would keep her arms free for a pull to safety if the space became too cramped to continue.

The question remained: What would she find beyond the bend? Was there a turning to jackknife her body around? Or once through, would another awkward move be necessary? All of it easy enough for these seal creatures with their flexible spines.

She was wasting air on indecision.

*Leave it.*

But for once she ignored the interior warning. Quickly she pulled off her fins and looped them over her arm. Then she unslung her air tank, careful to keep a tight grip on the mouthpiece, and shed her dive vest. She intended dragging the fins and tank through the hole after her; an inflatable dive vest in the narrows of whatever lay ahead would be more hazard than help. Needing both hands, she shut off the light and hooked its lanyard over her neck.

Slowly, using her feet to feel her way in the darkness, Kits wormed backwards into the narrow crack.

Fortunately, there was only one direction to go.

Moving her hips in a corkscrew motion, she forced herself more deeply in, thighs following feet, torso, and finally, with arms outstretched, her entire body.

The tinny sound of her own breath seemed louder now, and she felt the rhythm quicken with exertion. The trick was to keep her breathing even and light. Already the narrowness of the walls seemed to be increasing their pressure against her. A siege of panic and she would swell like a human blowfish, leaving herself trapped, too tightly pinned to move in either direction.

Upon reaching the bend, she pushed her feet through and found that it took the wrong direction for the attitude of her body. Working in a darkness so total as to be absolute, she rotated herself slowly around from belly-down to belly-up. She used the light once, shining it toward her feet, but managed only to frighten a small squid that locomoted within inches of her facemask to disappear in the direction she'd come. Lucky squid.

On her back she advanced still more deeply into the passage. Pushing with her hands, she allowed her feet and legs to lead blindly as she dragged the air tank along behind.

Her legs made the turn, then her body. With an inward sigh of relief, she found herself in a widening of the channel. Here she could crouch, embryolike, back pressing tightly against the jagged roof with each breath she took. Carefully she brought the air tank next to her to ease the strain on her jaws, then again explored with the light. Another fissure, much like the one that had brought her into this small rock cell. But was it truly an exit? Or did it lead her more deeply into a labyrinth of ever-narrowing channels that would finally so cramp her movement there would be no return.

At that moment a small gray head appeared in the angry slash of rock and was forced back by the light.

At least whatever was beyond was seal-sized. And again Kits maneuvered herself around. Feet-first, she crabbed backwards into the narrow fissure, feeling it turn slightly upward.

The increase in grade served only to make the items she dragged with her heavier and more cumbersome. Somewhere she'd lost a fin, but no matter. She was still at the point where she could pull herself back into the small, cell-like chamber, do a somersault, and return the way she'd come, she *thought*; it was a word the scientist in her hated.

For a long few seconds she was frozen in inaction. *Move, damn you! Do something.* But even as she grunted in anger, she felt something nudge her leg. Then again: the nose of a seal, cold and leathery against the bottom of a foot. A signal? Nonsense. *Come ahead, you'll be all right.* Absolute nonsense.

Almost against her will, she pushed herself more deeply into the tight fissure, a human cork hoping to slip through the narrow neck of the bottle.


"Trouble," said Basso, scanning the narrow V-shaped ravine with the binoculars. The plate-sized beach at its base was Conacci's pickup point.

Basso again tried the radio. Conacci had failed to make his last scheduled report, and now time was up. For all of them.

Fighting to hold the *Marie-Hélène* into the wind, Stone said, "We can't wait for him."

"A little longer."

"Kits is due out of the cave. She has only so much air, and it's nearly finished."

"But, David," implored Basso, his voice wrought by the contradictions, "something is wrong. You know. I know." His hands flicked skyward, asking the gods what they knew.

"We can't wait," said Stone, and put *Marie-Hélène* on a course back along the coast toward the channel mouth.

Again, Basso raised the binoculars to scan the empty beach they were leaving behind.

Like some skulling, pre-human creature, Kits rotated her body 180 degrees to back into still another angled crawlspace.

She had no way of telling how far she'd come—fifty feet or twice that. She was beyond retracing herself. Once past the small intermediary chamber, she'd found no place large enough in which to turn. To try going back head-first would mean pushing the heavy air tank before her. She was numb with fatigue, fatigue and the beginnings of deep chill.

For a moment or two she tried to ignore it. Then she allowed it as evidence: another factor she had to take into account, along with the certainty that her reservoir of air was reaching exhaustion. *Nerve, girl.* Burt calming her on their first deep dive together. Nerve. She had a sudden vision of Burt during the last seconds of his life, and wondered if anyone had nerve enough then.

She'd received a letter from him three days after he died; posted two days before the accident. He was working a diving bell in the North Sea with another diver he'd already brawled with twice. No one had any true idea of the nerve it took just to pass the day in the cramped quarters of an undersea environment, let alone a diving bell where men had to labor and earn their way. Burt said that he and his partner managed undersea. It was the topside crew that worried him. "Madmen I can take. Fools I can't abide." The last words of his letter.

She was losing her thread of concentration, another

sign of fatigue. Maybe death by suffocation was merciful after all. She hoped so. She hoped Burt had reached that stage quickly after the crew on the platform lost the hookup and dropped his diving bell into fifty fathoms of water. By the time a rescue team was sent down, it had been too late. Burt would have liked Stone. They were different as fire from flint, but natural men with an element in common: each felt things deeply, but distrusted words. She had loved one, and now loved the other, and it was a helluva place to learn that the time in between, what had passed with Mark, was a life only half-lived. Dreaming . . .

Forcing herself to concentrate, she realized that for the first time her feet found nothing to touch. The constriction of the rock walls about her torso was tight enough to make her scream, but her feet had reached space and the promise was wonderful.

Using her right hand, she reached back over her head to draw the air tank along the passage.

One moment it was moving smoothly, brought carefully forward by the air hose. The next instant the tunnel exploded with air bubbles as something unseen snagged, then severed the hose.

Fighting the natural instinct to take one more breath, she closed off her throat against the water flooding into her mouth, and immediately pushed with all of her waning strength, forcing her hips through the narrow passage into the open space her feet had already found.

Her hand clawed at the light. At most she had twenty, thirty seconds of air in her lungs. She shined the light about her, first in one direction then another, only to find herself surrounded by rough walls of slimy grass. She had escaped into a narrow rock cubicle from which there was no exit.

Her body began to shake with the understanding that

she was trapped. She was to die here in this narrow rock coffin. She made an instinctive lunge for the air tank buried deep in the tunnel, her lungs burning painfully as the scant air in them gave up its oxygen. She met the seal coming out. It glided gracefully past her shoulder, made a ninety-degree turn toward the vertical, and sailed through the vent, unseen, directly above her head.

Following the seal, she sprang from the bottom. She clawed her way through the opening, as sharp rock tore at her wet suit, as if trying to hold her back until her lungs involuntarily took that single spasm of breath that would fill them not with air but liquid.

Then she was through into deep water, all around her, deep and luscious and free—the grotto. Upward she swam, tapping the last strength in her body, willfully fighting to keep her lungs from crying out for air. Muscles began to cramp, but still she reached upward, trying to embrace the surface.

The explosion seemed to erupt in the exact center of her body. A sudden compression as exterior force hammered the last of the air from her lungs in a bubbly gasp.

Too soon.

She took in a great inhalation of seawater, even as she felt herself churning upward, drawn by something unseen. And somewhere, far short of the surface, the world behind Kits's eyes turned from yellow to black.

# Chapter 33
## Flight

*Ah, David, beware the courage of drunks and cautious men.*

In the rising wind that struck the *Marie-Hélène* stern on, Stone could almost hear Le Pic's warning. Always too late, Stone, you with your caution. Ready to give all for a lost cause or someone loved, but never sensing when the right moment to act had come and gone.

For the tenth time in as many minutes, Basso avoided his gaze, absently working the action of the Bren gun.

*When?*

*Not yet.*

Again, Stone brought the *Marie-Hélène* around to recross the mouth of the channel.

This time no need to glance at his watch. Kits's self-determined limit had passed, and then again by half.

*Take no chances.*

*David, don't worry.*

*No chances. I need you.*

But he hadn't said that.

Whatever they tried, whenever, it was already too late.

\* \* \*

Her first sensation was smell; the odors mixed but separately identifiable.

Kits turned her face away as the sharp bite of ammonia crawled down the back of her throat. Two rough hands pulled her upright. Her eyes opened to find the scarred, tired face inches from her own.

Seeing she was conscious, he eased his grip, took a step back. He wore a soiled uniform and worn officer's cap, with an eagle and wreath above the visor.

David's U-boat captain, Bunnerman.

"We don't have time," he said in English. "No time, you understand?"

She moved her head painfully to take in the small wardroom. Two other men watched her, one older, unsmiling, in dirty white dungarees. A younger one, with straw-colored hair, carelessly balancing a metal object, olive drab: a hand grenade, she thought.

She tried to let herself go faint again. But Bunnerman pulled her around.

"The truth, madame, and you may survive the next few hours. What brings you here?"

*The truth, then.*

"I'm a marine scientist. I was looking at the cave."

"Past the gate? Impossible."

Kits said, "Captain, my being here is proof it is not impossible."

Bunnerman reached out and slapped her sharply. "Don't be smart with me."

"I found a tunnel and lost my air tank getting through." *Talk, keep talking, give David time to arrive.* "I was trying to reach the surface when something exploded."

Bunnerman released his grip. He nodded toward the young man with straw-colored hair. "Manfred fishing for breakfast in his usual expeditious manner. Closer with the hand grenade and you would have died in the water.''

"I'm not holding you to blame," said Kits.

"How kind," replied Bunnerman.

"I'm well enough to go back now. I'm sorry I trespassed, I truly am." She tried to sound innocent and not too bright, but the dull look in the old German's eyes told her she hadn't fooled him in the slightest.

"So am I," he said slowly, and spoke to one of the sailors. "Bring in the farmer."

A moment later the man she recognized from her previous visit to the Enzo farm looked in at her from the doorway. He wore darkly stained knee breeches and carried a canvas game bag.

"That's her," he said. "The one who came snooping."

"So," said Bunnerman. *Zo*. Patience exhausted, Bunnerman asked, "Now, again. What brings you here?"

"A preliminary look at a cave," she insisted.

Bunnerman sighed. "And him? Why did he come here?"

Kits frowned. "Who?"

"Him."

At Bunnerman's signal the farmer emptied the contents of his sack onto the wardroom floor.

A furry animal, thought Kits, curled and raw in death. A ridge of ginger-colored hair.

"Oh, no."

"Him," said Bunnerman.

It was Conacci's head.

Watching the woman's face confirmed the worst: discovery.

"Lock her below." Bunnerman's command was to young Manfred.

"But she knows."

"Must I do everything myself?"

Manfred recoiled at the sting in his captain's voice. He wanted only to please the man, to prove he would have been a good soldier during the better times he'd never see. Glorious times. He'd been born thirty years too late.

He took Kits by the arm and forced her ahead of him along a short corridor and down narrow metal stairs. The pain in her legs reminded her that she had survived both explosion and that torturous hell of a crawlspace. She'd already died once that day. What worse could these people do?

With the woman gone, Bunnerman turned to the farmer, the sequence of what must be done ordering itself in his mind.

"Get ashore," he told Enzo. "And take your grisly souvenir with you."

"You're leaving the island?" He seemed neither pleased nor relieved.

Ignoring him, Bunnerman turned to Shreck. "Tell Schrammel we're getting under way. We won't wait for the second tide. Have him ready two detonators, one for thirty minutes, the other for three. Then report to the bridge. Bring machine pistols for you and Manfred."

He spun and entered the cramped captain's cabin. He dug out a clean, white uniform blouse with shining insignia on the lapels. He would have preferred a leisurely shave, but didn't have time.

Instead he took a long pull from the bottle of *grappa*, and found his navy Luger in the drawer at bedside.

Feeling like a man of twenty, charged with purpose and command, Horst Bunnerman climbed to the *Sea Fox's* bridge.

* * *

Descending the ladderway, with the young German at her back, Kits heard the deep rumble as first one and then the second of the vessel's diesel engines turned over and caught hold.

She was halted before an iron hatchway. The German opened it, pushed her inside, and slammed it shut behind her.

In the semidarkness, Kits's attention was first drawn to the two portholes, small eyes of light, little more than vents. No lamps, the smell of diesel oil and something else. Littered about what must once have been crew's quarters were dark, blanket-covered forms. With the sound of the latch being slid home, one of the blankets moved. Then another.

"Polly?" Even as she called out, the deck beneath her lurched and the boat began to move. The sound of the engine, rising under power, filled the cabin.

"Polly," she called again, and saw a slender shape rise unsteadily to its feet.

"Mother." But a stranger's voice. "Mother?"

# Chapter 34
## The Fire Ship

Standing behind Shreck at the wheel, Bunnerman blinked as the *Sea Fox* passed through the cave mouth and into the bright morning sunlight.

Immediately the wind tossed the prow high in a flume of spray. "*Gott*," growled Shreck, wrestling the wheel to keep the boat centered in the narrow channel. "*Mein gott*," he repeated, in a strident, fearful tone that Bunnerman couldn't account for. Shreck had surely seen worse, plenty of it, from the rigging of a nitrate ship on the Chilean coast a half-century before.

Shreck's arm lifted, pointing to starboard.

Bunnerman's first assessment was a vessel in distress: the clean graceful lines of a French *pointu*, mast down, run aground in the channel mouth.

Then he realized the boat was under power, moving toward them along the first leg of the channel. At that same instant he saw the muzzle flashes from the foredeck, as all around them windows shattered, spraying the wheelhouse with bits of wood and glass.

"So," whispered Bunnerman, thrusting Shreck aside to take the wheel himself. In his mind it was one of the paintings of naval warfare he'd so admired as a child: the wind-whipped sea in broad colored panels, murky green running to sapphire blue beyond the small, courageous vessel pressing home its foolish attack. For a moment he was outside himself, a witness who would faithfully report the steadiness of the *Sea Fox*'s captain under fire, record for history his crisp commands.

"Return fire," he ordered Shreck, "you and Manfred. If machine pistols aren't enough, then I'll use this boat to cut that pirate in two."

A classic example, thought Stone grimly, of arriving too late with too little.

Even as he threaded the *Marie-Hélène* into the narrow channel, he saw the high stubby prow of the *Sea Fox* slide from the cave. A scant two hundred yards away, it gained speed, moving along the inner leg of the channel. In profile it looked the size of a destroyer.

"The wheelhouse!" he shouted to Basso. "Work the wheelhouse."

But already the ex-para was squeezing off controlled three- and four-round bursts from the Bren. The first took the starboard windows, then moved right in search of whoever aboard the *Sea Fox* that day had the lean good fortune to be at the wheel.

Stone pushed the throttle forward and immediately heard the *Marie-Hélène*'s engine take on a new note.

Their original plan, makeshift at best, had at least *been* a plan: enter the cave, use the *Marie-Hélène* to block any escape, and press home their attack with automatic weapons and the inflatable boat.

Now the best Stone could hope for was to somehow prevent the *Sea Fox* from reaching open water. Somewhere aboard was Kits, he prayed, taken prisoner. Kits, Polly . . . he wasn't sure of any of it.

As Basso changed magazines, Stone saw a figure in dirty whites take advantage of the lull to bolt from the *Sea Fox*'s wheelhouse with a short automatic weapon.

Then came the dull *ping* as 9mm slugs began tearing into the *Marie-Hélène*'s hull, joined immediately by a second machine pistol firing from farther aft.

Ignoring the incoming fire, Basso again opened up on the wheelhouse. Basso, the surgeon, probing with his special tool.

Stone grabbed a machine pistol, and fired a one-handed burst over the top of the cabin that brought a howl from Basso.

"Please, *cher ami*," he shouted, looking around at Stone, wide-eyed, "I am not the enemy."

Noting the angle of fire, Stone realized that his own salvo had narrowly missed Basso's head.

Then, belowdeck, the sound of breaking glass and a shrill hiss as a bullet ruptured the propane tank in the galley; it should have gone over the side, but he'd forgotten.

Still fifty yards short of the bend in the channel, Stone knew the *Marie-Hélène* would arrive a poor second. As the range between the two vessels closed, Basso, with icy poise, tipped a fresh magazine into the Bren. But as he rolled into firing position, Stone saw his body jerk from the impact of something unseen, the deck around him flecking crimson.

"Take cover," Stone shouted. "Forget it."

Ignoring him, Basso fired again as, dead ahead, the *Sea Fox* slowed enough to take the bend in the channel.

Then the bow wave deepened. With a clear and beckoning course to the open sea, the vessel put on full speed; in its path was the *Marie-Hélène*.

Even as he judged that the *Marie-Hélène* would be crushed like an eggshell in a contest with 120 tons moving at speed, Stone saw that the turn of the vessel had bought Basso a few seconds of time. At the new angle of approach, bows on, the two men firing from the starboard deck were screened by the wheelhouse from a clear shot. In that brief instant, the advantage swung to Basso, and when a man in white dungarees appeared, crouching to squeeze off a burst, it was shorter than he ever intended.

Basso, too, reasoned that the men with machine pistols would need new firing positions and had lowered his point of aim, shifting it left. As the smudge of white appeared, Basso fired, the Bren thumping back solidly in recoil. He didn't have to fire a second time, for the man flung an arm across his eyes, toppled sidewise, and was gone.

But as Basso shifted the Bren's muzzle, Stone heard him yell, saw blood spread from a second wound in his thigh. Shouting at Basso to stay down, Stone again fired wildly in an attempt to divert the remaining gunman's attention. Slowly, with the deliberate movement of a creature designed to perform a single task on earth, Basso tipped the final magazine into the weapon's receiver. But this time he didn't fire.

He waited.

Setting the wheel, Bunnerman ducked low to dart the few paces into his own cabin. A moment later he was back with a small shaving mirror. Risking a look, he eased the *Sea Fox* into the final leg of the channel, and paid for it as a burst of machine-gun fire took out the remaining windows and a sliver of glass grazed his neck.

Dropping to the deck, he shouted "Full speed" into the intercom and, creature of routine, cranked the command into the engine-room telegraph.

Then sitting and facing astern, he used the small

mirror as a periscope to keep the *Sea Fox* on course. It worked less than ten seconds, the exact length of time it took the law of probability, as managed by the anonymous hand on the trigger of a machine gun, to catch up with him. A bullet shattered the mirror and tore away his second and third fingers. In the flash of pain, Captain Horst Bunnerman made his decision: he did not intend to die sitting on the floor of a wheelhouse, playing the game of war in the manner of a child.

To hell with it, reasoned Stone. Bunnerman could have his victory.

Less than a hundred yards distant and closing at the combined speed of both vessels, Stone made his own choice. If Kits or anyone else was being held prisoner aboard, the most likely place was in the large crew's cabin forward. A head-on collision would take its greatest toll there.

He was about to spin the wheel and put the *Marie-Hélène* onto the reef when Basso yelled. A figure was stepping into full view in the shattered frame of the wheelhouse window, and in mid-shout Basso fired—a short, steady burst that produced instantaneous effect. As the figure dropped from view, the *Sea Fox* heeled sharply in response to a sudden pull on the wheel.

At full speed the boat swung to port, crossing from the channel into copper-brown water above the reef.

For a moment Stone thought the boat would make it— that the upwelling caused by the wind had given the *Sea Fox*, with her shallow draft, enough water to reach the open sea.

Then the ugly rasp as coral brushed wood. *Sea Fox*'s bow rose in seeming triumph, as the sound reached them above the noise of the wind. Below the waterline something caught, and the vessel's own momentum tore open the hull.

Engines still pounding, the vessel ground to a canted halt. Aboard the *Marie-Hélène* Stone backed off the throttle, easing the boat gently toward the reef edge. Hastily he dumped anchors fore and aft, knowing that to reach *Sea Fox* he would have to wade the last fifty feet across the reef.

"Go," shouted Basso, waving away Stone's look of concern. He hugged the Bren to his cheek, sighting on the *Sea Fox*'s bridge to cover Stone's assault.

Taking a machine pistol, Stone plunged into the tepid water as, for the second time in his life and with greater reluctance, he made ready to board the disabled *Sea Fox*.

As the *Sea Fox* struck the reef with fierce impact, the young German, Manfred, was thrown heavily against the back of the wheelhouse. When he understood they were no longer moving, he crabbed toward the ladderway, keeping the wheelhouse between himself and the devil with the machine gun aboard the approaching boat. He had to reach Bunnerman. The captain would have orders, would know what to do.

He pushed open the wheelhouse door and gagged in horror. Bunnerman sat on the deck, his back braced against a bulkhead spattered with bits of his own flesh. He was conscious, but the eyes that fell on Manfred had lost interest. A navy Luger was held limply in a clawlike hand minus two fingers.

"We've failed," he whispered. "A lifetime of failure."

Frantically, Manfred risked a glance, saw the man wading toward them from the small boat, a machine pistol held above his head.

"They're coming."

"It's done, my young Trojan, finished."

Before Manfred's terrified eyes, Bunnerman bent his head forward, pressed his right temple to the upturned muzzle of the automatic pistol, and managed to pull the trigger with his three-fingered hand.

Ten yards from the *Sea Fox*, Stone heard the gunshot, and the shrill girlish scream that followed it. From behind him, Basso opened fire, spraying the wheelhouse as a blurred figure slipped past one of the shattered windows and disappeared. Someone alive and still in action.

Stone tried to run, but in the surging chest-deep water, pulling, turning his body, it was the drugged dream all over again: arms and legs thrashing, he seemed to draw no closer to the *Sea Fox*. He damned each second lost at the top of his lungs.

In the engine compartment, the engineer Schrammel shut down the last electrical circuit, leaving only the emergency lighting in operation; he needed it to work by. Twice more he tried the voice communicator to the bridge, the silence clearly telling half the story.

The other half was told by the sound of inrushing seawater, already ankle-deep in the engine compartment.

Leadenly, Schrammel went to the explosive charge rigged next to the hull. Like driving a spike into a dead man, but still he followed orders. He looked thoughtfully at the two pencil detonators. A younger man might have been able to put himself clear enough of the ship to allow use of the three-minute pencil; but he was no longer young. He chose the thirty-minute detonator, pushed it into the gray explosive, and crimped the soft metal tip.

As the chemical igniter began its work, he lit a cigar and slowly mounted the ladder toward the rear hatch.

Forty years late, Seaman Schrammel was ready to surrender.

Pushing shut the heavy door to the wardroom, Manfred stopped a moment, trying to fight down the panic. The orders had made everything so easy; without them he was lost.

When the captain's words came back to him, a smile filled with relief crossed his handsome young face.

*They must not talk.*

With the sureness of a man given absolution, Manfred descended the iron ladderway and went forward to the crew's quarters. Pausing at the bulkhead door, he reached with one hand to pull it open; in the other, ready, was the hand grenade.

With the first frightening sound of machine-gun fire, Kits told the girls to stay down and cover their heads with their arms. When the craft veered suddenly off course she barely had time to brace herself as the hull scraped over the coral. Then the horrible tearing sound, and she knew they'd run solidly upon the reef.

For a few seconds the engine's vibration shook the entire vessel; the silence that followed was anything but reassuring.

"Don't anyone move until I have a look," she warned, creeping toward one of the portholes. As she raised her head, a shot rang out above them, followed by the chattering of the machine gun.

"What is it?" cried Polly.

"The cavalry to the rescue, I think."

A moment later the hatch opened, but the man who stood there was no savior. It was the young, straw-haired German. When he smiled, she thought it might somehow be all right. He was still smiling when, with an easy swing of his arm, he lobbed a small, sputtering object at them, and pulled the hatch closed with a slam.

Stone was in the wheelhouse, standing over Bunnerman's body when he heard the explosion.

The sound seemed to come from two directions at once. From below, deep in the hull, he heard a resonant *crumph*, with a thinner reverberation beyond the boat's hull. Stone ran through the wardroom and met the blond man at the top of the ladderway.

There was no time to use his weapon except as a battering ram. Stone clubbed the young German with it, the impact of their collision driving Manfred back against the railing. He went down with a croak, but Stone was already past him and leaping down the ladder.

It took three strides to reach the hatch to the crew's quarters. Bracing himself, he pulled it open, afraid of what he'd find inside.

It was what the behavioral scientists call generalizable experience—the reason why people good at one dangerous thing are often good at others. The chief element was habituation. You learned more about yourself and sharks, for example, in five seconds of facing one than in a lifetime of theorizing. It was Kits's years of experience in undersea dangers, of controlling her nerve, that had enabled her to survive in the underwater crawlspace. And by the narrowest margins it nearly saved her from the hand grenade.

For a frozen second she stared at the sputtering object rolling across the floor, trying to make an identification. A veteran of infantry combat might have immediately registered *hand grenade*, and, it was this hesitation, just that much time, added to what came next in the sequence, that beat her. Her reaction was quick, as efficient as a healthy neuro-muscular system could be uninhibited by indecision.

She scooped up the grenade, a sputtering thing alive in her hands, and sprang to the nearest porthole, some eight feet away. Precious instants were lost as she lifted the deadly weapon to eye level, another instant gone as she decided to fling it instead of merely dropping it through. She wanted it away. From herself, from Polly. Away.

The grenade went off less than a foot beyond the porthole. Most of the hundred or so hot metal shards spattered harmlessly against the ship's wooden hull. All but the two that managed to find the six-inch oval porthole.

As she turned her face away, a single tiny fragment tore through Kits's lower lip, shattering two teeth before it lodged in her jaw. The second missed her temple and an easy penetration to the brain. A miss by an inch. Instead, it entered through the corner of the left eye, shredding the retina in transit. Splintering on contact with the bony separation behind the nose, a single tiny fragment nudged into her brain while the other sliced through one millimeter of optic nerve behind her right eye and came to rest against the inside of her skull.

For a narrow part of a second, she felt little except a sharp sting behind her eyes. When the short period of grace was over, an explosion of pain erupted in the center of her skull.

She turned to tell Polly she was hurt, but her mouth was full of blood and bone. Her last clear sight before she passed out was of David Stone standing in the open hatchway of the *Sea Fox*; her last clear sound, the scream of her daughter filling her ears.

# Chapter 35
## The Serpent

The clinic was Rome's finest. Its doctors had repaired a wounded Pope and patched more than one knee-shot politician. The staff had great experience in cases of this kind, the surgeon general assured Stone a bit too casually. Death, human wreckage: hazards of the times, like smoking or driving too fast.

"I'll flip a coin to see who goes in first," offered Polly.

"We could go together," Stone said.

Polly considered it while a nursing sister waited patiently for one of them to follow. Three weeks had passed since Kits had been air-lifted from the island by helicopter.

Polly said, "I think it would be easier for everyone one at a time."

"Then you be first."

"Don't chicken out, David. You haven't changed your mind?"

"Not at all. But she might like hearing it from you."

In the cool, darkened room, Kits held Polly a long time while she tried to find the threads of things she'd been saving to say.

"And the other girls?" asked Kits.

"There were more police and questioning than anyone wanted. But Christian sort of worked it out."

"Christian?"

"David leading us off the boat was the worst part. Blood everywhere, and people dead."

"Not Basso?"

"No, he's here. I've visited him plenty."

"We should be thankful."

"But the minute we were aboard the *Marie-Hélène*, there was an explosion. The other boat just sort of cracked in two."

"And sank, I hope."

"Partway, Mother. You can still see it on the reef."

Sitting up, very still, Kits said, "Why don't we make it 'Polly' and 'Kits.' "

She badly wanted to tear down the last of the wall between them. There was something in Polly's voice—a forced cheeriness that wasn't right.

Polly hesitated. "I think I'd prefer 'Mother' for a while longer. If that's all right."

"Of course, it's all right, darling. It's all, all right."

In the hallway Polly spoke brightly to Stone. "You don't have to worry. Mom's as good as she could be." She looked away. "You know, I keep thinking about what she did."

"Aboard *Sea Fox*?"

Polly nodded. "Watching the way she reacted, so sure she could make it. It was like, maybe, in a couple of seconds I really learned everything my mother is."

She was a big girl, with square swimmer's shoulders and fine wide-set eyes a shade paler than her mother's. She was on the verge of becoming a startling young woman. In the past weeks Stone had come to appreciate her intelligence and strongmindedness, her mother's admirable legacies. There was only one disquieting thing. He hoped he was exaggerating it, but he'd noticed the way she avoided even the most casual male touch.

She hesitated. "David, I didn't tell her. I couldn't, not about her eyes. I never got around to our trip. Only that I would be staying around awhile."

"She said yes to that?"

Polly grinned. "She didn't say no."

It was left to Stone to tell Kits she was blind and probably always would be.

"The retina of the right eye was destroyed, Kits. Nothing to be done. The doctor can tell you exactly what else happened."

"I'd rather hear it from you."

She'd wanted to add the word, *darling*. But it made too many presumptions, claims no longer valid.

"The optic nerve of your left eye was cut a third of the way through. Like the retina, it's—"

"Irreparable. I know."

"The rest of the nerve was severely traumatized, shocked. When it begins to function again, there's a good chance you'll regain partial vision in the left eye. There's a metal fragment in your brain that doesn't seem to be bothering anything, and they want to leave it for now. So much for Doc Stone's interim report. Better news next time."

"I'm glad you didn't sugarcoat it," said Kits after a long while. "You'd have disappointed me."

"I've been on the telephone to several hospitals Stateside. All sorts of new surgical techniques: lasers—"

"And the eye is one of the toughest parts of the human body," she interrupted him. "Did you know?"

She felt him come close then, not a trace of pity in his embrace. She could feel the heat of his body, and the steady strength in his arms told her what she needed to know.

Later, in a tone of confession, he said, "I'm afraid Polly and I have been scheming."

"Have you now."

"We've planned a little cruise. Nice and easy along the coast, just the three of us. How does that sound?"

"Lovely," she said, with a distant smile that quickly faded. "But nothing more about the *Sea Fox*. Promise?"

"Nothing but sunshine, wine, and song."

She reached out suddenly, gripping his arm. "David, what do I look like?"

"Like you've been in a fight."

"Ugly."

"You could never be ugly."

"Don't play with words, damn you. Don't do that to me."

"You look fine," he insisted. "Or will, after some sun and fresh air and a new pair of teeth."

"Truth, you swear it?"

"Truth."

She held him again. "It's not the end of everything then?"

"No," said Stone, something coiled and deadly in the back of his mind. "Not the end at all."


Two weeks later Stone again met Christian in the bar atop Nice airport.

Christian looked up blankly from a large cognac as Stone approached. He was a dead man walking; they both knew it.

"I've given it my best," he said, slumping defeated. "Nothing more to be done."

"The police can't tie Michaelis in?"

"Because there is nothing to tie. Oh yes, his henchman Rico was on the island about the time Bunnerman received his order to scuttle the *Sea Fox* with the girls aboard. But Michaelis never left Paris." Christian sipped mechanically at his drink. "The young one who threw the grenade escaped."

Stone appeared to accept that. "Did the police learn anything from the German sailor who gave up?"

"Only that their connection was the man called Yank. Brought the girls in via a fast Italian powerboat and took delivery of the dope. Interpol has issued bulletins on him and his male-bait partner, Pino. They may be in Brazil, anywhere. Or dead."

Below, an airbus flight from Paris was debarking passengers. Stone caught sight of a red-haired woman ducking into a terminal bus. It could have been Sophie, but the distance was too great to be sure; doubtful.

Christian was saying, "The authorities found the missing policeman, Labatt. Him and his wife, and the child. Shot. Then *carbonisée*, as the French so graphically put things. Kerosene."

"Where were they found?"

"The basement of his house. Does it matter?"

Labatt's worst fear, the long arm of punishment, and Labatt had waited for it to strike. The thought angered Stone. Had it, in truth, reached from Michaelis?

Sensing a lingering doubt, Christian said, "He remains untouchable. All of it done by remote control, don't you see? Nothing to tug the conscience, if the devil has one. He makes a mockery of the whole legal system."

"Not if he's innocent."

Christian's eyes rounded. "You say that after all he has put you through? The man is a fiend, Stone. A well-mannered, exquisitely tailored man of charm and culture. But evil, violent, and corrupt. You don't know how seldom the true villains look their part."

"I know you believe it," said Stone, "proof or not."

"And so should you," whispered Christian. Rising, he took a card from his pocket and handed it to Stone. "A telephone in London where I may be reached for the next few days. After that . . ." He didn't finish.

They parted as they'd met, without shaking hands. Stone turned to watch Christian go; labored and unsteady, each step a separate battle.

# Chapter 36
## Respite

From Cannes they sailed west along the coast in a *Marie-Hélène* sporting new paint to cover her recent patchwork. Short days of sailing, long nights in the small jeweled bays of the Esterel. Then San Raphael, and on past Port Grimaud to St. Tropez in time for Polly's sixteenth birthday.

Ashore, Stone led her and Kits through the narrow streets to a small restaurant near a dusty square hung with colored lights.

Basso was waiting.

Polly ran to him. But as she was about to fly into Basso's arms something caught and Stone saw the inner reluctance again as she shied from his touch. Basso didn't appear to notice, just held her at arm's length and sighed.

"Ah, to be sixteen again. No, I take that back. To be twenty again. And all the girls sixteen . . ."

A strange pained look passed behind his eyes when Kits reached up, searched his face with her fingertips, and gave him a kiss gentle enough for a small child.

"We've missed you, Basso," she said. "Truly missed you."

"Come," said Basso quickly, his face reddening. "The chef here is a thief, but the food he steals isn't bad."

That night Basso took command, presiding as Le Pic might have done. Watching him hover over Polly and Kits, Stone more than once observed the change. A great weight had lifted from his muscular shoulders, something to do with squaring things on Le Pic's behalf, Stone supposed.

Later Bosso told them that he and a few friends intended to rebuild the Bar des Marines. "A man needs a place to go, a real place. Not one of those plastic horrors along the Croisette. A place Le Pic himself would have been proud of."

"For Le Pic, then," toasted Kits.

"For all of us," said Basso, raising his glass.


West from St.-Tropez the days lost number. Already Kits was moving around the *Marie-Hélène* as surely as if she had a blueprint of it in her mind. By committee decision, and Kit's badgering, Stone and Polly ceded her the galley during the second week.

The only point of real stress was their sleeping arrangements. Stone had left the main forward cabin to Kits and Polly, while he bunked on the narrow bed near the galley. But when Kits was close to him, the sexual electricity was powerful enough to light neon. More than once he caught Polly watching them with a fixed, unsmiling appraisal he couldn't interpret.

One night over the cleanly picked bones of a *chapon* Polly had speared for dinner, she tapped her wineglass with a fork. "I have something to say."

"Sounds official," said Kits.

"It is. For the mental health of all hands."

"I may need a cognac," Stone said, starting to rise.

"No, you don't," said Polly firmly. "Come on, David." She waited until he lowered himself back into his chair. "The point is, I really don't mind if you two bunk together."

Kits opened her mouth, but couldn't quite put together a reply.

Polly continued, "I mean it would be better for me than watching you two mope around like a couple of lovesick hounds. Agreed?"

After a moment Stone said, "Agreed."

"Mother?"

"Of course, darling."

Polly sighed. "I'm glad that's settled. I've noticed people your age have a rough time talking about certain things."

By the time they reached the bay at Cassis, the days were visibly shorter, and the nights as sharp and dry as the flinty local wine.

They anchored farther on at one of the *calanques*, a narrow, steep-sided bay, almost fjordlike, and crested by sharp limestone bluffs.

Watching Kits swim a widening circle around the boat one afternoon, Polly smiled approvingly and said, "A boat was a good place for her to begin. She's already talking about new projects, things she can still do, things she's never tried."

"What do you think?"

"The important thing is wanting to do *something*, and she doesn't seem bitter about what happened to her. I mean, it could be the kind of thing that sort of paralyzes you."

"And you?"

She looked up sharply, making Stone feel as if he had

just broken some unwritten rule. Her eyes slid away. "It's like I've just come out of a dark place. A place where bad things happened to someone I knew. Every once in a while I slip back in, know it was me. But with a little time . . ." She smiled quickly and a little too broadly. "With a little more time I'll be fine."

Take stock, Stone. Glass in hand, icy cold, and heavy on lemon and gin. Half empty. Or half full, depending on level of optimism. Say half full.

Le Pic had wanted him to plunge. And this was it, with no doubts, no brass bands needed to spread the word. A quiet, sure thing, inside, something he and Kits shared.

Curled sleeping beside him, a nice face to look at anytime, very rare. Girl ashore, lean and browned, on the mend from previous ordeal. Look around you, Stone. And be thankful for all of it. Because the change in the air is telling you something. Fall will come on suddenly as it does in these parts. Add in vague yearnings—for new work, a new boat, he didn't know. Not important yet. But it would be.

*Face it, it's time for the cruise to end.* He'd propose same over dinner that night, a giant spiney lobster Stone, at great peril, had bagged himself.

He heard the sound of the engine as the gray launch edged its way into their core. It was making straight for them, and Stone recognized the Cassis port commander's boat.

Vague stirrings, but let the serpent sleep.

Closer, he could make out the tall, silver-haired officer who had stamped them into port a week and a hundred years ago.

"Monsieur Stone," he called out, "a message. *Urgent.*"

Kits was awake now, her head cocked to catch every word.

"From who?"

"A Monsieur Christian. By telephone, half an hour ago. You must make a call. Life and death, he said."

"I guess that could qualify as urgent."

Stone eased a thoughtful glance toward the head of the cove, a half-mile distant. Polly had taken the new inflatable Avon in to do some exploring ashore.

"I've a passenger ashore and one on board," Stone called out. "I can't leave them."

"You can come with me," the officer said. "Very fast, my boat."

"Go on, David," Kits urged. "Polly will be back soon, and I'll be all right."

Stone started to protest, but remembered that part of the exercise was to build Kits's self-reliance.

"I'm not going to drown," she laughed. "It must be important."

"Suppose you start dragging an anchor."

"I'll give it more line. Don't treat me like a child."

"I've left the radio on, set to Cassis marine."

"David, don't worry."

"I'll be back as soon as I can, sunset latest."

"I'll be here," she replied.

# Chapter 37
## Ambuscade

The number left by Christian had a Paris prefix. Stone called it from the port commander's office on the Quai des Moulines.

Christian's message fitted his flair for the melodramatic, but Stone didn't doubt the urgency.

At the tenth ring, Stone put down the receiver. The port officer shrugged.

Stone shrugged in return, staring a moment at the waterborn traffic moving in and out of the narrow port.

"I'll wait and try again," he said.

Polly had picked out the trail from the water. A narrow path fit for goats, that switchbacked up the steep side of the *calanque* from a rocky beach. The crest was several hundred feet above.

She ran the Avon ashore, unwilling to return to the *Marie-Hélène* just yet. She needed time alone to deal with the confusion sealed up inside her.

She debated leaving the boat unattended. She'd seen no one on the trail, or anywhere else, and decided the risk wasn't great.

She pulled the boat high up on a beach of fine shingle so it wouldn't float off with the tide. Then, swapping her boat shoes for a pair of tennies, she started up the trail.

It took a hard twenty minutes to reach the crest. Below, without the wind, the blue-green water looked solid enough to walk on, and she had a sudden impulse to try putting it all onto canvas, working the mixture of colors until it was just right. A picture that could always remind her of something clean and peaceful. At anchor, the *Marie-Hélène* looked like a perfect toy. It took her a moment to notice the other boat, crusiing idly into her picture: bigger than the *Marie-Hélène*, bigger and sleeker, and familiar.

"Stinkpot sailor," she muttered with proper derision. Easing toward the *Marie-Hélène*, the second boat swung around, changing her angle of vision.

When it came to her, a terrible fear constricted her throat. "No," she gasped. "Oh, no." Turning, she plunged back down the trail, running for all she was worth.

In the office of the port commander, Stone again tried the Paris telephone number left by Christian.

No answer.

Time, moving on the back of a snail.

*Life and death*.

He fought to keep his voice even when he said, "I need to call London."

Predictably, the officer's eyes glazed over. Stone held out a five-hundred-franc note. "This will cover it."

The officer looked at the note, and held up his hand in refusal. "Do what you must."

Stone found the card Christian had given him and dialed the number direct. It was a club in the city; the voice on the other end asked Stone to hold on while Christian was paged.

Stone waited, the rhythmic pounding of blood loud in his ears.

"Christian here."

"You're not in Paris."

"Stone? How could I be in Paris? I told you."

"No call from a Paris number."

"What in the world . . . ?"

Stone dropped the phone and whirled to the wide-eyed port officer.

"I have to call the *Marie-Hélène*. Quick, man, an emergency."

In the radio room Stone tried, but no answer. Aboard he'd left the set on and tuned to receive, the gain on high.

Stone's glance shot toward the port officer. "Someone wanted me off the boat."

It sounded feeble. When they mattered, explanations always did.

"But why, monsieur?" The port officer regarded Stone with open suspicion.

*Don't doubt me, you bastard.* Stone didn't have the patience to explain what suddenly added up to Michaelis reaching out for revenge. He told the port officer to notify the police.

"From your launch radio," he appealed. "I must get back to the *Marie-Hélène*."

It took a quarter of an hour at top speed. A mile distant, Stone could make out the shape of a sleek Italian motor cruiser, drifting a hundred yards or so off the *Marie-Hélène*'s stern.

Stone scanned the decks, saw no one aboard, and for the moment dismissed it.

He jumped aboard the *Marie-Hélène* as the launch drew alongside. Near the wheel the power cord dangled from the radio; blood spattered the deck nearby. He went below to find the interior a shambles. Topside he could hear the port officer already on the radio to the harbor police. No disbelief now.

"Urgent . . . urgent!"

# Chapter 38
## The Depths

Above the marine chatter from the radio transceiver, Kits had heard the low rumble of powerful engines.

"Ahoy there," a voice called out. A man's voice. "Ahoy, the *Marie-Hélène*."

She went up on deck, cocking her head toward the sound.

"Is that scoundrel Le Pic aboard?"

Less than thirty feet away, the voice calling down from a higher angle—the flying bridge of a motor cruiser. Strange that anyone who knew Le Pic, knew his boat, would have heard nothing about the bombing at the Bar des Marines. Sharp warning prickled the skin at the back of her neck.

"I'm afraid not," Kits said, remaining perfectly still.

"I'm a friend from over toward Marseille."

The rise and fall of engine pitch, closer now as the boat maneuvered in.

"What do you want?" said Kits, without any pretense of friendliness.

"Want?" Now laughter, amused but mean. "Hell, I don't want for a thing, Mrs. Maitland."

*Mizz-Mait-lun*.

Mentally, she was visualizing the path to the radio. There were spear guns, a knife in the forward lockers.

The jolt as hulls touched.

"You do not have permission to board," she stammered, feeling utterly helpless. "Do you understand?"

Engines backing and again that rough laugh.

"Well now, isn't that polite—*po-light*—all nice and formal. Just like a real sailor."

"It is not a request, whoever you are."

"I think you might know if you thought about it. I do believe that old Rico was right for twice in his life." She felt the *Marie-Hélène* dip with his weight as he stepped aboard. "You can't *see*."

She took a step back, away from the sound of his voice.

"Get off this boat!"

"Oh, I'll be gone soon enough, you can count on that."

The voice had moved closer, close enough so she could smell the rank alcohol on the man's breath. Suddenly a rough hand encircled her wrist.

"As soon as we finish the little thing I came for."

Descending from the bluff top, Polly fell twice as calcareous rock broke away under her feet. Both times she cried out in pain, tumbling down the incline like a newborn colt. Each time she rose, oblivious of the abrasions, to continue her plunge on down the path, toward the beach and inflatable boat.

She would speed back to the *Marie-Hélène*, warn them, and go on to Cassis for help.

She hadn't a shred of doubt that the sleek motor cruiser she'd seen from the clifftop was the same one she'd boarded with Yank and Pino. Stupid. It made her ill now to think of the things she'd let Pino do. Things no one had ever done before, most of which she'd liked before the whole thing turned from pleasure to pain. She'd wanted to fight, but hadn't. That had been her mistake. You had to fight for yourself the way her mother had fought aboard the *Sea Fox*.

She descended the last few feet of trail, digging in her heels to keep from stumbling. She was sure there had been only one trail. She halted, wondering at her mistake.

The inflatable boat was gone.

She walked slowly to the water's edge and found the stones leveled smooth where she'd dragged it from the water. Then she saw it, the clean gray fabric breaking the surface in shallow water. She waded out and dragged the boat to shore. The aluminum oars were still tacked down. Whoever had done it, hadn't even bothered to steal the engine. Then she found the slashes in the fabric from a knife or razor.

*And she knew*.

"Hey!"

From the scrubby brush beyond the beach Pino straightened, grinning in that way she would carry with her for a lifetime. He was shirtless, in jeans, and when he came toward her, she was conspicuously aware of the masculine bulge in his trousers—Pino's trademark.

"Hey, Pol."

He stopped a few feet away, letting his eyes wander over her body. She could remember him pressing down on her in the darkness, then the sting as the needle went home. She told herself to run. She wanted to, but in some strange manner Pino drained away her will.

"I wouldn't have believed it, Pol. Been watching you for days out there, swimming, walking around. You're looking fine."

His eyes were watchful now. As he took a step closer, he withdrew a straight razor from the pocket of his jeans and laid open the blade with a little whiplike movement of his wrist.

"Are you going to kill me?"

"Oh no, baby. I promise. Just . . . mark you a little."

"You've already marked me."

"I have to, Pol. Easier if you just let me, cleaner you know. Here . . ." He held out a hand, beckoning her. "It's something I have to do. You understand?"

"Yes," said Polly, reaching out. "I understand."


"Sonofabitch," breathed Yank, trying to pin down the body writhing beneath him on the deck.

Nothing like a good rape if you could pull it off, but he was having first doubts. Again he tried to press her shoulders to the deck, grabbing at her blouse front to tear it away. Something eerie in those flat sightless eyes turned up toward him. The muscles in her arms were like thin cables.

He whacked her once, good, a big hammy fist across the face. She went limp long enough for him to strip the blouse away. Brown, brown all over, except for her angry red nipples, and the sight of them began to arouse the thing in him that had been a source of growing concern for a would-be rapist. Old cockadoodle-don't.

Hell, it wasn't his idea.

But as he went for the waist of her jeans, her knee came up, hard bone against the gristle of his button nose. By the time the tears cleared, she had twisted away and was crawling toward the wheel. Except it wasn't the wheel she was after. When he understood what she had in mind, he made a lunge but was too late.

Perfect timing she had. Pulling loose the fire extinguisher, she swung it around in a wide arc as Yank reached for her.

The valve raked across his cheek an inch below the eye, laying it open to the bone. Yelping in pain, Yank lashed out blindly, but already she was on her feet. She took a sure step backward, down into the main cabin, spraying $CO_2$ in his direction and every other. By the time he'd ducked away and recovered, the cabin door was shut and he heard the snap of a storm latch.

So much for round one.

"Except with me," Yank cackled, "you don't get no minute's rest."

He tore the power lead from the radio, found the fire axe next to the extinguisher mounting, and began smashing through the cabin door.

Kits knew she couldn't let herself be trapped helpless belowdeck. As the first blows fell on the teak planking of the cabin door, she ran forward, past the head, to the lockers with their diving gear. She found the new spear gun with its trident spear, exactly where Polly had left it, and reached in for her diving knife.

*Gone.* As she rummaged through the locker for it, she heard the cabin door splinter and knew there wouldn't be time.

She went farther forward, dragging her fingers along the paneling to determine exactly where she was in the boat. She stepped into the narrow forward cabin and turned. From this point to the main cabin door was just over twelve unobstructed feet. She leveled the spear gun, and took a slow breath.

She fired when she heard the man grunt his way through the wrecked planking, felt the pointed shaft spring away. When it struck, a hollow *thunk*, not what she'd prepared her mind to expect, but the most awful scream as something heavy crashed to the cabin floor.

She slammed shut the door, bolted it, and waited. Five seconds, ten . . . then, ear against the door, she listened.

Nothing.

*Get out of here.*

Standing on the bunk, she pushed open the hatch that led to the foredeck and hoisted herself topside. She took in a breath of air, and started aft, for the radio. She managed a second step before he caught her, an arm circling her waist. A rough laugh gargled up from deep in his chest.

"I may be stupid, lady," he whispered savagely, "but I ain't blind."

The remark pulsed anger through her, and she butted her head toward the voice. She felt the sharp pain as her forehead broke teeth away.

For the barest instant his grip loosened, and in that moment, it was Kit's's arms that encircled his abundant girth, this man who had come to extract payment for something it wasn't hers to pay.

As he gasped in surprise, Kits lifted with all of her strength. It was not enough to take his feet from the deck, just enough to teeter him off-balance. As she felt the imbalance, she filled her lungs with air and crabbed her leg around his.

They went over slowly, Yank's foot catching the lip of the deck. A second later, locked in a lovers' embrace, they struck the water. Before he could take much of a breath, Kits pulled him under, thrusting now with her muscular legs.

Kicking, tugging with all that was in her, Kits took him deeper into the place she knew as home.

# Chapter 39
## The Kill

It was finished in less than a minute.

In those first seconds underwater, he must have vomited. Quite before she expected, she felt him convulse and begin thrashing like a speared fish in the final, oxygen-burning spasms of life.

Twice he went for her throat. Each time, as his hands found her, she pulled him deeper. Then the survival systems of his brain became dominant, and the hands loosened as he tried to claw upward toward the surface, dragging the weight of the two of them.

When he could no longer keep from taking a breath, she felt a second great spasm wrack his body. All control gone, his back arched, and even underwater she heard a sound from within like nothing human.

When he no longer thrashed or tried to pry loose her fingers, she let the body drift away. Later, the absence of emotion would trouble her; she'd found this killing so terribly easy.

But with the burning sensation in her own lungs, Kits found herself thinking not of one man but two. Polly'd mentioned *two* aboard the boat used to take her and the other girls.

She kicked powerfully to the surface. She treaded water long enough to feel the current moving about her, trying to read the subtle differences in the sounds of land and sea. Given the narrowness of the cove, she could easily find shore. But could she find Polly?

Gambling on her orientation, Kits began to swim.


"Make it easy, Pol. For the two of us." Pino took a step closer, slowly reaching for her hand. A reassuring grin showed his beautiful teeth. "Come to Pino," he said softly, and she had the sudden vision of a skittish horse she'd often ridden at school, a creature that always needed gentling before it would give up control.

Maybe Pino sensed what she would do because, springing suddenly, he lunged for her. As he did, she made a little move with her shoulders toward the water, and when Pino took the feint, she ran in the opposite direction, toward the foot of the trail.

"Bitch!" he cried, going for her ankle and missing by a finger-length.

But as she reached the bottom of the trail she heard him behind her, harsh breath wheezing out between clamped teeth like a crazy man.

*Don't look back. Climb, keep climbing.* Both hands clawed the crumbly earth to pull her still higher. Her feet lost purchase, slipping back before they dug in again. *Higher, climb faster.* It was fear that drove her now, no longer paralyzing but charging her body and flowing freely within her.

Reaching for a handhold, her fingers touched a mug-sized stone. Instead of plunging on, something planted deeply in her mind made her slow. Imagining her arm held a tennis racquet, that her swing was really no different than practice on a school court, she turned from the waist. A low, flat swing with the stone in her hand, just as Pino reached her.

As his arm raised to fend off the blow, she connected with his elbow.

It was enough to put him off-balance and she hit him again. She heard the gravel slide loose beneath his feet. He went back down the path flat on his stomach, bobsledding bare-chested a good twenty feet.

When he came to rest, he didn't get up, didn't even move.

*Careful, he's full of tricks.*

Then she heard him whimper, a pitiful little cry for help.

She could run now, escape.

Keeping the stone ready, she edged back down the path.

His eyes were open, slits just wide enough to show the whites. The odd angle of his right arm meant broken. He couldn't have held the razor with an arm like that.

She searched the brush nearby, but couldn't find it. Too bad. Better if she had found the razor.

She threw away the stone and walked back down to the beach. She went straight to the collapsed inflatable boat. She unsnapped the Velcro binding over the emergency oars and lifted one out. Blades of stamped aluminum, soft enough to take an edge against the outcropping of limestone at the foot of the path.

Pino was still there when she climbed back up the trail carrying the oar. He looked up at her, eyes open, but still not able to focus clearly.

"Can you feel, Pino?"

He made a sound congested with pain.

He tried to move; but as he did, she put a shoe down

firmly on his broken arm. She felt the bone shift beneath her foot as Pino screamed and lay back.

"Can you, Pino? Can you feel me?"

When he merely groaned, she reached down and used the sharp edge of the aluminum oar to cut off the top button of Pino's jeans. Ever so carefully she pulled him free. Poor little thing. Poor dead bird.

"Feel me, Pino," she said, "feel me." And began to work with the blade.

Stone found them on the dark smudge of beach. Approaching aboard the port commander's launch, he saw the two of them, Kits and Polly, hunkered down on the pebbles, side by side. Kits sat with her arms around Polly, a tight embrace to battle the tremors that shook the young girl's body.

"*Mon Dieu*," breathed the port officer.

When they grounded the boat, Polly's head turned mechanically to observe them. If she recognized Stone, she made no sign. Closer he saw an animal wildness in her eyes that turned him cold. It told the story well enough; in the hours since he'd seen her last, something had swept away her fragile defenses, drawing Polly Maitland back into darkness.

# Chapter 40
## Lawman

Christian stared into the deep, soothing amber of his second brandy and declined the offer of a third. The request from the club barman, and Christian's firm refusal, was a ritual highly polished over the years.

As the white-coated barman turned away, Christian raised his arm to call him back, but caught himself in time.

That was the point exactly, a precise metaphor of the quandary the Maitland woman had forced upon him. Did a man abandon principle when the choices facing him struck at his core? What good was self-discipline in the absence of a true test? He felt like a man rediscovering his faith in God on the edge of the grave, a faith that, although frequently ignored, had remained the bedrock of his being. Quite simply, even under the stress of the past weeks, Christian found he still believed in justice. Not some theoretical abstraction, but the everyday justice of the law, even as it was so often administered by fools and the self-serving.

It was the act of a revolutionary to totally throw aside the past to embrace something new. For Christian, it would mean rejecting a legal system he himself was part of. Robert Christian, revolutionary? Unthinkable.

The irony was that unless Christian now chose to break those lifelong rules, deal with Michaelis at his own base level, the man would go unpunished.

Until that afternoon he'd thought the Stone affair finished. True, the Maitland woman and her daughter had suffered grievously. But their recompense was beyond Christian's power, legal or physical. He had done his best, they must understand that.

At four o'clock he'd taken the call in his office. His desk was clean now, the drawers emptied. He had spent hours there these last days, hands folded, finding comfort in routine. Two days until he entered the hospital; he no longer had the will to postpone the inevitable.

"David's gone," he had heard Kits say. The connection with the south of France was the clearest he could remember.

"Gone?"

"I want you to find him, Christian. Stop him."

*I can't*, Christian wanted to scream. *I couldn't aid a falling infant.* Nothing in his voice betrayed his own helplessness. "Stop him from what?"

"From killing Antoine Michaelis."

Stone spent the nine-hour train ride reviewing each intended step.

In Paris he checked into a small, overpriced hotel on the Rue Jacob that traded heavily on the claim it was once favored by Hemingway. What would Hem have liked in the place? Stone wondered. Location, perhaps. Around the corner from the Brasserie Lipp and a good sobering hike from the cafés of Montparnasse. For Stone, it was within striking range of Antoine Michaelis.

In the week past he'd devised plans worthy of the

Borgias, and then considered no plan at all: a frontal attack, guns blazing. A part of him had ceased to reason; another part, the true survivor buried deeply within him, was pure animal cunning. By the measure of the David Stone he'd been two months before, he was peeled bare to the elementals—a creature striking out in reflex to protect his own. Primitive man. He should have carried a club and spear.

Lifting the telephone at bedside he gave instructions to the desk clerk, identical for the fourth consecutive day.

"Wake me at three p.m. sharp."

He lay down then, fully dressed, thinking of those plain-faced assassins, the ones who stalked presidents and pop idols, waiting for their time. Outsiders with personal histories of impotence and failure. Until they made the grand discovery: a stalker was all powerful, God himself, for the moment of death was his to administer.

Stone had considered and rejected Christian's plea to rely on the law to mete out punishment. What evidence was there? A few initials on some documents in a Swiss lawyer's office. A bodyguard whose name escaped the lips of a thug while he tried to carry out Michaelis's dirty work and ended up at the bottom of an ocean. *The name Rico, your honor, a common name, filling half a column in the Paris phone book.*

Judged by the evidence? Innocent.

*But we must protect society, Stone. You and I, each of us must try.* Christian making his final appeal.

The abrasive buzz of the telephone at bedside pulled him from a shallow sleep.

"Three o'clock," the impersonal voice said. Stone rose.

Brilliant plans: photographs, close-up, of Michaelis, slipped beneath his door at night. Proof to Michaelis that

Stone had been close enough to use a weapon. There would be no escape.

Kidnapping: Michaelis's fourteen-year-old son. Perfect replica of his father. *Leave me and mine alone and you can have him back.*

*Your word of honor?*

*I promise.*

And what then?

How much distance between him and Michaelis's people would be enough? How much was enough for those federal witnesses who testified against former mob friends? Off with new identities to anonymous small towns. They still ended up dead, or making midnight phone calls to the Godfather begging forgiveness, anything to stave off the axe hanging over their lives. Ex-Nazis unearthed to this day in Paraguay, their time spent waiting for the past to arrive. The policeman Labatt.

Stone went to his suitcase. No spear or club. Only a small automatic pistol. Alloy frame, small magazine, big bullets: .45-caliber hollow-points, 185 grains of lead and copper that blew bone and tissue ahead of them.

*What choice have I been given?*

He took the pistol, cocked and locked it, slipped it into his jacket pocket.

The waiting was over.


Her name was Winnie Mullen.

Her apartment was a *grand studio* with balcony on the seventh floor of a high-rise building in Neuilly, the kind Parisians complain is blighting their skyline. Yet from one corner of her living room she had an unobstructed view of the Eiffel Tower, had she chosen to look. But the visual splendors of The City of Light interested Winnie not at all. She was twenty years old and English, as were most of her fellow Blue Belle Girls. She passed the larger part of her time in the small apartment gazing at her reflection in a magnified, neon-lighted mirror, examining each pore and blemish for signs of age.

Her most marketable features, she thought, were long legs and modestly sized (but perfectly shaped) breasts. Her back was straight, her carriage statuesque. She was not a dancer, she was quick to tell people. The costumed elegance of the Blue Belle Girls drew the crowds to the Lido, not the dancers. Even if the crowds these days were mainly Japanese businessmen in large orderly groups, smiling nervous gold-filled smiles and puffing their cigarettes like little machines. In the hard light of day she was tall, ordinary, a pretty girl who seldom turned heads on the streets. A nice girl, Mum was still sure, bored with filling empty days in a city that wasn't her kind of fun. Haughty and aloof the Parisians were, even with each other. And Winnie enjoyed a good chat.

Stone found her approachable, and most helpful.

"I love horses," she confided, "and I'd love the races, really."

They'd met in a *crêperie* within sight of her apartment.

"We'll go Thursday," Stone suggested.

"Um, can't on Thursdays. Besides I go to work at seven."

Stone smiled at the hint they'd need more time. "Never on Thursday?"

She regarded him slyly. "You're not a snoop, are you, David?"

"We all have our little secrets."

A few minutes after three, Stone was waiting when Andre Rico and his sullen girl friend exited a hamburger joint on the Boulevard St. Germain. Cigarette dangling at his lip, he said a few curt words to the girl before she walked away with no goodbye. Rico watched her go, flicked away the cigarette, spat for effect, and climbed into a large tan Peugeot sedan double-parked at the curb.

Ordered lives and comfortable routines. *Bless the French*.

Stone didn't bother to follow him. It would take Rico at most a half-hour, even in stagnant rush-hour traffic, to reach Michaelis's apartment.

Stone had considered making the move there. A good sixty feet separated building entrance and street. But the single time Stone *did* follow him, Rico'd had his mind on business. Out of the car to open the rear door smartly. Michaelis's passage was brief, and then they were off again, no time wasted. A few seconds' exposure, but still, with surprise, a possibility.

But Stone could no longer count on the element of surprise.

Two nights before, he'd returned to his hotel room and found Christian waiting in the darkness, inside.

"If I found you, so can Michaelis." When Stone reached for the switch, he raised his hand. "No, please, leave the light off."

In the faint glow from the street, Christian's face was even more drawn and skull-like than usual.

"Give it up, Stone."

"I want an ending. And not a time and place picked by someone else. Ask Labatt . . ."

"But we're moral men, you and I. Not necessarily good men, but moral, however much we pretend to the contrary. We still believe the law is better than each man being his own judge, jury, and executioner."

"The law can't touch Michaelis. It's your tune, Christian. All sad violins."

"It might someday. You can't throw aside what is right."

"The law has its limits, and every cop will tell you so.

When it comes down to my own life and those around me—either him or us—Michaelis loses."

Unsteadily, Christian crossed to the window. His bent shoulders diminished his height, gave him the look of a withered tree.

Slowly, in the tone of a confessional, Christian said, "I telephoned Michaelis. I warned him you've come to Paris to kill him. For you, Stone. I've taken away the temptation that even a moral man will give in to if he thinks he can escape retribution."

"Like America and Russia. If we both have a thousand Nukes or ten thousand, as long as it's equal, both sides are powerless."

"Exactly," said Christian.

"It takes the mind of a politician to believe that," said Stone. "You missed your calling."

"You may have a gun, Stone. But you won't pull the trigger. I know you."


At 3:30 p.m. Stone took the Métro, changing trains at Chatelet, toward Pont de Neuilly. Just now the leggy Blue Belle Girl, Winnie Mullen, was leaving a cool salon near Port Maillot, returning to her apartment. Her toenails would be trimmed and lacquered, her feet plained smooth and creamed. Thursday, 2:30–3:30. Pedicure.

At 3:40, Stone climbed the steps from the Métro and turned along a busy side street. The table he picked in the *crêperie* had a clear view of the entrance to the apartment building. By counting windows along the seventh floor, he found Winnie's apartment, curtains already discreetly drawn. He ordered a sea-salt *crêpe*, a glass of cider, and waited.

At 3:58 the large tan Peugeot turned into the street. It stopped at the building long enough for Antoine Michaelis to duck out. A big man, barrel-thick at the chest. He said something to Rico behind the wheel, then walked quickly toward the apartment entrance. The concierge opened the door for him, nodding in recognition.

Thursday, 4:00 to 6:00, Winnie Mullen entertains gentleman caller, in the person of Antoine Michaelis.

As the Peugeot sped off, Stone turned his attention to the *crêpe*. Nothing to do quite yet.

At 5:10 p.m. Stone entered the florist's. The potted *palmier* ordered the day before was ready, artfully wrapped with bright metallic paper. He added a note to the palm, paid the clerk, and left, carrying it with him.

As Stone pushed his way into the vestibule of the apartment building, the concierge looked up from behind a glassed-in enclosure.

"For Madame Bercy," Stone said.

The concierge's eyes slid from Stone to the plant and became heavy-lidded with boredom. Oddly enough, Stone had most worried about gaining entrance to the building.

"Crazy that woman," said the concierge, coming out from behind the glass. "Her apartment is a jungle." He led Stone to the elevator and pushed the call button for him. "Plants everywhere. Even the balcony."

"I've noticed."

Inside the elevator Stone pressed eight and checked his watch—5:40. Pray Winnie is in good form this afternoon, and patient.

At the sound of the door buzzer, Stone heard the yip of small dogs inside Madame Bercy's apartment. A moment later the heavily made-up face of a woman in her late sixties peered at him suspiciously over a thick chain across the door, a face from old French movies on TV.

"I didn't order that."

"A gift, madame."

"Who would give me a gift?"

"An admirer, perhaps."

"My admirers have been dead for years. All dead."

"I'll just leave it here."

He placed the palm near the door. Suspicious eyes followed him until the elevator door closed off her view.

Stone pushed five.

At the fifth floor, he stepped out and reached back in to touch eighteen, sending the elevator empty to the top floor. If below, the concierge was watching the elevator's movements, let him try to unravel it.

Stone walked up one flight, checking out the emergency stairs, then back along the sixth-floor hallway to the elevator door.

One floor below Winnie's apartment. Stone looked at his watch again. He was ready.

At 5:56 the signal light above the elevator door blinked on. The elevator descended from the eighteenth floor, past the floor above, and continued to the foyer.

*Passengers entering.*

An instant later the elevator rose to nine, stopped, then descended from nine to seven. One floor above, someone got in. On the dot.

Stone's hand tightened on the pistol in his pocket, as with his free hand he pushed the DOWN button.

When the elevator door opened, he stepped in quickly, prepared for Michaelis.

He found instead an attractive blond in tight white pants with a girl of eight or nine. The speed of his entrance startled them both. The woman glared. Stone smiled.

"Up?" he asked, pointing.

"Down," said the woman, managing in a single word to let Stone know what a simpleton he was.

"Sorry."

He backed from the elevator breathing an apology.

At 6:03 the elevator again rose to Winnie's floor. Waiting, Stone nudged the call button, praying Michaelis hadn't found Winnie's pleasures worthy of a second go-around.

When the elevator topped, Stone stepped in, avoiding the eyes of the lone occupant: Antoine Michaelis.

Stone pushed five.

When the door opened, he held it back with his hand. He'd considered using the STOP button to halt the elevator between floors, face Michaelis there. Twice, he'd tried it in other elevators and been greeted by a loud alarm bell.

He didn't want bells.

On the fifth floor he looked into the empty hallway, and pointed the pistol at Michaelis's chest.

"Out."

Below thick eyebrows, the dark eyes fell to the gun.

"Robbery?" Something uncertain behind the eyes, but no fear.

"Not even close."

"Ah."

"Yes, ah."

"It's Stone, isn't it?"

Floor below someone buzzed, then impatiently buzzed again.

Michaelis's head shook a slow refusal. "If you really intend to use that gun, you've already made a mistake by not using it quickly. I won't make it easier for you."

It was a resonant voice, sure and full of power.

"Then here will do."

"You've made a mistake. Perhaps you've thought of that. The reason you didn't shoot."

"No mistake about what happened to my boat. Or about the ladies, or you running dope. Tell me how innocent you are."

Below, the hand leaned steadily on the buzzer.

"Why would I bother, Mr. Stone? I'll tell you only that the trade in hashish isn't worth my time. A bulky product of low value. The endless middlemen, informers, high costs—and to earn what? A few million dollars in a business that within a decade will wither from legalized competition."

"What *is* worth your time?"

"More profitable enterprises."

"Hard drugs?"

"Things I don't intend to name and would never admit to. Businesses that produce real money, Stone. Cash. In bundles and bags, a volume that needs bill-counters and computers and lawyers. Not a worn-out boat to move a few girls and earn what? A million, two million?"

"But you know."

Michaelis managed a thin smile. "Because my driver Rico used my name in a venture I knew nothing about. What is done is done, and what am I to do?"

His hands spread wide in resignation, and he waited. Perspiration beaded his forehead.

Stone had measured every word. Michaelis was either an inspired liar, or he was handing over his driver Andre Rico in sacrifice. What Michaelis was or wasn't, Stone didn't know. Hardly an innocent, in any event. Stone had needed to come here, give himself the pleasure of looking the devil in the eye.

Stone took his hand off the elevator door. As the elevator started down, Michaelis said, "You've proven your point."

"What point is that?" *That Christian was right*, he thought. He wouldn't use the gun.

"That it doesn't matter these days," said Michaelis, gesturing vaguely toward the world beyond. "Bodyguards, island hideaways. Useless. If someone wants you dead enough, it will happen. We are all vulnerable."

"All I want is to be left alone."

"As do I," said Michaelis. "It's to my advantage and profit, wouldn't you say?"

When the elevator door opened on the ground floor, it was Michaelis who held it back.

"I'll talk to people, Stone. You'll be left alone. You have my word."

He said nothing more. Michaelis's word, by his rules the best he could offer and solid gold. Maybe.

Giving Stone the full breadth of his back, as though offering him a target, which not taken advantage of would seal their bargain, Michaelis walked past the concierge.

The gun stayed in Stone's pocket, as Michaelis pushed his way through the outer door. Farther along the street, headlights blinked on. As he started toward the curb the tan Peugeot came forward to meet him. All neat, practiced, efficient.

Except Michaelis didn't make it.

# Chapter 41
## The Clapper

Physically, the woman was unremarkable. Later descriptions ranged in age from early twenties to late forties. They varied in height six inches. Her dress was variously identified as black, mauve, and navy blue. She may have worn glasses, but then again . . . They all agreed upon one thing, though: her hair. Dark. Very dark. Black as pitch.

As Michaelis walked from the building, Rico left the motor running and slid from behind the wheel of the tan Peugeot. He circled the car and opened the right rear door, eyes scanning the area nearby.

Whether Rico was momentarily confused by the observable contradictions no would ever be sure. The first contradiction was Stone. Rico picked him out through the lobby window. Doubtless Rico knew of Christian's warning that Stone intended to kill Michaelis.

Yet Michaelis had just left Stone behind and was moving toward the automobile in neither panic nor flight.

If not confused, surely distracted.

For Rico failed to pay any attention to the tallish, dark-haired woman walking toward him along the sidewalk.

In no hurry, she kept easy pace with the early-evening pedestrian traffic.

She knew exactly what had to be done.

Step one: take out the protection.

Michaelis was still ten feet from the rear door of the automobile when the woman passed between him and Rico.

For a narrow second Stone wasn't sure they were gunshots at all. Four or five sharp, metallic snaps in rapid order, and Rico was sliding down the auto's rear fender holding his face. Small-caliber automatic, range less than three feet.

Even before Rico hit the concrete, the woman spun about, bringing up a long-barreled weapon to take more careful aim. All too fast, too smooth even for Michaelis. He hesitated, then, understanding, he ducked to one side, causing the first shot to miss. The bullet punched a neat hole in the glass outer door of the apartment building.

With the sound of splintering glass, the concierge, too inexperienced with assassination to give everything proper value, yelled murder.

With the first shot gone wild, Michaelis sprinted to his right. The woman pivoted with him, firing as he ran, like a shooting-gallery slick pumping lead into the rabbit. Michaelis managed about three giant steps before he tripped on nothing and slid head-first into the sidewalk.

He tried to get up, blood oozing from a half-dozen places. By then the woman was at his side. *Poor man. Yes, she was there to help.* She bent close to Michaelis, said something only he could have heard, and shot him twice more in the forehead.

She straightened then, took a quick look at the handful of passersby to see if any posed a threat. Then she walked calmly to the big Peugeot, climbed in, and drove it off into the Paris night.

Fifteen seconds at the outside.

Later they'd find the car, and the gun, because the pros didn't get caught carrying. And the black wig, too, which Sophie had chosen to cover the bright red hair nobody would have mistaken.

Stone didn't wait for the police. He walked the city that night, thinking of the dark things he'd learned about himself and hoped he wouldn't have to learn again.

A moral man; but Christian had never fully understood how frightened. Frightened for those around him. He'd wanted peace, but under attack he'd gone for the most efficient weapon available. He'd been aware of Sophie on his tail from the beginning. Had flagged Michaelis for her in Day-glo pink. Sophie with no qualms about pulling a trigger. No mental baggage to make her think twice. Purpose and pure talent—the Sophies of the world, kept tucked in their closets, out of sight, while people pretended they didn't exist. Until they were needed again to do the dirty work of moral men.

Crossing over the Pont du Carrousel, Stone paused long enough to drop his gun into the Seine.

Then he caught the 10:41 back to the south of France. To his ladies, each damaged in their separate ways, but no worse than he. They'd survive, and more. They all would.

# LEWIS PERDUE

**THE TESLA BEQUEST**
A secret society of powerful men have stolen the late Nikola
Tesla's plans for a doomsday weapon; they are just one step away
from ruling the world.
☐ 42027-7 THE TESLA BEQUEST                                    $3.50

**THE DELPHI BETRAYAL**
From the depths of a small, windowless room in the bowels of
the White House, an awesome conspiracy to create economic
chaos and bring the entire world to its knees is unleashed.
☐ 41728-4 THE DELPHI BETRAYAL                                  $2.95

**QUEENS GATE RECKONING**
A wounded CIA operative and a defecting Soviet ballerina hurtle
toward the hour of reckoning as they race the clock to circum-
vent twin assassinations that will explode the balance of power.
☐ 41436-6 QUEENS GATE RECKONING                                $3.50

**THE DA VINCI LEGACY**
A famous Da Vinci whiz, Curtis Davis, tries to uncover the truth
behind the missing pages of an ancient manuscript which could
tip the balance of world power toward whoever possesses it.
☐ 41762-4 THE DA VINCI LEGACY                                  $3.50

# SHOCKING TRUE CRIME STORIES

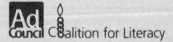
## Join Pinnacle in the fight against illiteracy!